Unbroken Promises

Some promises are meant
to be broken.

To Cindi,

For being the strongest woman I've ever known.
I am honored to call myself your daughter.

Twenty-five years you lived with cancer, yet you never allowed
it to take a single day of your life away. You may not be here
anymore, but your love will always be with us.

PROLOGUE

Cole

TEN YEARS OLD

BEEP.

Beep.

Beep.

I hear the beeping of the machines before I even walk into the room. Beeping is a good sign, though, right? Beeping means she's alive. I open the door all the way and immediately spot my mom lying in her bed. Her shoulders are shaking from crying. Tears are rushing down her face. When she notices I'm in the room, she looks up. I want to scream, but I hold it in. Both of her eyes are bruised, and her face looks like someone beat her up.

"Oh, Cole, come here my precious boy." She tries to hold her arms out for me, but they fall to her sides, so I run over to her and wrap my arms around her belly. She groans in pain, and I feel bad for hugging her too tightly. It's just that I'm so glad she's alive. Grandma told me on the way here that my parents were in a car accident. She said Dad died before he could get help, but Mom is still alive.

"Mom, are you going to die too?" I ask, but she doesn't answer.

"Come here and sit with me. I want to tell you something," she says, her voice sounding off. I climb onto the bed and carefully sit next to her.

"I love you so much, Cole."

"I love you too, Mom."

"You're so young." More tears fall down her face, and I try to wipe them up. I hate when my mom cries.

"I'm not young." I shake my head. "I'm ten years old."

She laughs softly, but when I look at her, she's not smiling. "I know, sweetie, but you still have so much life to live. I want you to promise me something. Promise me that you will be happy. I want you to make good friends and enjoy your life. Go to college and find out what your passion is."

"What's *passion*?" I ask, confused.

"It's when you're so excited about something, you always want to do it. Like how I love to make clothes. It's my passion." I don't know a lot about what my mom does, but I know she makes clothes for older people to wear, and she sells them in the big stores.

"I love basketball." I play it every day—on a team and with my friends in my neighborhood.

"Yes, you do. It might be your passion one day." She kisses my forehead. "I want you to find that passion and hold onto it with everything you have. I want you to one day fall in love just like your daddy and I did." Her voice cracks.

"I miss him," I admit.

"I know, baby, I miss him too, and I know he misses us

as well. But you know what? We might not be able to see him anymore, but he's looking down on us from heaven."

"Do you think he'll be able to watch my basketball game this weekend from heaven?"

"I would like to think so."

"Then I'll make sure to score more points for him."

"Oh, Cole." My mom cries harder, and I don't know what I said to make her even more upset. "Your father and I love you so much. You're our entire world." Her hand comes down to mine, and she squeezes it softly. "I want you to promise me that when you're older and you fall in love, you'll never let her go. Love her and marry her and spoil her rotten, just like your daddy did with me."

"I'm never falling in love. Girls are gross."

Mom laughs even though she's still crying. "Oh yes, you will. Girls won't always be gross. Trust me. One day you will meet a pretty girl who is going to make you laugh and smile, and she will make your heart beat faster." Her hand comes up to my chest before it falls back down. Her eyes close and then open again. "Marry her and spend your life loving her. And one day, if the time comes and you two have a baby, I want you to remember to be the best daddy, just like your daddy was to you, okay?"

I don't understand why she's saying all this, but I don't ask her. She's crying so hard, and I remember one day when she was really upset and I wanted to ask if I could go to my friend's house, Dad said not to ask for anything while she's upset. I waited until she was happy again and she said I could go. I'll just wait until she's happy again to ask her.

"Now, promise me, Cole. Promise me that you will love your life and your wife and your babies." *Babies? Does that mean I have to have more than one?*

"I promise."

"Good boy. Now give me a kiss." I lean over and kiss her cheek, careful not to hurt her even more. "I love you, Cole, more than anything in this universe."

"I love you too, Mom."

"I'm going to rest for a little while. Why don't you go find Grandma?"

"Okay." I scoot off the bed.

"And Cole?"

"Yeah."

"Give Grandma a big hug and kiss for me, please."

"Okay," I say, climbing off the bed and running out of the room to find my grandma.

Part One

CHAPTER ONE

Delilah

"I DON'T WANT TO GO." MY BODY DROPS ONTO THE OVERSIZED MAKESHIFT haybed that is covered with thick winter blankets to keep the straws of hay from poking through and pricking us. My arms cross over my chest, and I let out a loud huff, well aware that I sound like a petulant child.

"You say this every year, Delilah, and every year we tell you everything will be okay. It's been four years, and every year you worry for nothing." My best friend Cole plops down on the same haybed as me and pulls me into his lap. "Just go, get the news that everything is fine, and then come back so we can celebrate our eighteenth birthday and the fact that we've made it through our first week as high school seniors."

"Ugh! But I don't want to go." I pout, and my head falls into the crook of his neck. I inhale deeply, immediately feeling the calmness that I can only find in the arms of Cole. I don't know what I would've done the last six years without him—without his positivity and comfort—and I don't ever want to find out.

"Well, you have to go," another voice demands. "I have a rare twenty-four hours of no practice, and we need to do both your birthdays up right."

I lift my head and turn to find my other best friend, Xander, standing in the doorway of the old barn that my parents should've torn down years ago but never did because they know how much I love this place. Pushing myself off Cole, I stand and sprint the short distance to Xander, and without warning, I jump straight into his awaiting arms. He, of course, catches me—my legs wrapping around his waist and holding onto him like he's my lifeline. Because he is—both he and Cole are. I feel his chest rise and fall as he chuckles over my dramatics. He may only be forty minutes away at Texas University, but it feels like he's moved to another planet. I can't wait until the three of us are at the same school again—only nine more months to go.

"I missed you too, sweet girl," he murmurs into my ear. I always smile when Xander calls me *sweet girl*. Anybody who knows him, knows he's rough around the edges. While Cole is sweet and wears his heart on his sleeve for the world to see, Xander keeps his locked up tight from everyone besides Cole and me. I love that I'm privy to that small piece of Xander others don't get to see.

Xander drops me back down and walks over to Cole to give him one of those weird handshake-hug things guys always give when they see each other. When they're done, they both turn around to face me while I stand against the wall, facing the two of them, in a stare down that I already know I'm going to lose. This is the life I've been dealt and Cole is right. Every year I go and everything is okay, but it doesn't stop me from feeling the nervousness in the pit of my stomach over the fact that it already happened once, and it can easily happen again. As I glare at my two best friends, I remember the first time I met them. It was right here in this same building. I don't think any of us knew it at the time, but the two of them stumbling into my barn would forever change all of our lives in so many ways.

CHAPTER TWO

Delilah

SIX YEARS AGO

I CUDDLE UP WITH MY DOWN COMFORTER AS I LAY IN THE HAYSTACK BED I made, looking up at the stars in the sky through one of the barn's skylights. I watch and wait for a shooting star to appear so I can make a wish on it. It's January in Texas and a bit chilly, but my thick blanket keeps me warm. I would rather be laying out in the grass, but I promised Mom and Dad I'd stay inside the building. I close my eyes as a wave of nausea hits and wait for it to pass. Once it does, I open my eyes to continue watching above. There are so many stars in the sky, but the only ones that matter are the ones I can make a wish on. The first night my parents found me outside behind the barn, they yelled and screamed and demanded I never run off again without telling them. I knew they weren't really mad at me, though. They were just scared like I was, like I am. When they saw that I was crying, they stopped yelling and pulled me into their arms.

They held me tight and told me how much they loved me. Then they assured me that they would be with me every step of the way, while I cried until the tears ran out. They didn't make any promises, though, and that scared me because even in my young twelve-year-old brain, I knew if they weren't making any promises, it must be bad.

After I stopped crying, I asked if I could please sleep in the barn. I just needed to breathe the fresh air. It reminded me that I'm alive. I've always preferred the outdoors over being cooped up in our home, even if our house is one of the biggest ranches in Brenton, Texas. My mom wasn't thrilled about it, but my dad said he would fix it up so I was safe. The next several weeks, whenever my dad wasn't working on our cattle ranch, we spent our days turning the old barn into my very own home away from home. We rebuilt the ladder leading up to the second level and laid down new wood floors. We replaced the old skylights with new ones, and my mom helped us turn barrels of hay into a makeshift bed for me so I could lay under the stars from inside. They got me a cool mini-fridge to fill with drinks, and my mom fixed up the bathroom. My dad insisted they install a monitoring system, but I didn't mind. I knew they were worried about my current condition and wanted to make sure they could two-way with me any time. On the nights it's raining or is too cold, they put their foot down and make me sleep inside the house, but on the nights like tonight when the weather is perfect, I get to sleep out here.

Feeling another bout of nausea hitting, I close my eyes again, willing it to go away. Only this time, when it doesn't, I jump off my haybed and run to the garbage can that my mom put up here for this very reason. I reach it just in time and throw up my dinner. Knowing that once I start, it usually happens again, I don't move from my spot. And sure enough, a few seconds later, I'm throwing up all over again.

"Are you okay?" I hear someone call out from below. Before I can answer him, I throw up a third time, only this time I'm just dry heaving since there's nothing left in my stomach.

"Are you okay?" he asks again, his voice sounding closer this time. He must've walked up the ladder. Grabbing the wet wipes my mom keeps for me next to the garbage can, I wipe my mouth before I turn around to face him. Only when I turn around, there's not one but two boys standing in front of me.

"Who are you?" I demand, tilting my chin up to show I'm not scared in case they're here to hurt me.

"I'm Cole Andrews," the first boy says, and I recognize his voice as the one who was asking if I was okay.

"And I'm Xander Thompson," the other boy adds. While I've never seen Cole before, I do recognize Xander. I've seen him at school, and I know he lives with the Carson family on their ranch along with the other foster kids they've taken on. The Carson's property backs up to ours with only a wood fence to show where their property ends and ours begins.

I reach into the fridge and grab a bottle of water. It's important to stay hydrated so I don't get weak. After I take a sip, I say, "I'm Delilah Cross." I grab a piece of gum off the wooden shelf and pop it into my mouth to get the nasty taste out, then I offer them each a piece. They both take it and thank me.

"I've seen you around," Xander admits. "I was showing Cole your cows when we heard you puking. You have cancer, right?"

I nod. "Yeah, I have cancer."

"Wanna help me show Cole around?" Xander asks as if I didn't just admit to having a life threatening disease. Most kids who know I'm sick don't want to be around me. Even though everyone knows cancer isn't contagious, they act like it is.

"I'm not really feeling well," I admit.

"We could ride one of your UTVs. I can drive." Xander grins and his smile has me smiling as well.

"What's a UTV?" Cole asks.

"You don't know what a UTV is?" I question.

"He's from the city," Xander says with a laugh.

"It's like a golf cart but for the ranch," I explain. "It can drive through anything."

"Cool!"

"Yeah," Xander agrees. "So, let's go!"

"I don't know if I should leave. I'm supposed to stay here."

"What are your parents going to do? Ground you?" Xander shrugs. "You have cancer. Nobody grounds their kid when they're sick. C'mon, let's go."

We spend the next hour riding through the fields and showing Cole a few of the nearby ranches. Xander wants to take him through the back of town, but I tell him no. My parents will definitely ground me if I'm seen on our UTV riding around. On the way back, Cole tells us how his parents died in a car accident a little over two years ago on their way to dinner for their anniversary. His grandma stepped in to take care of him, but she was old and died from a heart attack in her sleep a few months ago, and because she was the only family he had left, he had to go to foster care, which is why he's now living at the Carson's house with Xander.

Xander, in turn, tells us that his dad is in prison for the

rest of his life for killing someone on purpose, and that he never knew his mom because she took off right after he was born.

Hating that they have no family, I don't talk about mine or tell them that I have a good family. Unlike a lot of kids my age, I actually like hanging out with my parents. I love hanging out with my dad on the ranch after school and baking with my mom on the weekends. We go on a lot of trips together as a family, and my parents are always finding reasons to kiss no matter where they are or what they're doing. It's kind of gross but also nice. I hear a lot of stories from kids at school about how their parents fight a lot or are divorced.

On the way back, I think about Cole and Xander being without a family, and how even though there's a chance I might not live a long time, I could be their family. Plus, my parents always wanted to have more kids but couldn't. It took them over ten years just to have me. I bet they would really like Cole and Xander. I've only just met them, but I already like them a lot. So, when we pull back up to my barn, I tell them what I've been thinking. "I know you live with the Carson's and we just met, but if you want, I can be your family, and I bet my parents will like you too."

Neither of them say anything at first, and I'm afraid what I said was stupid. But then Cole smiles and pulls me into a hug, and Xander nods, and I'm not sure but I think they're both my family now.

Once Xander parks the UTV in the shed, I try to say goodbye but they insist on walking me back to my barn. When I ask them if Mrs. Carson will care that they're out this late, they both laugh and say that as long as they don't get into trouble, she doesn't care where they go or what they do. Her only rule is that they must be home before bed, and apparently their bedtime is way later than mine because it's already almost ten o'clock and they don't have to be home yet. According to Xander, Mr. and Mrs. Carson have five other foster kids to look after, so they don't have time to watch their every move.

"This place is really cool," Cole says, eyeing my haybed.

"If you lay down on it, you can see the stars," I tell him. Cole and Xander lay down on my haybed, and I watch the two of them look up at the dark sky. For not being related, they look similar. Like me, they both have brown eyes and brown hair. The only difference is, where Xander's and my hair is light brown, Cole's hair is darker—closer to black. They're both the same height, and I'm shorter than both of them.

"Hey look!" Cole yells. "A shooting star!"

"What?" I fall onto the haybed next to him, trying to see it before it disappears, but I'm too late. "Darn it."

"What's wrong?" Cole turns his head to face me.

"Nothing." I shake my head to emphasize my point.

"Tell me."

"It's stupid."

"Tell me and I'll tell you if it's stupid."

"Fine." I huff. "Every time I see a shooting star, I make a wish."

"What do you wish for?" Xander asks from the other side of Cole.

"I don't want to say because then it might not come true." Tears build up in my eyes, but I quickly wipe them away, not wanting the boys to think I'm a baby.

Cole stares at me for a moment before he says, "I don't think that's stupid, but you don't have to tell us. I think I know what you wish for anyway."

"We better go," Xander says, and the boys both stand.

"Are you going to school tomorrow?" Cole asks. Tomorrow is the first day back to school after winter break and everyone will be returning but me.

"No, I'm stuck being homeschooled because I get sick too much."

"How long will you be sick for?" Cole asks.

"I have to do chemo for five more months. So if I'm still alive when it's all done, I'll go back to school next year."

"Cool," Xander says.

Cole walks closer to me. "You're not going to die."

"How do you know?" I ask. He's the first person to ever say that to me since I found out I have cancer. My doctors can't say it because if I die, they can get in trouble for lying, and my parents never say it because they don't make promises they can't keep.

"Because you're my family now." He shrugs. "And there's no way God would kill more of my family."

"I don't think that's how it works," I say, trying to remember what our pastor says at church every Sunday. He's old and speaks really loud and fast, and usually I fall asleep during the service—until my mom nudges me awake and glares.

"Well, I think it is," Cole insists, and this time I don't argue.

Both boys climb down the ladder and tell me they'll see me tomorrow. I don't really think they mean it, but the next day when my mom isn't looking, I steal some more blankets and pillows from the hall closet, and after having one of my dad's ranch hands bring some more hay up to the second level, I make two more hay beds, placing them right next to mine.

The next night, both boys show up just as they said they would, and when they see I have three haybeds, they each lay down on an outside one. Cole is technically laying on mine, but I don't say anything. Instead, I lay down on the middle one between them. We spend the night watching for shooting stars, talking about their first day of school, discussing who their teachers are, and which kids are cool and which ones to stay away from. Xander is the same age as Cole and me, but because his birthday was in the beginning of the year, he's a grade ahead of us. Even still, I know more people than he does since he's only been living here for the last year while I've grown up in this town. My parents have the biggest cattle ranch in Brenton, and my grandparents own a bunch of stores in town.

While we're hanging out, I have to get up a couple times to throw up, but neither of them say a word about it. They stop talking while I throw up, and once I'm done and lay back down, they go back to talking like nothing happened.

And this pattern continues every night for the next several months. Even on the nights when it's too cold for me to be out in the barn, they sneak in through my bedroom window and hang out in my room with me. We usually watch television or sometimes a movie. While my parents never mention the boys sneaking into my room, I know they know they're there. Mom always makes sure to leave leftovers in the fridge, and she never says anything when they're all gone by the next morning. Dad doesn't comment on the fact that there's a ladder outside my bedroom window, and even though that same ladder was always stored in the shed, now it stays against the side of the house.

One night when they come over, I tell them to go away. So much of my hair has fallen out that my mom felt it's time to shave it. She bought me some wraps to cover my head. They're pretty and in a bunch of different colors, but they don't make me feel any prettier.

"What? Why?" Cole asks from the top of the ladder.

"Because I'm bald and ugly!" I cry out.

The boys come up anyway. "You might be bald, but you're not ugly," Cole says.

"And plus, your hair will grow back," Xander adds.

The next night when they show up, both of their heads are completely bald. None of us say a word but it makes me love them even more.

When the chemo is over and I get to go back to school, we continue the same routine. The three of us are inseparable. It doesn't matter if we're at school or at home, we're always together. They're there the day I find out the cancer is gone, and they're there the day we celebrate six months of me being in remission.

The years pass by, and we grow up. Xander starts high school, and a year later, Cole and I follow. Both of them play basketball, and I cheerlead for their team. The guys have their friends, and I have mine, but at the end of the day, nobody comes before my boys, and I know they feel the same way about me. We've created a friendship that I know will stand the test of time.

CHAPTER THREE

Delilah

PRESENT DAY

GET IN THE WATER, DELILAH!" COLE YELLS. HE'S WAIST DEEP INSIDE THE lake and is trying to splash hard enough to get me wet, but it's not working because I made sure to position my blanket far enough back so I won't get splashed. Brenton Lake is located in a deserted field just outside of town. It's where everyone comes to swim and party on the weekends. There are probably two hundred kids here with us celebrating our birthday, which is pretty much our entire Junior and Senior Class. Most are swimming and some are laying out in the grass. A few are dancing to Luke Bryan—who's singing about kicking the dust up—which is blaring from someone's truck speakers. And I'm pretty sure a bunch of teenagers are in their vehicles or hidden in the fields, making out.

Usually I would be in the water, but today I'm laying out on my blanket staring up at the sky. It's not quite dark enough yet to see the stars but it will be soon, and I have a bunch of stars I need to wish on tonight. The song changes to *If I Die Young* by The Band Perry, and I force myself not to cry. Clearly the person singing this song never experienced the real possibility of actually dying young, because if she had, she wouldn't want to wait for people to know her thoughts until after she was gone when she could tell them how she feels while still alive. But then again, maybe she doesn't have all the people I have in my life who want to hear me. Maybe she's alone and scared that nobody will be interested in what she has to say until after she's gone. *How sad.*

"What has you so quiet?" Xander asks, sitting down next to me. He has a beer in each hand and offers me one. If the parents knew what their kids get into out here, they would skin us alive, even though they all did the same thing growing up. It's the life of a small town.

"Just thinking," I say, taking the beer from Xander. "How's school and basketball going?" I ask, changing the subject.

"I love it. I love living in the dorms and playing basketball every day. There are parties happening all the time. The classes are kind of hard, but I'm handling it. I can't wait for you and Cole to join me."

My head falls against his shoulder as I try to imagine what it will be like if I make it to Texas University. "You know I'm here to help you study," I point out. Xander has always had a difficult time in school, but I've always been there to help him along the way. I hate the thought of him forty minutes away and struggling.

"I know, sweet girl," he murmurs, and I can feel his lips press against my hair. "Now, do you want to tell me what's going on?"

"It's probably nothing, but Dr. Morton ran my blood

like he does every year, and usually that's it, but this time he requested more blood and a CAT scan. So now I'm worried that my cancer might be back."

"And if it is, we'll handle it together, the three of us, just like we did last time." I love how much of a realist Xander is. If I were to tell Cole how I'm feeling, he would promise me it would all be okay. Xander just promises he'll be there.

"C'mon!" Cole yells, walking over to us. "Get in the water!" He reaches down and cups the water, splashing it at us.

"Okay! Okay!" I yell, putting my beer down. "I'm coming!" After taking my shirt and shorts off—leaving me in my red bikini—I grab Xander's hand and pull him up. He's already in his board shorts sans shirt, so he drops his beer into the sand next to mine and lets me lead him into the water.

When we're deep enough, I dunk down under the water and come back up, brushing my wet hair out of my face. I look up just in time to see it, a shooting star. Closing my eyes, I make my wish, and when I reopen them, I see Cole eyeing me. He knows there is only one reason I wish on a shooting star.

"I'M SO SORRY, DELILAH. I KNOW THIS IS A LOT TO TAKE IN, BUT WE HAVE A plan put together to help you beat this."

Breast cancer. I'm eighteen years old, and I have stage two breast cancer. According to the oncologist, only one in a million teenage girls get breast cancer, and of course, I'm that one. I tune out Dr. Morton while I think about how two weeks ago I was celebrating my birthday with my friends, and now I'm being told I have breast cancer. Everything

I had planned for my senior year won't be happening anymore. I can't cheer when I'm sick, and really, who wants to watch a bald, sickly girl shake her pom-poms anyway. I can't party because being around crowds of people will only hurt my chances of beating the cancer when I end up sick with an infection, and drinking alcohol is a definite no-go. The ski trip that the guys and I wanted to take during winter break, and the road trip we mapped out for spring break, won't be happening. For one, my parents will never let me out of their sight, and even if they did, I have to stay away from public places because my immune system will be messed up. Now, the only thing my Senior year will consist of is me trying to stay alive and—

"...single mastectomy."

My thoughts are interrupted at those two words. "Excuse me? What did you say?"

"We'll need to do a single mastectomy."

"I'm only going to have one breast?"

"Sweetheart," my mom coos. "You can have breast reconstruction done, but the important thing is that we get rid of the cancer."

I'm aware of how extremely vain it sounds to be worried about losing a breast when I just found out I have cancer, but I'm an eighteen-year-old teenager who's about to have a breast removed my Senior year of high school. It's bad enough I've been known around this town as cancer girl my entire life, the last thing I need is another reason to stick out like a sore thumb.

"How long will I have to go with only one breast?" I ask Dr. Morton.

"You'll be able to schedule the reconstructive surgery after the chemotherapy is over. The treatment plan we've put together will start with surgery. We'll go in and remove the breast and cancer. Once we've confirmed it hasn't spread to any other parts of your body, we'll schedule chemotherapy. You'll come in for your IV every other week for six months."

"Chemo again?" I question, my hand coming up to my hair. The hair I've spent the last four years growing back and it's only just below my shoulders.

"Yes, we feel taking an aggressive approach is the best option, especially since this isn't your first time with cancer." When he says 'we' he's referring to his team. While Dr. Morton is my main oncologist, there is also Dr. Burger and Dr. Stone. The three of them have been my doctors since I was diagnosed with cancer when I was twelve, and they're who I see every year to get checked to make sure the cancer hasn't come back. Now they'll be the doctors who hopefully make it go away once again.

"What are my chances of surviving?"

This time Dr. Burger answers. "You know we can't answer that as everyone is different, but statistically, the five year survival rate for a woman with stage two breast cancer is about ninety percent."

"So, I still have a ten percent chance of dying."

"That's a very low percentage," my dad says encouragingly, but it doesn't help.

"I had a one in a million chance of getting breast cancer, and I have it," I point out, and the room goes quiet.

"When's the surgery?" I ask.

"We would like to schedule it as soon as possible." Dr. Morton looks at his computer. "I have Monday open."

"This coming Monday? Like in three days?" A lump forms in my throat, and my breathing becomes labored as I come to the realization that in three days my entire life is going to change, again. Three days isn't enough time to prepare. Abruptly, I stand and the chair hits the wall.

"Delilah?" My mom turns to face me, her voice laced with concern. I glance around the room at my parents and doctors, and my hand comes up to my throat as I fight to take in oxygen.

"I need..." I struggle to speak. "I need to go."

"Sweetheart." My mom stands.

"Please," I say, pleading for her to understand. "I just need time to process this."

"Okay." She reaches over and pulls me into her arms for a hug. "We'll be at home when you're ready to talk."

My dad stands and, pulling me out of my mom's arms, brings me in for a hug. "We love you, kiddo."

I nod into his chest before I back away and run out of the office. I sprint down the stairs then out of the building. I don't stop running until I get to my car. I drove to the doctor's office myself since I'm supposed to meet Cole afterward for dinner. I turn the ignition on and take off down the road. My mind is racing and my heart is thumping against my chest. I have cancer again. I beat it once, but what are the chances of beating it a second time?

"Damn it, God!" I scream. "Why me?" I hit the steering wheel with my palm so hard I feel the pain radiate up my arm. My tears fall in bucketful amounts down my cheeks as I drive to my safe place. At one point, I'm crying so hard I can barely see, but I can't stop driving. I need to get to the barn.

When I finally arrive, I throw my car in park and run inside. "Cole! Xander!" I yell. I wasn't planning on meeting them here, but I was hoping to find them here, which is stupid since they don't even know what's going on. Xander is most likely at school since he lives in a dorm on campus, and Cole is probably at home waiting for me to go to dinner. The barn is quiet as I climb up the stairs and throw myself onto the large haybed—what used to be three separate ones, over time has turned into one large one that we share. My cries get harder, more out of control, as I think about everything I might not live to see or do: going on my first date, going to prom, graduating from high school, going to college. I might never get married or have kids. Oh my god! There's a chance I'm going to die before I even experience my first kiss or have sex! I'm not sure how long I'm crying for when I hear my name being called.

"Delilah." I can barely see Cole through my blurry eyes, but I feel him pick me up and place me in his lap, just like he did two weeks ago when he told me it would all be okay. Right before I went to the doctor and they asked to run more bloodwork and do a CAT scan. When I was done, I came back here, celebrated our birthdays, and tried to pretend like I wasn't worried. Three days later, they did a biopsy on my breast, and now it's been confirmed.

"How did you know I was here?" I ask through my sobs.

"Your mom called me. She was worried about you and asked me to find you and make sure you're okay, but she wouldn't tell me why."

"I have cancer again," I whisper against Cole's neck, and I feel his hold tighten around me. "I didn't tell you before, but when I went to my appointment, my blood test came back abnormal, so they did a CAT scan. They found a lump in my breast and biopsied it, and it came back positive for cancer. There's a chance I'm not going to live." I pull my face back and look into Cole's angry eyes. I can see the unshed tears he's holding back as he glares at me.

"You are going to live, Delilah. Don't say that shit!" he yells.

"There's a ten percent chance I'll die!"

"Ninety percent chance you'll live!"

"The odds aren't in my favor, Cole. I'm the one in a million chance of getting breast cancer."

"You had cancer before and you beat it, and you'll beat it again."

"What if I don't? What if my luck has run out? What if I never make it to prom or to graduation? What if I never get to go on a date or be kissed or even have sex?" I repeat every thought I was thinking, out loud.

"Stop it!" Cole yells. "Stop saying—"

But before he can finish his sentence, my mouth crashes against his. My tongue plunges through his lips as my arms go around his neck. I kiss my best friend with everything in me as I try to convey every emotion I'm feeling in this moment: anxiousness, sheer panic, desperation. It's my first kiss and it's nothing like I imagined. I always pictured it to be soft and sweet, but this isn't that. It's hard and rough, fear pouring out of the both of us. Cole takes over the kiss, and before I know it, we're breaking apart only long enough to pull each other's clothes off. We should be thinking about the consequences but we aren't. At least I'm not. The only thing I'm thinking about is wanting to feel something other than fear. Needing something to numb this pain. Take my mind off the tomorrow and live for today because there's a real possibility that *tomorrow* may not come for me. Cole lays me down on the haybed, and I pull his face toward mine, our lips pressing against one another.

"Cole...Delilah." Xander's words stop us in our tracks. We both look at him, hurt evident in his face as he stands there, his eyes darting back and forth between Cole and me.

"You asked me to meet you here," he says to Cole. "What's going on?"

"I have breast cancer," I choke out, and Xander pales. He doesn't need any further explanation. He knew this was a possibility when we talked by the lake the night of our birthday party. He cuts across the room and pulls me out from under Cole, hugging me tight.

"It's okay, sweet girl. We're here for you."

"I'm scared," I murmur into Xander's chest, ignoring the fact that I'm completely naked in his arms.

"Have you guys been together before?" Xander asks, and when I glance up, I see he's looking at Cole for an answer.

"No," Cole says, "it just happened." He swallows hard, looking from Xander to me. "It was a mistake," he says softly, clearly not wanting to hurt my feelings.

"I have to get a mastectomy on Monday. I'm going to have a breast removed before I've even gone out on a date. My hair is going to fall out from the chemo and no guy is going to want to date me...if I survive."

"You will survive," Cole growls out.

"But there's a chance that I won't and I don't want to wait until it's too late. I don't want to die before I get to live and experience things like having sex."

"So you want Cole to be your first?" Xander asks, and it hits me that had Xander shown up instead of Cole, I would've just as easily attacked him the way I did Cole. It wasn't about who I was kissing, but why I was kissing him. I feel like my life is spinning out of control, and I'm just trying to grab ahold of something—or someone—to steady myself. Cole and Xander have always been the ones to keep me stable when I felt like I was going crazy. For the last six years, no matter how far I'd fallen into that dark abyss, they'd been my light to guide me back out. And right now, I just really need them to hold my hand.

"I want to have sex"—I clear my throat so I can finish my sentence—"with both of you." I'm looking at Xander when I say it, and his eyes widen. Then I glance over to

Cole, who is still naked, and he's just as shocked.

"You're my best friends, and I love you both equally. On Monday, my entire life is going to change, and I'm terrified I won't get a chance to live past my teens. I'm going to have my breast removed. I just...I just want to experience what it's like to make love to someone—for a guy to touch me while I'm still me." A tear escapes and Xander catches it halfway down my cheek.

CHAPTER FOUR

Cole

PUT YOUR SHIRT BACK ON WHILE I TALK TO COLE FOR A MINUTE," XANDER says to Delilah, setting her down on the haybed. She nods, and grabbing my shirt instead of hers, pulls it over her head. I swipe my boxers up from the ground and put them on. Xander grabs me by my arm and pulls me over to the corner. "What are you thinking?"

"I'm thinking we're going to do whatever she asks because she has fucking cancer and there's no way we'll deny her anything she wants." Xander nods thoughtfully, and I ask him, "Are you okay with this?"

His eyes meet mine, and I can see he's at war with himself over this, but I'm not sure why. Since the day we met Delilah, we've made it a point to give her anything she wants or needs, and not because she demands it or expects it, but because she deserves it. She deserves everything life has to offer, especially when that same life she's simply trying to live has dealt her a shitty fucking hand. We might not be able to control the cancer and whether it kills her, but we can help make sure that while she's alive, she's living her life and is happy. I never want her to live—or die—with regrets. Watching her fight for her life when we were younger made us all realize how fragile life really is, and that it can be taken from us in a blink of an eye. *She* can be taken from us in the blink of an eye. Not a day will ever go by that Delilah doesn't know just how loved she is.

"Okay," he finally agrees, "If this is what you want to do, then I'll do it."

"So...how do we do this?" I ask.

"We both make love to her like she wants." Xander shrugs then walks past me over to Delilah, and I follow. "We'll do it," he tells her, "but we need rules."

"Okay." She nods her understanding.

"Only this once," Xander says. "We make love to you and then you fight like hell to beat this shit." She nods. "Nothing changes between any of us. After tonight, we go back to being friends. We don't discuss it with anyone." He looks from Delilah to me. "Agreed?"

"Agreed," we both say. People in this small fucking town already talk shit about how close the three of us are. The last thing we need is to confirm their rumors are no longer fiction.

"How do we decide who goes first?" I ask.

"She'll flip a coin."

"Really?" I laugh humorlessly.

"It's the only way to keep it fair. If she decides, she's choosing one of us. No sides."

"Okay," Delilah agrees.

Xander pulls a quarter out of his pocket. "Call it," he says to me.

"Heads."

The quarter flies through the air and after spinning

several times, lands on the ground.

33

CHAPTER FIVE

Delilah

I CAN'T BELIEVE THIS IS ACTUALLY HAPPENING. I'M ABOUT TO MAKE LOVE FOR the first time and it will be to my two best friends. When I mentioned the three of us being together, I thought for sure at least one of them would turn me down, but they didn't. I should probably be more nervous about this, but I'm not. As a matter of fact, being with the two of them for my first time feels right. They've been there for me every day for the last six years. They've seen me at my worst—throwing up, bald, and crying—and they still love me. Being with them for my first time makes complete sense.

I watch Xander as he unlaces his shoes and kicks them off. Then he undoes his jeans and pulls them down. He grabs his wallet from his pocket, opens it up and pulls out the condoms he has stored in there. He throws one to Cole and drops the other one next to the bed. He throws his pants to the side then reaches behind him and pulls his shirt off, leaving him in only his boxers, exposing his chest and abs. My eyes dart from Xander to Cole. Both of them are similar in height. Both lean and muscular from years of playing basketball and working out. I've seen them a million times without their shirts on when we go swimming or when they're helping my dad on the ranch, but I've never actually *looked* at them. Now, as I stand here with them in front of me, it hits me that my two best friends are both gorgeous.

"Have either of you done this before?" I ask, even though I'm almost positive I know the answer. We've heard the rumors but choose to ignore them. The ones where jealous girls who get turned down by Cole and Xander try to say I'm having sex with one or both of them. I know they just say it because they're mad that two of the most popular basketball players at our school don't date anyone and they're always seen with me. Since the not so quiet speculations don't seem to bother Cole or Xander, I just let it go and let people think whatever they want.

"No," they say in unison.

Xander takes control by walking up to me and pulling Cole's shirt back off my body, leaving me once again naked. "Lay down, sweet girl," he murmurs softly, and I do as he says, laying down on the haybed.

"Cole," Xander says, and Cole comes over. "We need to get her ready." Xander parts my legs, leaving me wide open and vulnerable. I should be embarrassed, but I'm not, and not for the first time, I think how lucky I am that my first time will be with my two best friends. Cole and I watch as Xander ducks his face down, spreads my pussy lips, and licks up my slit, his warm tongue eliciting a shiver down my spine and straight to my core.

After a couple laps of his tongue, he murmurs, "Holy shit, you're soaked." He looks up at me, and I can see the wetness sparkling on his beautiful lips. His tongue darts out to taste my juices and the muscles at the apex of my thighs tighten. His gaze meets Cole's, and he gives him a slight nod before he looks back down at my pussy and slowly inserts a single finger into me. He pushes it in and then pulls it out a few times before he adds another one. He stops for a second and gives Cole a heated look before he inserts a third finger.

Cole's gaze leaves my lower half and his mouth and hands go directly to my breasts, massaging and sucking on them tenderly. Xander continues to fuck me with his fingers, and I can feel something in me building, my body shaking with need. His fingers stop, and I hear myself let out a sigh, wanting him to keep going. But before I can verbalize my complaint, his cool breath is once again against my entrance. His tongue landing on my clit as he pushes his fingers back into me.

I moan loudly, but I'm quickly silenced as Cole claims my lips. One of my hands go to Xander's head, my fingers running through his hair, silently pleading with him to never stop doing what he's doing to my body. My other hand grips the back of Cole's neck as he continues to kiss me passionately, and before I know it, my body is built so high, wound so tight, I have no choice but to let go and fall, and holy shit what a fall it is. My entire body trembles and my pussy spasms. I feel like I've lost all control, as I come all over Xander's fingers and tongue. It's not the first orgasm I've ever had, as I've given myself a few while experimenting, but it's definitely the most mind blowing.

While I'm still coming down from my orgasm, I notice Cole's eyes meet Xander's. Something must be silently communicated between the two of them because Xander stands and comes to the side of me while Cole pulls his boxers down and rolls the condom on. I notice his hands are shaking as he parts my legs.

"Are you okay?" I ask, and his eyes meet mine.

"Yeah." He runs his fingers through his hair like he always does when he's nervous. "I'm sorry if this isn't good for you." His lips twitch into a handsome smirk.

"I'm with the two of you. It will be good no matter what," I insist.

"If it hurts too much, just tell me, okay?"

"Okay," I agree.

With one hand gripping the inside of my thigh, Cole lines his dick up at my entrance. Xander doesn't make a move to touch me, so I make the move instead. Pulling his boxers down, I grip his dick and tug his body towards me. His shaft is hard but dry at first, so I lick the palm of my hand to lubricate it. And as Cole slowly pushes himself into me, I focus on stroking Xander, afraid of the inevitable pain I'm about to endure. When I start to feel the head of his dick pushing into me, I gasp out loud. Xander leans down, and removing my hand from his dick, he takes both my hands into one of his and holds them above my head as he kisses me for the first time.

His tongue swirls with mine as Cole continues to enter me. The further he goes, the more it hurts, and the harder Xander kisses me. I feel it when Cole pushes past the barrier of my virginity. My mouth opens to gasp in pain but Xander's kisses swallow it down, and he doesn't stop kissing me as Cole slowly pumps in and out of me. With every thrust, the pain begins to subside little by little, and when it's finally just tolerable, Cole stills, and even through the condom, I can feel the warmth of his release.

He pulls out, and Xander stops kissing me. Both guys stand and switch places. I watch as Cole removes his condom and tosses it into the garbage as Xander rolls his on.

Xander kneels in front of me, and his eyes lock with

mine, silently asking if I'm sure I want to do this. But he was right in what he said earlier. I can't choose. I need to be with them both. I give Xander a small nod, and he pushes into me. I try to keep from wincing in pain, but I can't help it. I'm already sore from being with Cole moments ago.

Xander's not quite as gentle as Cole, but he isn't rough either as he thrusts slowly in and out of me. Realizing I'm giving all my attention to Xander and none to Cole, my eyes leave Xander to look at Cole, and that's when I notice, he's frozen next to me, staring at Xander.

Needing to touch him in some way like I did with Xander while Cole was in me, I intertwine my fingers with Cole's. He glances down at our hands and smiles sweetly at me for a moment before he leans over and kisses me. I can feel it when Xander is about to come, because unlike Cole's steady thrusts, Xander's turn frantic like he's losing control. His fingers dig into the flesh of my thighs, and I let out a low moan. Cole breaks our kiss, and as Xander comes, my eyes are on Cole, while his are on Xander.

THE THREE OF US ARE BACK IN OUR CLOTHES AND LAYING IN OUR HAYBED. MY face is snuggled into the crook of Xander's shoulder with his arms around me, and Cole's head is resting on my belly— his fingers trailing up and down my side while my fingers thread through his hair. If I could freeze a single moment in time, it would be right here, right now, with my boys. My body might be sore but it only serves as a reminder that I've just made love to my two best friends. My hair is still full, my breasts are still intact, and I don't feel sick or weak. I feel whole. I feel complete.

"Why is it that I feel more scared now than I did when

I was twelve?"

"Because when we're kids, we don't understand fear. It's why parents have to hold their toddlers' hands while crossing the road, put fences around the pools, and remind them to chew completely when eating," Cole answers. "The day we met you, you were sick and weak, throwing up more than not, yet you were still so strong and brave. You had no fear because you didn't really understand what it would mean to die."

"We're going to be with you every step of the way," Xander adds. "I know I'm at TU, but I'm only a forty minute drive away, and Cole is right next door. Just like six years ago, we're here for you. And when you get through this, you're going to go to college and join some girly sorority and have the time of your life. Your hair will grow back and your breast will be replaced, and years from now, you will look back and this will all just be a shitty memory. Just a small moment in time."

"I don't want to join a sorority. I want to live with you guys."

"I have to live on campus the first two years because of basketball, and if Cole plays he'll have to as well, but once you guys are juniors, we'll make it happen. I promise," Xander says. "Just get through this, please."

CHAPTER SIX

Xander

"HEY MAN, I'M GOING TO GRAB A SHOWER!" I YELL TO MY ROOMMATE AND teammate, Tim. We've just gotten done with practice and all the guys are planning to go to the cafeteria to get dinner. The dorm I live in is strictly for the athletes. It's one room to two people and we share a bathroom. The room isn't huge but it's decent. Like me, Tim is majoring in business. A common major for athletes. Because we're freshman, we're only taking the general education classes right now, but holy shit, college is nothing like high school. I'm only a month into this semester and I'm already struggling in several of my classes. If it wasn't for Delilah helping me, I don't know what I would do. I've never been a good student, but luckily I have her, and she's damn smart.

"All right, I need to finish and turn in an assignment anyway," Tim says. "I'll jump in the shower after you." He sits down at his desk and starts typing away on his laptop.

Grabbing a change of clothes, I bring them into the bathroom with me, and after undressing and making sure the water is hot enough, I jump in the shower. The steady flow of the water beats against my aching muscles, and I roll my neck in an attempt to loosen them up. Squirting some soap into my hands, I lather up and start washing down my sore as hell body. One thing I've quickly learned about college ball is that the coaches don't play around. We're up every day at five a.m. for our morning workout, and when we aren't in class, we're practicing. We're already halfway through the season and still undefeated. The guys are supportive of each other, and we all get along. They're even great about lending me their car occasionally so I can drive down and check on Delilah. She's had her surgery and is recovering. They've checked and believe they've gotten everything, which is a good sign. If all goes well, she'll be starting chemo soon. Thankfully, Cole and her parents are around, so she's never alone.

One of the things I miss about home is playing ball with Cole. For hours, we would shoot hoops and bullshit. While the guys on the team are great, I miss our friendship. Lately, though, I've been thankful for the time apart. Since we hooked up with Delilah, I've replayed that night several times, and while that would seem like a normal teenage thing to do—fantasize about the beautiful woman I had sex with—my problem is that my fantasies aren't about Delilah—they're about Cole.

And just the thought of him has my dick hard as steel. My soap-covered hand instinctually grips my hard shaft as my thoughts go back to that night. Cole buck naked, standing between Delilah's creamy thighs. Watching him as he stroked his long, thick cock a couple times before he sheathed himself.

My hand strokes my own cock as I remember watching, mesmerized, as he pushed himself into Delilah. I was so turned on watching him thrust in and out of her, I had to force myself to kiss her. And then when it was my turn to be with her, my eyes locked with Cole's for a brief second, and I could be wrong, but I'm almost positive I saw the same look of want in his eyes that I felt.

My fingers tighten around my shaft, my dick now fucking my fist as my eyes close and I come to the memory of Cole as he dragged his eyes down my body, landing on my cock, and watched me fuck Delilah until I came. And in this moment, I know I have a major fucking issue. Because whether I like it or not, I am falling for one of my best friends—and it isn't Delilah.

CHAPTER SEVEN

Delilah

"COLE IS KILLING IT," MY DAD SAYS FROM NEXT TO ME, AND I SMILE IN agreement. My parents and I are sitting in the bleachers of our school gymnasium, watching Cole's last basketball game before winter break, which begins in three weeks. Our basketball team is undefeated, and Cole is a lot of the reason for that. Xander might not be on the team anymore, but Cole has stepped up and the colleges are definitely taking notice. I hate that I was forced to miss several of his games this year, but I'm excited to get to watch him play today, especially since it might be the one and only game I attend this school year.

It's been three months since I had my mastectomy, and thankfully it went smoothly, but I was in a lot of pain and stuck at home while recovering. Just as I feared, I feel like a vital piece of me is now missing. I'm extremely grateful to my mom who ordered me padded bras and a silicone insert for when I leave the house, but no amount of padding or silicone helps ebb the brokenness I feel as a woman. I'm aware one breast missing doesn't take away my womanhood or make me any less of a woman, but knowing that doesn't stop me from still feeling that way.

I'm officially on hospital homebound—meaning I'm still a student but I'm doing my schoolwork from home—which sucks but I'm feeling okay for the most part. Dr. Morton is allowing me to wait until after New Year's to start my chemo, and they're going to be using a newer drug that will decrease my chemo time by one-third. From what I've been told, there's only a fifteen percent chance of me losing my hair—although, I try not to focus on percentages, since they never seem to be in my favor.

There's only two minutes left of the game and we're down by six. Cole has just stolen the ball from the other team and he's dribbling down the court. Even after all these years of being best friends with Cole and Xander, I still have no clue what's going on in the game other than the fact that they make a lot of shots into the hoop every game.

The other team is coming after him, and when two of the players try to stop him, he weaves around them both. Everyone screams and yells as he makes it almost to the basket. An opposing team player stops in front of him, his arms outstretched to block Cole from shooting. Cole looks like he's going to go to the right but instead starts running to the left. He makes it barely a foot in that direction, when he stumbles and falls to the ground. The crowd gasps and the coaches go running toward him.

"What's going on?" I ask my dad as I try not to think about the worst. It's hard to see Cole with everyone surrounding him, so my mind is conjuring up horrible thoughts.

"It looks like he tripped, but he's not getting back up," my dad says. I stand, trying to get a glimpse of Cole, but

I can't. I feel my phone ringing in my pocket and when I check to see who's calling, it's Xander.

"Hey, I'm at Cole's game and he fell."

"I know. I got back from practice and was studying. They were playing the game on ESPN. The commentators are saying he might've torn his ACL or MCL. He was holding his knee."

"I don't know what that means," I say dumbly.

"It means Cole might be badly injured. He might be out the rest of the year."

"Oh no!" I gasp. The EMTs show up and put Cole onto a stretcher.

"Delilah," my dad says, "Let's head over to the hospital. Cole is eighteen, so you know the Carson's won't be going."

"Hey Xander, we're going to go to the hospital."

"Alright, please keep me posted. I have a game tomorrow, or I'd find a way down there."

"I'll text you with any information we get. Stay focused and play safe."

"Will do. Bye."

We hang up, and my parents and I head over to the hospital. Luckily, Cole had put my dad down as his emergency contact, so we're able to get updates. Cole tore his ACL, and as soon as the swelling goes down they can do the surgery. The issue is, with his state insurance, the surgery isn't covered.

"I'll cover it," my dad tells the doctor.

"Sir, even with the surgery, there's a chance he won't play the same, and the chances of tearing your ACL again are even higher."

"Basketball is his life," Dad tells him. "Does he need the surgery to have a chance at playing again?"

"In my professional opinion, yes."

"Then do the surgery. I'll give billing my information." I watch as my dad heads over to the billing department, and tears fill my eyes.

"He's going to be okay, sweetheart," my mom coos.

"I know. I'm just so lucky to have such amazing parents." I give her a hug. "He's not your guys' responsibility, yet you're paying for the surgery."

"Cole and Xander might not biologically be ours, but they're your best friends, and they have no one. They're family."

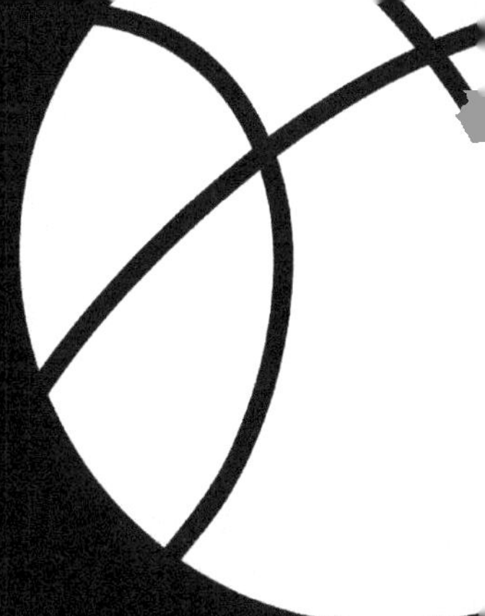

CHAPTER EIGHT

Cole

"MERRY CHRISTMAS!" DELILAH JUMPS ONTO THE COUCH, AND I GROAN IN PAIN. "Oops! I'm sorry." She shoots me an apologetic look before sitting at the opposite end. I've been confined to this damn couch for the last four weeks since my ACL surgery, so to say I'm not exactly feeling festive right now might be an understatement. All this "rest" is driving me mad. I'm finally able to apply light pressure to my knee, and in a few more weeks, I'll begin physical therapy. According to my doctor, I'm looking at a minimum of eight to twelve months of no basketball, which means I won't be getting picked up by any decent college to play, and even if I did, there's a high chance of me getting reinjured. Fuck! Look at Derrick Rose. The only reason why the Bulls kept him on was because he had already proven himself. Me? I haven't proven shit, and now I more than likely won't have the opportunity to do so.

Since Mr. and Mrs. Carson pretty much made it clear they don't have the time to deal with my injury, Delilah's parents stepped in and insisted I come and stay with them while I'm recovering. Delilah's mom even mentioned that she's glad I'll be here when Delilah starts her chemo next week. We both have a long road ahead of us, but at least we'll be under the same roof.

"Ho! Ho! Ho! Merry Christmas," Xander's voice echoes through the house, followed by the front door closing. Texas had a game yesterday, so he's just now arriving, and since they don't have a game until after New Year's, he's staying for the week. Because he has no vehicle, John, Delilah's dad, insisted on driving to TU to pick him up. It's times like these, when I remember what Delilah said about us becoming her family and know she wasn't kidding.

"In here!" Delilah yells. John walks into the living room, followed by Xander, who is holding a small stack of presents. "Ohh! For me?" Delilah jumps back off the couch to snatch them, but before she can grab the gifts, Xander lifts them over his head where she can't reach them.

"Hey!" She giggles. "Give me!" She jumps up and down, trying to reach Xander while he shakes his head, laughing.

"Xander, be nice to my little girl," Joanne chides, walking over and giving him a kiss on his cheek. "Merry Christmas."

"Merry Christmas," he says back, then lowers the gifts, handing one to Delilah, to her parents, and then to me. "It's not much." He shrugs.

"Oh, stop," Delilah says, sitting down on the couch opposite of me with her parents. When she opens the box, she gasps. "Oh, Xander!" Tears pool in her eyes as she lifts the framed photo out of the box. It's a collage of pictures Xander has taken over the years. They're all in black and white, and all of the three of us. When we were thirteen, Joanne was cleaning the house and pulled out the boxes of photos of Delilah. Xander mentioned he doesn't have any photos because his dad never gave a shit enough to take any. The next day Joanne gave him a camera and told him it's time he starts making memories. From that day forward, the camera went pretty much everywhere Xander went.

Delilah sets the gift down and stands up, throwing her arms around Xander. "I love it. Thank you."

Joanne opens up their gift next and it's a beautiful photo of Delilah and her parents from the Fourth of July barbeque they threw last year. "Thank you, sweetheart," Joanne says, giving Xander a hug.

"Maybe you should consider majoring in photography," John points out, also giving Xander a hug.

"Nah, that might take the fun out of it," Xander jokes as he sits down on the same couch as me.

I open my present, and just like everyone else's gift, mine is a framed photo as well. It's a single image of Xander, Delilah, and me. It's from the day Delilah found out she had cancer again, when Xander came up so we could be there for her. We made love to her that day, the three of us losing our virginity together. Afterward, Delilah insisted Xander take a photo of the three of us. She said she wanted one last picture before her life changed. In the photo, Delilah is grinning at the camera, and to those who don't know her, she looks happy. But because I do, I can see the worry in her eyes and the fear written all over her face. Her cheeks are flushed from just having had sex. Xander is also looking at the camera, his broody-ass barely smiling. And me, I'm glancing at Xander. My stomach knots as I stare at the photo and force myself to shake off the feelings that overtake me every time I think about our one time together. We agreed it would only be once and we'd never talk about it again, but since that day, all I can think about is being with Delilah—and Xander—again.

"Thank you, man," I say to Xander, praying my mixed

emotions aren't seeping through into my words.

"You're welcome." He nods slightly and gives me a small smile.

"Okay!" Delilah yells. "Let's open the rest of the presents."

CHAPTER NINE

Xander

"HAND OVER THE BOTTLE, MISTER." DELILAH LIFTS HER HAND AND BENDS HER fingers in a come-here gesture. Cole takes a swig of the expensive-as-fuck vodka that Delilah swiped from her dad's liquor cabinet then hands it over to her. Delilah's parents left a few hours ago for a business associate's party in the city. Because it's New Year's Eve they decided to book a hotel room for the night, so they won't be back until tomorrow. John is driving me back to my dorm in the morning since I have a practice in two days, a game in three, and my classes start back up next week.

"Do you think it's wise to drown your sorrows in a bottle of liquor?" I ask as Cole takes the bottle back from Delilah and guzzles down a shot's worth of alcohol.

"Um...I don't really care." Delilah shrugs and takes a sip. "I have one breast, and I start chemo in three days."

"And I won't be playing basketball for the foreseeable future. Life sucks." Cole goes to take another sip but I grab the bottle from his hand before he can.

"Well, I only have one night left here before I go back to school, and I'd rather not spend it watching you two getting completely toasted." I set the bottle down on the table.

"I'm barely tipsy!" Delilah giggles and leans over Cole to grab the bottle. She misjudges her reach and falls off the couch and into my lap.

"Really?" I ask dryly. I know she's only had a couple shots worth but it's clearly going straight to her head. "Let's watch a movie."

"Okay, fine," Delilah says. "I'll go make the popcorn." She jumps up and runs into the kitchen while I go through the movies on the television, trying to find one to order. When I come across one that looks interesting enough,—something about a guy who is a champion bull rider—I ask Cole if he wants to watch it. When he says it sounds good to him, I click purchase.

Cole moves to the end of the couch to make room, and when Delilah comes in with a large bowl of popcorn in her hands, she sits in the middle, so I sit on the other end of the couch.

"Oh! I wanted to see this movie when it came out a couple years ago!" Delilah exclaims as the movie starts.

WE'RE PROBABLY A LITTLE MORE THAN HALFWAY THROUGH THE MOVIE which turned out to be some ridiculously sappy love story—I should've known better since there was a guy and girl in the image—when the main characters, Luke and Sophia, start removing their clothes. They end up in the shower, with the guy fucking her against the wall. The three of us are watching, and while none of us are saying a word, the sexual tension in the room is palpable.

"Am I the only one who wants to do it again?" Delilah blurts out, and my head whips around to her at the same time Cole's does, our eyes locking.

"Do it again?" I ask, even though I know exactly what she's talking about.

"Have sex," she clarifies. "I mean...I know I'm missing a breast, but I could keep my shirt on." Her voice is soft, insecurity dripping from each word. "I just...I enjoyed being that close with you guys. It hurt but at the same time it felt good, and I read that the next time won't hurt."

Turning my entire body to face her, my hand cups her cheek. "It wouldn't matter if you had no breasts, you'd still be beautiful." And it's the truth. Delilah is a naturally gorgeous woman. She has beautiful brown eyes that shine with every emotion. Her body is beyond sexy with a soft yet flat stomach and a round, perfect ass. And her plump, kissable lips leave you wanting to press your mouth to hers over and over again. She's never paid attention at school, but so many guys over the years have wanted to get between her legs. Cole and I have threatened the shit out of several of those fuckers who'd talk about wanting to take her out, knowing they just wanted to get in her pants.

"You're just saying that because you're my best friend." She rolls her eyes and her fleshy lips turn into a pout. Without thinking, I lean in and press my lips to hers.

"You're beautiful," I say again. "I've thought about us all being together again more times than I can count, but do you understand if we do this, it will change everything?"

"Maybe that's okay," she says and turns her head to look at Cole. "None of us are dating anyone, so we aren't hurting anyone." She shrugs. "Sex is supposed to be with someone you love, and I love you two, and no matter where life takes us, I know I will always love you both."

I glance over at Cole and see he's frozen in thought, so I say what I'm thinking. "I love you too, sweet girl, and if this is what you want, I'm down, as long as we make one promise."

"What's that?" Cole asks, finally speaking.

"All of us or none of us." My eyes lock with his.

"Agreed." He nods his head, his gaze still on me.

"I agree as well," Delilah adds.

"I can't do shit now," Cole says, looking down at his knee. "I'd have to wait until I have more range of motion in my knee."

"Or..." Delilah says, bending over and rubbing her hand across Cole's crotch. "You can sit right here while Xander and I do all the work." Her voice is soft and seductive, and my dick twitches—only I'm not sure what I'm turned on over: the fact that *Delilah* is rubbing on Cole's cock, or that she's rubbing on *Cole's* cock.

Instead of trying to figure out my feelings, I focus on Delilah as she lifts her legs up onto the couch and gets on all fours—her ass popping up in the air—while she undoes Cole's belt.

My hands move to her hips, and I pull her tiny shorts down, taking her panties with them. She wiggles her ass playfully, and I slap one of her cheeks with my palm. It immediately turns red with my handprint as she lets out a low groan, telling me she likes what I just did. As a teenage guy who's only had one sexual experience, I've watched my fair share of porn, so as I look at Delilah's round ass in my face, my mind goes to every video I've ever watched, wanting to know if what I've seen in the videos will work in real life. If I spread her cheeks and lick her asshole, will she like it? Or if I separate her thighs and dip my head down, licking right up her slit, will she come as hard as the women in the videos? The last time we were together, I ate her out just like I'd seen, and holy shit, did Delilah come.

My eyes glance around her body to Cole, and I see his dick, hard as granite, in her fist. Her head lowers toward his cock and blocks my view, but that doesn't stop me from imagining her lips wrapped around the head of his dick, sucking him off. And that thought alone has me wanting to be inside her tight cunt. But first, I need to get her off, because every video I've ever watched, every movie I've seen, has the guy making sure the woman is taken care of before he gets off.

Flipping over onto my back, I move my body towards Delilah. I'm too fucking tall so my feet are hanging off the arm of the couch, but that's the least of my concerns right now. "Spread your legs, sweet girl," I tell her, and she obeys, spreading her thighs for me. I back right up under her pussy, and with my hands gripping the globes of her ass, I get to work eating her out. I can't see anything as I tongue her clit, but I can hear her moans and feel her losing control as she rides my face, her dripping cunt grinding against my mouth. My fingers come up and swipe at her juices, gliding them up to her ass. Then slowly, I push a single finger into her tight-rimmed hole. She grinds against me harder, moans louder, then she comes all over my goddamned face.

Lifting her leg, I move from underneath her just in time to see her swallow Cole's entire dick. I lift her body up and move her in between his thighs. She continues to suck him off while I roll the condom on. Then tilting her ass up slightly, I push into her warm, wet pussy, and fuck if she isn't just as tight as I remembered. Using her hips as leverage, I pump in and out of her. My gaze meets Cole's just before he closes his eyes and throws his head back.

"I'm getting close," he murmurs, his words causing me to fuck Delilah harder. Wanting to get her off once more, I reach around and find her clit. She bucks against my fingers, but I don't let up, massaging that little fucking nub until she's screaming out her orgasm, her legs shaking and her already tight pussy squeezing the shit out of my dick.

"Hol-y fuuuck!" Cole groans, his eyes opening and meeting mine. "I'm coming," he warns her, his gaze never leaving mine, as we both come inside Delilah at the same time.

CHAPTER TEN

Delilah

"YOU HAVE THE OPPORTUNITY TO PLAY BALL IN MICHIGAN. WHY WOULDN'T you take it?" Cole and I are sitting at the dinner table with my parents, discussing college. We're a month away from graduating, my chemo has finally ended—I'm thrilled to say while my hair has thinned, I didn't lose it—and I'm hoping in the next month or so, I will be able to have my reconstructive surgery, so I can go to college whole again. Cole and I were accepted to a few different colleges, but unfortunately while Cole was accepted to TU, it was based on his grades and not to play ball.

"I haven't played in close to six months. I love playing, I do, but I'm not Xander. I'm not going to the NBA one day. I'd rather go to the same college as you two, then go off to Michigan just to sit on a bench."

"I agree with him, sweetheart," Mom chimes in. "Michigan is far away. He would have to fly home and pay out-of-state fees because they didn't offer him a full scholarship." I know she's right, but I hate that he's giving up his dream to play ball. For years, that's all he and Xander talked about.

"What will you major in?" I ask.

"I've been thinking I could major in physical education. Teach sports at a high school and possibly become a basketball coach." He shrugs. "I would still be following my dreams—it would just be in a different direction."

"That's a good goal," Dad says. "Maybe we can have you and my daughter return after college to teach locally." My dad shoots me a wink, knowing that my dream has always been to teach elementary school here where I grew up.

"So, it's settled," Cole says, "Texas University here we come."

CHAPTER ELEVEN

Delilah

ONE YEAR LATER

"WE'RE CELEBRATING! YOU ARE *OFFICIALLY* ONE YEAR IN REMISSION, YOU'RE tits are even perkier than before, we're about to begin our sophomore year of college"—Cole slams two twenty-four packs of beer onto the counter—"and we're living in this awesome fucking condo thanks to your parents."

Generally, freshmen are required to live in the dorms their first year, but because of my cancer, I was allowed to live off campus, since my parents submitted a medically necessary form to the university. They rented me a small one bedroom apartment walking distance from campus. I was glad for that, but it also meant Cole and Xander lived on campus while I lived on my own. Now that they're able to live off campus with me, my parents purchased a three bedroom condo for the three of us to share, also in walking distance from campus.

"I agree!" Xander adds, carrying the last of the boxes

into the living room. "A huge blow-out celebration is in order." He sets the boxes down and leans over to give me a kiss on my cheek. "But first, I believe a smaller, more intimate celebration is in order." He waggles his eyebrows playfully, and I laugh.

"The beds aren't even put together yet!" I joke, knowing full well I'll never turn down being with my guys. Even during my lowest point during my treatments—when I felt ugly with only one breast, scars from the surgery, no meat on my bones from throwing up, and my hair thinning like crazy from the drugs—the guys made me feel like I was whole again. They made love to me like I was their everything, and that's more than most girls can say about the guys they've slept with.

"We've done it in worse conditions," Cole points out. "Like that uncomfortable as fuck haybed."

"Oh, fine!" I roll my eyes and let out a fake annoyed huff. "But don't you dare make fun of my haybed!"

Cole chuckles, then picking me up, he throws me over his shoulder and carries me down the hall to my room. I look up and see Xander following us down the hallway.

When Cole throws me onto my bed, which is still on the floor, he pulls his shirt off and crawls over my body, bracketing me in his arms and placing a soft kiss on my lips. "I'm so glad you're here, Delilah." He kisses my nose. "You're healthy and alive, and your heart is beating." He runs his nose down the middle of my chest and gives my breast a kiss over my heart. This is something he's said and done several times over the last couple years. It's almost as if he needs to remind himself I'm not going anywhere.

"And those tits," Xander adds playfully to lighten the mood.

"Yes, these tits are definitely a plus," Cole agrees, lifting my shirt up and pulling my bra down. His lips wrap around my hardened nipple, and he sucks. Since my left breast had to be completely reconstructed, I decided since my right one was small—barely a B cup—I would get them both done. Now I have full D cups, and my guys love them. While I have almost no sensation in my left breast, I can feel everything in my right one, and they make it a point to give it a ton of attention.

The bed dips down, and I look over at Xander who is lying next to me, in only his boxers. Pressing his fingers to my cheek, he turns my face towards him and kisses me. His tongue pushes through my lips and swirls around while my hand comes up and holds his face to me, deepening the kiss.

Cole pulls down my jean shorts and panties and pushes his fingers into me as Xander's lips break from mine. "Jesus, Delilah, you're always so fucking wet," Cole murmurs, pumping his fingers in and out of me.

"Always," Xander agrees, getting back off the bed and undressing completely. He comes back down to join us, his lips raining kisses all over my neck and face while Cole continues to fingerfuck me.

"My turn," Xander grunts, and Cole's fingers are replaced with Xander's. His fingers are rougher and go deeper. I glance down and see Cole's face dip down, his tongue darting out as he licks my clit. My hips buck in pleasure, and less than a minute later, I'm coming all over Xander's fingers and Cole's tongue. The feeling of them worshipping my body—simultaneously working together to make me come—is something I never want to lose. I can't imagine anyone making me feel more loved and cherished than Cole and Xander do.

"That's our girl," Xander says with a grin. He lifts his fingers up to his mouth and sucks on them. I glance over to Cole and see him give Xander a heated look and wonder if I asked Cole to lick my juices off Xander's fingers, if he would. But before I can voice my dirty thoughts, Xander speaks. "Now flip over."

I do as he says and flip onto my knees, my ass in the air. I'm not sure who does it, but one of them smacks my ass cheek—probably Xander—he loves to smack my ass—then another smack and another. I turn my head and see the two of them looking at each other as they take turns smacking my butt. My pussy clenches with each smack, and I let out a heady moan.

"Fuck, sweet girl, I love it when your ass is red," Xander says, massaging the globes of my ass with both his hands.

"I want to suck you guys off, please," I groan. I learned quickly how much I enjoy giving head. I don't know what it is about taking a man's cock into my mouth, but I feel like I'm in complete control. Maybe it's because I've had cancer twice, and both times it's felt like every decision that came with being sick was out of my hands. I'm not really sure. I just know that I crave the control I feel when I'm sucking them off and bringing them to their knees in pleasure.

They come around to the side of the bed, and Cole pushes his pants and boxers down. Both of their dicks are jutting straight out, and my mouth is watering at the idea of taking them both into my mouth. I start with Cole first, my lips wrapping around his swollen head, my tongue swirling over the tiny hole. My left hand comes up and fondles his scrotum while I take his entire length into my mouth. I feel his fingers weave into my hair, gently massaging my scalp. It doesn't matter what we're doing in bed, they both always make me feel adored and treasured. I pull my mouth off his dick and move to Xander. He likes it a bit rougher, so without any preamble, I take him all the way in, the head of his dick hitting the back of my throat.

"Fuck yes," he groans, grasping the back of my head and pulling me closer as he forces me to take him even deeper. My thighs squeeze shut, and I hear him chuckle. "I love that it turns you on when you fuck my cock with your mouth." He releases me, and I back up slightly, wiping the drool from my mouth that escaped, then I go back to Cole, putting him back into my mouth and fucking him slowly.

I feel Xander's hand on my ass, so I scoot slightly over, giving him better access. "I want this ass, sweet girl." I moan my approval around Cole's dick, eliciting a low groan out of Cole. I feel Xander spread my cheeks then feel lube dripping down my crack. After the first time Xander slipped a finger into my ass, I knew I would love ass play. The first several times they fucked my ass I needed to be prepped first, but now, every single one of my orifices are stretched to fit them perfectly. Xander pushes his dick into my tight hole, and I let out another moan. I start to fuck Cole faster and harder with my mouth, my rhythm matching Xander's. I can taste the precum on my tongue, but before he lets go, I'm pulled back.

Xander is on his back, and I'm on top of him, my feet planted on the mattress on either side of him and my hands using his chest to hold me up. I start riding him backwards, up and down, using his dick for my pleasure. "Fuck yes," Xander breathes as he pulls me backwards, closer to him, so my back is against his chest and his dick is nice and snug in my ass. His hands grip my ass as Cole climbs up on the bed and grasps my left ankle, holding it up in the air. I hold the back of my thighs up, and Xander takes over, thrusting in and out of my hole from the bottom. I watch Cole stroke his hard length as he watches Xander's dick go in and out of me, and when he can't take it anymore he says, "My turn."

Xander stops fucking me, pulls his dick out and lifts me up, placing me on Cole—who is now laying down next to Xander—so I'm straddling him. With my hands on either side of his face, Cole takes my breast into his mouth and sucks on my nipple. I turn my head to look behind me and see Xander coming up behind me. He takes Cole's dick into his hand and strokes it, and my pussy tightens as I imagine the two of them fucking. Once Cole's dick is hard enough, Xander guides it into my pussy. He stretches me wide, his dick hitting that special spot that is going to have me coming in no time.

Still watching Xander, I see him edge forward on his knees. Then he stands over us and pushes his dick back into me. His hands grip my ass, and both of them start moving. Cole is fucking me from the bottom, and Xander is fucking me from above. My second orgasm continues to build higher until I finally lose it—my pussy spasming violently around Cole's dick and my ass tightening around Xander's. Less than a minute later, and they both lose their resolve as well—warm liquid fills both my holes as they come deep inside of me.

They both still, catching their breath. Xander pulls out first and then Cole. My body feels like Jell-O, and I don't want to move, so I don't. Cole chuckles when he sees my body sag, and he gently flips me over so I'm lying on my comfy bed. They both leave to the bathroom to get cleaned up, and even though I can feel their cum leaking out of me, I close my eyes and fall asleep in a comfortable state of sated bliss. I'm almost positive life can't get much better than this.

CHAPTER TWELVE

Cole

sitting down at the table across from him. I pass him a beer and take a pull from mine.

"A few scouts have been by during practice to introduce themselves."

"I was watching Sport's Center the other night, and they said they're expecting you to get drafted in the first round if you decide to enter." Xander smiles and shrugs. The guy has always been like that. He's one of the top college basketball players right now and he acts like it's no big deal.

"If I go in..." He's only a junior this year, so he has to decide if he's going to stay for his senior year or enter into the draft. If he enters, anyone can draft him, and there's a good chance that for the first time in eight years, we'll all be separated—well, Delilah and I will still be here, but Xander could end up anywhere in the United States.

"I miss you on the court, man," he says, taking a sip of his beer, and I nod in agreement. Other than the occasional pick-up game, basketball has taken a back burner in my life. It sucks that I tore my ACL, but I'd like to think everything happens for a reason. And in this case, being injured allowed me to be there for Delilah through her surgery, chemo, and recovery. Oftentimes, I think back to the promises I made my mom and hate that I'm letting her down. But my hope is that once I graduate, I'll get a job teaching and coaching, and while it's not the same as playing, it's still following my dreams. Basketball is still my passion whether I'm shooting the ball or teaching someone else how to. Hell, maybe one day I could get a job coaching college ball, or if I want to aim high, maybe the NBA. Just because I'm not playing, doesn't mean I'm not following my passion. At least that's what I tell myself.

"Hey, you okay?" Xander asks, shaking me out of my thoughts.

"Yeah, just thinking. What time is everyone supposed to be here?" We're throwing a move-in party tonight at our new place. The guys from Xander's team will be here, along with the girlfriends Delilah's made, and the few friends I've made. For the most part it's the three of us, but we've added a few close friends to our circle the last couple years.

He looks down at his watch. "Soon, I'm going to go jump in the shower." He downs half his beer and tosses it into the trash before he heads down the hall.

THE MUSIC IS THUMPING AND THE CONDO IS FILLED TO THE MAX WITH college students. I haven't gone out onto the rooftop patio, but my guess is it's just as packed. Girls are dancing with guys, with each other, on the coffee table, in the corners. I would be worried about us getting kicked out if we weren't the only people on this floor. Delilah's parents clearly knew what they were doing when they purchased this place.

Several people come over to congratulate me on the new digs, and a couple women make passes at me, offering to help me break in my new room. Nobody knows that I'm technically taken. They don't know anything about the relationship I have with Delilah and Xander. Hell, sometimes I don't even think we know. Back in high school, people accused and assumed, but they were all lies. We were nothing more than best friends. Now, the things they accused us of are actually the truth, but in college nobody pays attention like they do in high school. Everybody is too busy with school or work.

I'm sitting on the couch with a couple guys who are talking about the upcoming football game this Sunday, and my eyes find Delilah. She's standing in the corner of the room with a beer in her hand. Her brown hair is long and comes down past her breasts. She was so sure she was going to lose it when she started chemo, even though the doctors told her there was a good chance she wouldn't. In the dark of the night, she'd cry in fear of it falling out—scared she would take a shower and it would all end up in the drain. She would tell me that her hair was the last thing she had left to make her feel beautiful, and that broke my heart. Because what she didn't realize was that it wouldn't have mattered if she lost it all and was completely bald. She would still be Delilah, the brown-eyed woman who has more reasons than most to give up on life, but instead chooses to wake up every morning with a smile on her face ready to fight for her life. And for those reasons alone, in my eyes she's the most beautiful woman in the world.

Tonight, she's wearing cut-off jean shorts and a Taylor Swift T-shirt she cut the bottom off of. Her tiny stomach is showing, and I can see her belly button ring glinting in the light. She got it last year after her last round of chemo was finished, at the same time I got my first tattoo.

As if she senses me watching her, her eyes leave the guy she's talking to and meet mine. She grants me a beautiful smile and the most adorable wink, and my heart feels so damn full. Her gaze goes back to the guy she's standing with, and I imagine what it will be like the day she realizes just how amazing she is and moves on with her life. When she wakes up one day and remembers why she fought so hard to survive: to get married and have kids. And when that day comes, my only prayer is that whoever she ends up with will understand why our relationship was like this and will still allow Xander and me to be a part of her life.

I take a pull of my beer, and as I set it down, my eye catches Xander. He's leaning against the counter in the kitchen with a barely clothed woman pressed up against him. She's laughing at whatever it is he's saying as her hands roam up his torso and over his chest. His eyes meet mine, and for a second, he freezes in place like he's just been caught doing something wrong—only he hasn't been. The three of us agreed: no sex with anyone but each other, and sex only when we're all together. We all promised if any of our situations change, we'll let the other two know immediately. If Xander wants to date, he can, and the same goes for Delilah and me. But have any of us? Not that I know of.

Needing to take a breather from this party, I excuse myself—even though I wasn't even participating in the conversation—and escape down the hall to my bedroom. The condo is three bedrooms and two bathrooms. Since Delilah is the reason we are all living here rent free, and because she's the only girl, she has the master bedroom and bath. Xander and I have our own rooms but share a bathroom—along with anyone who comes over.

Closing my door behind me, the music lessons but not much. We just finished moving in today, so my room is still filled with boxes. Sitting down on my bed—which is now put together—I reach over to the box on my nightstand that is marked fragile. When I open it up, I spot a couple of framed photos. The first one I grab is of my parents and me. I was ten in this picture. It was the last trip I took with them before they were killed. We're standing in front of a large aquarium and the three of us are smiling. Sometimes, my heart aches over how much I miss my parents. They were older when they had me. I was their 'oops' baby. After years of trying, they didn't think it would ever happen, and then at forty-two years old my mom found herself pregnant. She had a brother who died of a heart attack when I was little, and my dad was an only child. When my parents died, my grandma took me in, but she was already over eighty and not even two years later, she passed away.

I pull another framed photo out of the box. This one is of Delilah, Xander, and me this past summer. It's another photo Xander had printed. We drove from Texas to New York and back, stopping at various places along the way. In this particular photo, the three of us are standing at the top of the GE building. Delilah is in the middle, and she's cracking up laughing at Xander who is scowling because her hair is being blown by the wind right into his face—and me...I'm looking at them. While I would give anything to have my parents back, sometimes I wonder if everything happened the way it was supposed to. Had my parents not died, I would've never ended up in the Carson's foster home. It was a pretty shitty place to live, but I would live there for the rest of my life if it meant I would meet Xander and Delilah. Maybe it was God's plan for the three of us to meet at a time in our lives when we needed each other more than even our twelve year old selves could ever know.

"Hey." I look up at the voice and see Xander standing in my doorway. He steps inside and closes the door behind him. "You okay?" He sits down on the bed next to me and takes the photo out of my hand. He stares at it for a few seconds before he looks up at me. His tongue darts out to wet his upper lip before he bites down on the bottom one. He does this whenever he's worried.

"Yeah," I say, adverting my eyes back to the picture in his hand. "Just thinking about how good it is for the three of us to be living under one roof. Delilah is healthy and we have this next year for all of us to hang out before you have to decide if you're staying or going."

"Cole," Xander whispers, and I look up at him.

"Yeah?"

He licks his lips and bites down on his bottom lip again before he shakes his head. "Never mind." He chuckles softly and stands, handing me back the photo. "I'll see you back out there." He tilts his head toward the door then walks away. I place the photo on my nightstand and follow behind him.

Grabbing another beer, I spot a friend of mine that I met in health class last semester. "Hey man! Nice place." Darryl sticks his hand out to shake mine.

"Thanks. You ready for school to start back up this week?"

"Fuck no, but I'm ready to be one year closer to graduating."

"True. Did you do anything this summer?"

I'm listening to Darryl tell me about his various hookups and trips when my eyes lock with Xander's. He shoots me a lopsided grin that has me feeling shit I most definitely shouldn't be feeling about my best friend. This isn't the first time, though, I've had these feelings pop up. It's been happening for years, but I've chosen to ignore them. I tell myself it's because we're sleeping with the same woman. My body and mind are just confused. The problem is something deep down inside of me often calls bullshit on that excuse.

IT'S CLOSE TO FOUR IN THE MORNING WHEN THE CONDO IS BACK TO THE WAY it was before the party. Everyone has left, the beer is all gone, and it's quiet, aside from the soft music that's still playing, filling the silence. Xander is taking a shower in our bathroom, and Delilah is taking one in hers. Since I already took one, I'm lying in my bed playing my PlayStation. There's a knock on my door and in walks Delilah. She's dressed in her tiny cotton shorts and tank top. She lays down next to me, and like she does often when I'm playing my video games, she puts her head in my lap and watches. A few minutes later Xander joins, snagging up the other controller and sitting on the bed next to me. I switch the game to two players, and we play a couple games of NBA Live before we're both too exhausted to see the screen. I turn the PlayStation off, and when I look down, Delilah is softly snoring. Xander just shrugs, scooting down and wrapping his arms around one of my pillows. I pull Delilah up next to me and her head goes straight to my chest.

"I'm pretty sure this defeats the point of having three bedrooms," I joke as I slide down the bed, so I'm laying down.

"Nah." Xander chuckles. "We'll just rotate bedrooms, that way they all get used." He grins over at me before he closes his eyes, and as I watch my two best friends sleep, I can't help but wonder what is in store for all of our futures. I've learned over the years that if things appear to be too perfect, they probably are.

CHAPTER THIRTEEN

Xander

"HOW THE HELL DID YOU GET ME TO AGREE TO THIS?" I STEP OUT OF THE bathroom, and Delilah squeals.

"It's so perfect! This is awesome!" She steps closer and fixes the collar to my…"What the fuck is this? A cape?" I ask.

"No!" Delilah giggles. "It's a robe!"

"Whatever. I look like a nerd. I'm a twenty-year old college student. I'm supposed to look cool." I pout.

"We can look uncool together," Cole says, coming out of his room, dressed in the same robe as me. Only he's wearing an ugly as fuck orange wig. I crack up laughing.

"I guess it could be worse. I could be a carrot top." I nod toward his head.

"How about you go fuck yourself," Cole smarts back.

"You two…stop," Delilah chides. "Now hold still, Xander. I need to draw the lightning bolt on your forehead." She uncaps a marker, and standing on her tiptoes, draws on me. "There!" She steps back and stares at me for a second before she says, "Oh! Glasses!" She scurries into her room and comes back out with a pair of black-rimmed glasses. She places them on me. "Now you're perfect!" She jumps up and down, clapping, and when I look at Cole, he's grinning. He doesn't care how nerdy he looks. He loves making Delilah happy. We both do. I just wish I didn't have to do it dressed as Harry fucking Potter.

"We're going to be the best dressed, you know." Delilah says as we head down the hall to the front door. "How perfect is it? Hermione, Harry, and Ron...three best friends."

"I'm pretty sure the three of them didn't fuck," I point out, grabbing Delilah by the waist and pulling her into me, playfully.

"No, they didn't. But you know everyone was wishing they would've."

"Really? All the kids who watched the movies were hoping for a threesome?" I joke, pressing the elevator button. Cole laughs and shakes his head.

"Noooo, the teenagers and adults. C'mon, everyone felt the sexual tension between them, but the author had to keep it PG."

We arrive at the Halloween party that one of the houses on campus is throwing. Delilah immediately spots her friends, Summer and Kaelyn, who live here, and runs over to them. I spot some of the guys from the basketball team, and they call me over. As I'm walking over to them, I see Cole standing alone. He's been here for a year, but his entire focus has been on Delilah getting better and school. Sure, he's made some friends and several of our old friends from high school go here as well, but Cole has always been more of a loner. Even as one of the star basketball players at our school, with girls wanting to date him and guys wanting to hang out with him, he always chose to hang out with Delilah and me over everything else.

"Hey," I call back to him. "Let's go." He nods once and joins me. We spend the next couple hours drinking and playing cards with a bunch of other people.

"Ron! Harry!" We hear Delilah shout, and we both groan.

"I think she's a little drunk," Cole says with laughter as Delilah approaches. She plops down onto Cole's lap and wraps her arms around him.

"Did you know Hermione and Ron get married at the end of the last book?" she says, her words coming out slurred. Cole looks around her toward me and shoots me a *please help me* look. A drunk Delilah is a loose lipped Delilah.

"Alright, Hermione. Nobody is getting married tonight, but you know what you *are* doing?" I stand up and walk over to help her up.

"Casting a spell on you!" She points her finger at me and grins.

"Nope!" I answer, trying not to laugh at her antics. Cole, on the other hand, shakes with laughter. "You're going home and sleeping off your drunkenness."

Delilah flicks her wrist and yells, "Amortentia!" Then she backs up slightly from Cole and flicks her wrist toward him, repeating the word again. "There!" She claps. "I cast a spell on you both!"

Cole stands and places Delilah on the floor, holding onto her hips so she doesn't sway. "Oh yeah, are we going to turn into frogs?"

"Nope," she says, making a popping sound as she drags the word out slowly. She bends her pointer finger, indicating for me to come closer. I move towards them slightly, but she shakes her head, silently telling me to come even closer. When I'm close enough to her liking, she whispers, "It's a love spell."

"We already love you, sweet girl," I point out.

"I know that, silly." She giggles. "It's a spell to make you two fall in love! Duh."

I look over her shoulder at Cole and see his gaze is boring into mine. "Let's get you home. You've definitely had too much to drink."

"Fine, but don't say I didn't warn you."

CHAPTER FOURTEEN

Delilah

"Hand me the red nail polish," Summer says to Kaelyn, who is currently painting my nails on my right hand.

"Umm...it's actually called Seduction." Kaelyn laughs and tosses it her way.

"Oh...even better, since I plan to seduce a man tomorrow night and lure him back to my room." Summer waggles her eyebrows playfully. I met Summer and Kaelyn our freshman year in our English class. The girls were already friends, but they welcomed me into their tiny circle with open arms. I was worried that once I told them I had had cancer, they would shy away, or like my high school friends did, push me away out of fear of 'catching it.' They, however, proved to be amazing, supportive friends.

"I seriously love this view," Summer says, standing up from the lounge chair and walking over to the wall. "Every time we come out here, I never want to leave." We're currently sitting on my private roof patio that is accessible directly from my condo. My parents, knowing how much it means to me to be outside, made sure the condo they purchased had access to a roof patio. It's not as amazing as my barn, and it doesn't hold as many fond memories, but with a few lounge chairs, a large umbrella, and a table and chair set, it's a pretty awesome place to hang out and create new memories. The truth is I've probably spent more time out here the last several months than inside the condo. We even put a barbeque out here, and the guys grill often.

"You think you'll stay living here after we graduate?" Kaelyn asks.

*After we graduate...*There was a time I didn't even think I would be alive to graduate high school let alone attend college, and now there's only one month left of my sophomore year. The thought makes me smile.

"I'm not sure." As much as I love living here, my dream was always to get my elementary education degree and teach at the elementary school I went to, so I could live near my parents, but now so much has changed. Cole is officially majoring in physical education and is hoping to coach basketball, and Xander is majoring in business— even though he will most likely end up in the NBA. We never talk about the future, but I would love to be wherever they are. I'm just not sure if they feel the same way. For so long I was scared I wouldn't make it to the next day, so we never discussed a month into the future, let alone a year or five years. Xander and Cole helped me create an escape from the reality of my life, of my cancer, and they never would've asked about the future, knowing there was a good chance I might not have one. But now that I'm once again in remission—and have been for almost two years—I feel like maybe it's time to start planning my future again.

"Ladies," a masculine voice says, and I turn around to see Cole and Xander walking over. They're both dressed in their workout gear...if you can call it that—basketball shorts and tennis shoes. That's right, no shirt. I can't help but check them both out. While their bodies are both lean and muscular, both of them well over six feet tall, they wear their facial and body hair differently. Cole keeps his face clean shaven, never letting it grow past a light stubble. Xander, on the other hand, keeps a full face of hair—always edged and trimmed neatly. I love that when I kiss them it feels so different. Cole's chest is completely hairless. He doesn't wax it or anything, it's just the way it is. Xander, however, has a light smatter of chest hair along with a thick happy trail that begins just under his belly button and goes straight down to his—

"Ahem." I shake myself out of my thoughts. "You okay there?" Xander chuckles.

"Yeah," I choke out. "I'm just feeling a bit warm. Maybe we should head inside soon." This time Cole laughs.

"What are you two up to?" I ask, changing the subject.

"Just playing some ball and getting a workout in. Championship game is tomorrow night. You coming?"

I roll my eyes. "You already know I'll be there. Have I missed a single one of your home games this season?"

"I know...I'm just making sure."

"We can ride together," Kaelyn says, jumping into the conversation.

"Yeah!" Summer adds. "We're going to Club Matrix tomorrow night. You guys should come after the game."

"You're going to Club Matrix?" Cole questions with a frown.

"Yep!" Summer answers for me. "We're going to find some hotties to dance with." She winks at Cole, and both girls giggle. I'm not even sure Cole sees the wink, though, because when my eyes dart to his, he and Xander are both glaring at me. My stomach twists into a tight knot. I can't remember the last time, if ever, my boys were mad at me. I mean, they may have been, lord knows I'm not perfect, but when you've danced with death, people tend to look past anything you do wrong.

"Yes!" Kaelyn adds. "We're going to find a man for Delilah."

"And for us!" Summer laughs.

When the girls begged me to go out dancing, I tried to say no, but then they pointed out that I've been single for too long, and it's time to put myself out there. I tried to refuse but they weren't taking no for an answer, and since I can't exactly tell them I'm taken—kind of—by my two best friends, I didn't really have a valid reason for not wanting to go out dancing in hopes of meeting someone.

"So...you boys want to join us?" Kaelyn coos. Her hand goes to Xander's wrist, and I bite the inside of my cheek in an attempt to keep my mouth shut. I can't get mad at them for hitting on my boys. They asked me if I wanted to claim either one, and since I couldn't tell them I wanted to claim both, I said no. They held up their end of the girl code by asking first, so I can't say shit when they hit on them.

"We'll see," Xander says, backing out of Kaelyn's reach. "I need to take a shower."

"Same," Cole agrees, following Xander, even though there's no way they're *both* going to shower since they share a bathroom and never use mine.

Once they're inside, Summer and Kaelyn both gush about how hot the guys are and how they can't believe I live here with the two of them, and if they lived with them, they would be sneaking into their beds at night. I don't bother to tell them that I don't need to sneak because they welcome me willingly.

CHAPTER FIFTEEN

Xander

DELILAH IS ONE OF THE MOST IMPORTANT PEOPLE IN MY LIFE. I LOVE HER AND need her and crave her. But the thing is, while I'm sexually attracted to her, my need for her isn't because I'm in love with her. I would say my love for her is more like a brotherly-sisterly sort of thing, but that would be fucking weird since I stick my dick in her on the regular. My point, which I'm doing a shitty job at making, is that I love her, but it's not like someone who loves their lover, the person they want to spend the rest of their life with. I love her because I need her. She's the glue that holds us all together. She and Cole are my entire world. I crave Delilah because when I'm with her I feel complete. But all of that is only because with Delilah comes Cole.

So as I stood outside and listened to her friends go on and on about finding her a man, I wanted to tell them to shut the fuck up and kick their asses out. They don't realize that by pushing Delilah to move forward, they are inadvertently taking Cole with them. I know one day

Delilah will move on. I know she'll get married and have kids, and the relationship we have will change. It's inevitable. But I'm not ready for it to end yet, because when it does, I'll lose Cole. And I'm not sure I'll ever be ready to lose him. But just like Delilah, I know one day Cole is going to move on. He's going to marry some sweet woman who will give him a bunch of babies. He'll live in suburbia and drive a fucking minivan. And when that day comes, I'll have no choice but to watch them walk away. Even if it fucking kills me to do so.

Not able to listen to Delilah and her friends discuss her moving forward any longer, I made the excuse that I needed to shower. I could see Cole was pissed as well and gave the same excuse I did, following me into the house. The difference is, where Cole is in love with Delilah—and not like she's his sister—I'm in love with Cole. So, while he's pissed at the thought of losing her, I'm gutted at the thought of losing him. Which is ironic as fuck since I've technically never had him.

Without saying a word, we both walk down the hallway. When I see him go into his room, I go into mine. I fall onto my bed, covering my eyes with my arm, and think back to the day I knew my feelings for Cole ran deeper than being friends.

"Hey, man, how's it going?" I say, answering Cole's call. I'm seriously running late, but I always answer Cole's call, especially since it's been close to three months since I've seen him and Delilah. Not since winter break when I came home for the holidays.

"It's going. How are you?" he asks.

"I'm all right. How's Delilah?" I ask while tucking in my shirt. Once I'm done, I grab the jacket to the suit I rented for tonight. I had no clue how I was going to afford one, but

luckily one of the guys mentioned his father owns a tuxedo rental company, and he was offering to fit and rent any of the players a tux for free. While I'm here at Texas on a full-ride scholarship, it doesn't cover anything extra, and with me playing basketball, it's the equivalent of a fulltime job without any pay.

"She's okay. She had a rough bout of chemo the other day so she's home sleeping. Her mom is taking care of her." This statement shocks me because normally it's Cole who is caring for Delilah. Don't get me wrong, her mom dotes on her plenty. She's loving and caring, and protective of Delilah—everything I imagine a mom is supposed to be like, and nothing like Karina Carson, the woman who took care of Cole and me.

"Why aren't you there with her?" I hold the phone between my shoulder and ear as I try to tie this fucking tie. I glance at the clock and see it's almost 5:30. Shit! I need to get going.

"I have something more important to do," Cole answers, and I feel my stomach sink. Since when is anything more important than Delilah?

"Oh," is all I say. "All right, well I gotta go. I'll call you tomorrow and see how she is."

"Okay, man. Have a good night," Cole says, then hangs up the phone before I can even say goodbye. I look in the mirror and nod to myself. This is the best it's going to get. I should be excited for tonight. I'm a freshman in college, and I'm being awarded MVP at the team banquet. Most freshman don't even leave the bench, yet I'm a starter and kicking ass and taking names. Coach told me if I keep going the way I am, I'll be playing in the NBA before I can legally drink. I should've been ecstatic at that, but my first thought was if I get drafted, I'd have to leave Cole and Delilah.

While I should be excited about getting this award, the truth is I'm dreading it. The team banquet is also known as the family banquet. Normally I would've invited Cole and Delilah to go since they're my only family, but with Delilah going through chemo, she's not supposed to be out in public more than necessary, and Cole's mobility is still partially limited from his ACL surgery. Since Cole and I don't have a car of our own, that would mean he would have to borrow a car or take a cab, which is expensive. So, instead it's just me. I knew moving up here would mean being away from my friends, but I didn't realize just how lonely I would feel. Which is so strange to me since most of my life I was alone. I might've lived with my dad for the first ten years of my life, but he didn't exactly raise me. He was too busy robbing banks and shit to actually be a dad.

Grabbing my wallet, cell phone, and keys, I shove them into my pockets and swing the door open. And standing there, with a single crutch under his armpit, in a black tux, is Cole. He smiles at me and my heart does the craziest thing. It's like it skips a beat or picks up speed or something...I don't even know.

"You're here," I say dumbly.

"Where else would I be? You're getting a fucking MVP award tonight." His hand comes down to pat my shoulder and his touch has me feeling weird thoughts. Then he pulls me into a hug, and for the first time in my life, I feel not so alone. Tears prick my eyes and a lump gets stuck in my throat. He's here... Cole is here for me.

"How did you know?" I ask once I get my emotions in check and can speak.

"I subscribed to the Family of Texas Basketball Athletes newsletter a while back. I know you're busy, so I wanted to make sure I was kept in the loop. And it's a good thing I did, since you didn't bother to tell me you're getting an award tonight. I had to email the booster ladies and get myself a damn ticket." Cole smirks, and in that moment I know I'm in love with my best friend. Fuck!

My eyes water as I remember later that night after my banquet. He ended up spending the night in my dorm with me, and we talked for hours. It might have been the night I realized I was in love with him, but it was also the night I realized I would never stand a chance with him.

It's late. Probably three in the morning. After the banquet, a bunch of teammates threw a party, and Cole and I hung out there for a while. Once we had enough, we came back here to shower and go to bed. Since basketball season is over and it's Saturday night, my roommate is out for the night with his girlfriend. Cole is laying in my roommate's bed and I'm lying in mine. We've been talking for the last couple hours about everything and nothing. It reminds me a lot of the nights we spent together at the Carson's. I knew back then I had feelings for Cole, but I always chalked them up to friendship. Since I was old enough to understand the difference between the male and female anatomy, I've always been attracted to a sexy woman with a nice rack and a round ass. Not once did I ever look at a guy and think, "Hell yeah, I want that dick." When Cole and I are with Delilah, her pussy and ass feel like heaven gripped around my cock, so I know I'm still attracted to women. But at the same time, when I watch Cole fuck her, I find myself fantasizing about what it would be like for him to fuck me instead of her, or vice versa.

"Do you ever wonder if we made the right decision by being with Delilah sexually?" I ask Cole, trying my best to appear nonchalant.

He takes a moment before he answers. "That's a tough question. I try not to regret anything I do. My parents dying made me realize life is too short to live with regrets. I love Delilah. Aside from you, she's my best friend. When I moved in with the Carson's I was down. I had lost both my parents and grandma in less than two years. You and Delilah came into my life and made me feel like I once again had a family."

"You guys did the same for me," I admit.

"I don't think we made the wrong decision short term. I think the issue will come years from now. When she wants to accomplish everything she was afraid she wouldn't be able to, like getting married and having kids. In order to do that, we'll have to end. And whoever she meets is most likely not going to understand the relationship we had with her."

"It's not like we would continue to fuck her once she moves on."

"No, but Delilah's parents never keep anything from each other. We've heard them say on several occasions that the key to a good marriage is honesty. So, I'm almost positive that Delilah will go into a relationship with the same mindset. And once she meets someone she wants to spend her life with, she's either going to have to keep the fact that we've all had sex together from him or tell him. Would you want your girlfriend or wife hanging out with two guys she spent several years fucking... together?"

I try to imagine myself one day having a wife, but for some reason the only person I can see when I visualize my future is Cole. While Delilah choosing a boyfriend or husband over us would fucking suck, I can't help but do a metaphorical fist pump in the air that Cole is talking about her meeting someone else which means he doesn't see himself with Delilah in the future.

But just to confirm, I ask, "Could you see yourself with Delilah?"

"As my wife?" He tilts his head to the side and quirks his one brow up, and I have to hold back my grin at how fucking sexy he looks when he does that. "We agreed all together or not at all."

"I know what we agreed, but what if that wasn't a rule?"

"It is, so it doesn't matter." He shrugs one shoulder.

"Do you see yourself getting married one day?"

"Yeah," he admits. "When my parents got into the car accident my dad died instantly, but my mom actually survived. While she was in the ICU recovering from her surgery, my grandma brought me to see her, and even though the doctors thought she was going to make it, I think she had a feeling she wasn't going to, because she went on and on about everything she wanted for me in life."

"Damn, what did she say?"

"She made me promise a bunch of shit. Like to find my passion and hold onto it. And when I find the woman I want to spend my life with, to love her and treat her like my dad treated my mom. To be the type of dad he was to me. They were literally the last words she ever spoke to me.

"Not even an hour after I left the room, she died. It sounds bad, but with the way my parents loved each other, I feel like maybe they were meant to die together. Like she couldn't live knowing he was in heaven without her," Cole says.

"Like they were soulmates," I add softly, realizing there's no way Cole will ever give us a chance. In order to be with me, he would have to go against everything his mom wished for him on her death bed. And that's not the kind of person Cole is.

Feeling annoyed and defeated, I get back up, grab my towel from behind my door, and head out of my room to the bathroom. I pass Cole's room on the way and see his door's shut. I want to knock and ask him what's going through his head, but if I'm honest with myself, I don't really want to know. The three of us have been friends for over eight years—three of those years spent with us fucking like we're married. But other than the rules I established to ensure Cole and Delilah would never be together without me, we've never once discussed what we're doing. We're all apparently completely okay with living in our three-way-ignorant-bliss.

Lost in my thoughts, I swing the bathroom door open without knocking and freeze in my spot at the sight in front of me. Cole is standing in the shower, and while there's a shower curtain blocking me from seeing him, it's see-through plastic with yellow ducks all over it—Delilah's choice, not ours. I never noticed just how fucking see-through the curtain is until right now, as I watch Cole, with the water raining down around him and his cock in his hand as he jerks his dick. I shouldn't still be standing here. I'm like a Peeping fucking Tom, but I can't take my eyes off him. We've been together dozens of times the last few years with Delilah, but it's never enough. He's always right there in front of me, in reaching distance, yet untouchable.

It started out as Cole wanting to give her what she needed at the time. She had just found out her cancer was back. She wasn't sure if she was going to live long enough to be sexual with someone, and she wanted to feel something other than fear. When I walked into the barn and saw them about to have sex, I had a choice to make in that moment: beg them not to do it in fear of everything changing, or join them. Knowing Cole would do anything for Delilah—hell, we both would—I joined them. I knew I had feelings for Cole. I've had them for years. But up until that moment, when I watched him push his cock into her pussy, I didn't realize just how strongly I felt for him.

"Xander?" The baritone voice brings me back to the present, and I realize I'm still standing here in the fucking bathroom while Cole's in the shower. "Everything okay?" he chokes out, and when I look down I see his dick is still hard in his hand. He follows my gaze then quickly releases his cock. It bobs up and down, and I wonder how it would feel if I dropped to my knees and took him in my mouth. How he would taste. Would his cock swell at the feel of my mouth wrapped around his hard shaft?

"Yeah." I clear my throat. "I didn't realize you were in here. I saw you go into your room." My eyes go back down to his still hard length, and before I think about the consequences that could come from my words, I ask him, "Can I watch you?"

Cole's eyes widen and dart back down to his dick. He doesn't say anything for a long moment, and I'm almost positive he's either going to shrink back and cover himself or freak the fuck out on me. I mean, I pretty much just admitted I want him. But he doesn't do either one. Instead, his eyes meet mine as his hand reaches down to his dick. He grips it tight and starts to stroke it. My dick twitches at the sight, and my mouth waters at the thought of my mouth replacing his hand. But I keep control of myself. I'm in shock he's even stroking himself in front of me. There's no way he's going to let me wrap my lips around him and suck him dry.

As I watch him, I close the door behind me. I don't walk all the way into the bathroom, though, not wanting to spook him. Instead, I lean against the door and silently watch. The shower water continues to rain down over him, and I follow the droplets of water as they run down his face, over his muscular chest and down his abs, leading straight to his dick. My eyes follow the way his hand pulls at his shaft, and with slow and steady pumps, he fucks his fist. I imagine that his dick is moving in my ass. Would it feel good? Would it hurt? The first time we took Delilah's ass, even with it lubed up, she complained of it hurting. But after a few times, she started to really enjoy it. Hell, now she practically begs for it.

A moan releases from Cole's lips, and my gaze drags up to his face. His head is tilted back, and his eyes are squeezed shut. A few seconds later, he groans out, "Fuck, I'm coming," and I'd like to think he just said those words out loud for me. My eyes drop back down to his dick just in time to watch him come all over his fingers, the cum dripping off his hand as the water washes it away. He releases his dick, which is still semi-hard, and looks at me almost shyly. The moment is broken, and I pray to whatever God that's up there that I didn't just push my best friend away.

Before he can say a word, my hand reaches behind me and turns the knob, and with my eyes locked with his, I back out of the bathroom and close the door behind me.

"Hey," Delilah calls from behind me, and I practically jump out of my skin. I turn around to face her but can't look her in the eye. "Is Cole in the shower?"

"Um...yeah, I had to take a piss." I shrug.

Delilah's head tilts slightly to the side, not too much but enough to know she's contemplating whether she believes me. Then she walks up to me and, standing on her tiptoes, whispers into my ear, "If you never tell him how you feel, you'll never know if he feels the same way." Then she kisses me on my cheek, pats my chest gently, and walks away, leaving me standing in the hallway, fucking speechless.

CHAPTER SIXTEEN

Cole

"OKAY! I HAVE EVERYTHING WE NEED." I LOOK TO MY LEFT AND SEE DELILAH standing next to me, her hands full of junk food. "I got us two hot dogs." She attempts to hand me one, and I snag it before it hits the floor. "A bucket of popcorn." She juggles it with one hand, popcorn pieces falling to the ground, so I grab it as well. "Thanks." She grins. "Here's a soda for us to split." She hands me the drink. "And last but not least..." She pulls several bags of candy out of her back pocket while still holding her hotdog in one hand. "I got us M&Ms, KitKats, and Twix!" Her eyebrows waggle up and down, her grin getting wider.

"No cotton candy?" I deadpan, and she frowns. "I'm kidding! I think you got enough shit to last us ten games. It's only a forty minute game."

Delilah gives me a side-eye. "Yeah, sorry, buddy, that lie no longer works on me." She sticks her tongue out, and I chuckle, remembering the first game of Xander's we attended. We were still in middle school, and it was his first year of high school. Delilah asked how long the game was, and I told her the truth...thirty-two minutes. Two hours later, she was starving, had to go pee, and was as restless as a toddler on a sugar high. So, I might've forgotten to mention that a minute in sports is more like ten...sue me.

Delilah sits down and gets situated. A few minutes later the music starts up and the teams are announced, each player running out onto the court when his name is called. When the announcer yells, "Xander Thompson," the gym goes crazy. Women are screaming his name extra loud, the cheerleaders are cheering for him with extra pep, hell, even the guys are clapping harder for him. It makes sense since this is the final game of the season. The winners of this game will be named conference champions. And if Xander makes the decision to enter the NBA draft, the game tonight will be the last one he ever plays in college, and who the fuck knows where he'll end up.

My thoughts go back to yesterday with me in the shower and Xander asking if he could watch me jerk off. When I saw him standing in the bathroom looking at me, my first thought was that he needed to take a leak and walked in without realizing I was in the shower, but as I observed him standing there, a weird feeling came over me, like he wasn't just looking at me but instead assessing me. And when he asked if he could watch me finish, I didn't know how to handle it. Plenty of times when we've been together with Delilah, Xander has grabbed my dick to guide it into her. He's even stroked it a few times to make sure it's hard, but I never thought anything of it, but now...now I'm questioning everything, and I have no fucking clue what to think. I thought my feelings for him were safe because they were one-sided, but knowing Xander might feel the same way...*Fuck!*

"You okay?" Delilah asks, shaking me out of my thoughts. I nod but keep quiet. I've never lied to Delilah or Xander, but it feels like even simply nodding my head is a lie. The truth is I don't know how I feel. When I was jerking off and Xander was watching, I felt turned on. But when it was over, I almost felt...dirty, like what I did was wrong. Then when Xander walked out of the bathroom without saying a word, I felt guilty as fuck. For what? I have no clue. For not talking to him about it, maybe, or for doing it with only him in the bathroom when we all promised it was all of us or none of us, I don't know. I have no fucking clue what to think or feel.

But now as I watch him play his last game, I'm suddenly feeling nervous...scared even. What if he does decide to enter the draft? I need to talk to him, ask him what all that meant. Was it curiosity? Is he gay? Bi? He's clearly turned on when we're all together, but is it for Delilah or me? Aside from being with Delilah, he's never been with anyone else...but at the same time, neither have I. What started as a way to comfort Delilah has turned into something else... something more...something we never talk about. We just pretend like it's perfectly normal for the three of us to be friends by day and fuck buddies by night.

"Are you sure, Cole?" Delilah pushes. "You're awfully quiet."

"Yeah, where are your parents?" I look over at the empty seats next to her.

"They're on their way. My mom texted that there's an accident, so they will be a few minutes late."

"Okay." I nod.

"Cole," Delilah says, "I know something is on your mind. What's going on?"

"Do you ever wonder where we're going?" I blurt out.

"Going where?" she asks, confused. "To the club tonight?"

"No." I shake my head. "Do you ever wonder where the three of us are going with this relationship? I mean, what were we thinking? When do we end? When one of us meets someone else? What if the guy you meet isn't okay with the fact that you slept with your two best friends? Xander is going to be joining the NBA. There's no way this can all continue." I hear my voice rising and see the people around us glancing at me, so I lower my voice. "You're my best friend, Delilah," I whisper. "You and Xander...you guys are fucking *everything*. What if us all being together is what destroys our friendship?" I don't voice the concern niggling in the back of my mind as I recall Xander standing in the bathroom. *What if it already has?*

Delilah opens and closes her mouth several times like she's trying to form her thoughts into words, but nothing ever comes out, words aren't spoken, and just like we've all done for the last three years, we go back to pretending like everything is completely normal, sweeping it all under that proverbial rug. But you know what the problem is when you keep sweeping that dirt under the rug? Eventually, someone's bound to trip over that shit and fall flat on their face.

CHAPTER SEVENTEEN

Delilah

ONCE WHEN I WAS TEN, MY PARENTS AND I WENT TO CALIFORNIA ON vacation. We were hanging out in the hotel room, watching television and eating dinner that my parents ordered from room service, when out of nowhere the ground began to quake beneath us. The pictures on the walls shook and anything that wasn't tied down fell to the ground and broke. It happened so quickly we didn't even see it coming, and it was over before we could even comprehend what was happening. I was young, but I can remember looking around and wondering how something that only lasted a few short moments could bring such destruction to everything it touched. Luckily, it wasn't a huge earthquake, and we were all okay.

Now, as I sit here, in the living room of my condo, it's like experiencing that earthquake all over again. The only difference is, while the one in California silently destroyed physical property, the one I'm experiencing right now is not only silent, but to the visible eye, one wouldn't even know it's occurring. But I know it is. And I'm terrified how it's going to rate on the Richter scale. It may not appear bad, but I have a horrible feeling that lives are about to be destroyed, and as much as I would love to be able to blame mother nature, I am the only one to blame. I did this. I came in quietly, and before Xander or Cole even knew what was happening, I destroyed everything in our wake. But instead of dealing with the destruction, they chose to ignore it. They chose to love me and put me first. I'm selfish, and I don't deserve either of them, which is why I'm going to fix this. I'm going to clean up the mess I've created, and I'm going to earn their love.

"If you want to go out, you should go," Cole says as he grabs a beer from the fridge and sits down next to me. "Xander is going to be late. With them winning the championship, he's going to be giving interviews for a while."

"I know. I just don't feel like going out." I sit back on the couch and tuck my legs under me.

"Are you feeling sick?" Cole starts checking me out like he always does any time I mention I don't feel well. He's so afraid of the cancer coming back that at the first sign of any illness he freaks out.

"Calm down. I said I don't feel like going out, not that I don't feel good." I see Cole visibly sigh in relief. "Want to watch a movie?"

"Sure." He walks over to the entertainment center and holds up a couple of movies we recently purchased. I pick the romantic comedy, and Cole groans but puts it into the DVD player. He sits back down, and we watch the movie in silence. When it finishes, I have him put in another one. *Xander needs to get here soon...*

I couldn't even tell you what happened in the first movie

or what's going on in this one. I'm way too nervous. I came up with a plan to make everything right, and at the time I thought it was pure genius, but now that it's time to execute said plan, I'm not so sure anymore.

Just as I'm considering chickening out, the front door swings open and in walks Xander. He's dressed in his suit that he has to wear to and from all their games. He nods to both of us and starts to walk past us, down the hall, which is odd. Before he makes it too far, I call out his name. "Come and watch the movie with us."

He stops in his place, and since I'm paying close attention, I see his eyes dart to Cole before he looks at me. I can tell he's going to say no, so I add, "It just started. You haven't missed anything. Please."

Not able to say no to me, he says he's going to get changed and will be right back. While he's gone, I move to the middle of the couch so Xander will have to sit on the other side of me. A few minutes later, Xander comes back out, now in his basketball shorts and a cotton tee. He sits next to me, and it doesn't go unnoticed that he and Cole haven't said a single word to each other. Once Xander gets comfortable, I fake a yawn and lie down across the couch with my head in Xander's lap and my feet in Cole's. Xander's hand comes down and rubs the heel of his palm up and down my arm while Cole rests his hands over my ankles. After a few minutes of neither of them making a move to do anything, I realize I'm going to need to take control.

Rolling over onto my back, my breasts move to where my arm was, and Xander's hand rubs up against my nipples since I'm not wearing a bra. I let out a moan to make my interest known, and Xander looks down at me, one brow quirking up (Okay, my moan might have been a bit dramatic, but c'mon!). I push my chest out slightly and give him a grin that makes it clear I want him to touch me. Thankfully, he gets the hint this time. Using his fingers, he trails a line across my breasts and stops at my now erect nipple, tweaking it slightly. I let out another, more believable, moan, and it gets Cole's attention. His head turns from watching the movie and his gaze lands on Xander...not me, but Xander. It's only for a quick second, but I saw it. Immediately, his attention goes to me, and without me having to say a word, his palms run up my thighs to my shorts.

Cole edges closer and, without wasting any time, pushes my shorts and panties down my legs, while Xander helps me pull my top off. Cole spreads my legs enough so that he can stick his fingers into me. I'm not yet wet, so he spreads my legs further, moving down onto the floor and positioning himself between them. He spreads my lips and starts licking me. I look up at Xander and catch him watching Cole. When he sees me, he bends his head down, grips the back of my head and pulls me into a searing kiss. It's the roughest he's ever been with me, and it screams desperation. His teeth clack against mine, but he doesn't care. His palm massages my breast almost to the point of pain, and I let him. I don't know what's going on with Xander, but it's almost as if he's using my body as an outlet to take his aggression out on.

With Xander's mouth never leaving mine, I feel Cole spread my thighs wider, his fingers delving into my pussy and his tongue flicking at my clit repeatedly. We've all done this dance so many times, they can get me off in record time. I feel my orgasm approaching, and I can't help but buck my hips against Cole's mouth, his light stubble scratching against my pussy and causing friction. He holds my thighs in place, and when the flat of his tongue presses against my clit, I lose the last of my control. My moans are muffled by Xander's mouth, and only once I've finally come down from my orgasm do either of them stop touching me.

Before they can say a word, I jump up from the couch. "I want to suck you both," I demand, dropping to my knees. They both obey by pushing their pants and boxers down. Their dicks are hard but not hard enough for what I have in mind. Taking both of their dicks in my hands, I lift Xander's shaft and lick up the underside of his thick, long length before taking it completely into my mouth. Then I do the same thing to Cole. I lick, kiss, and suck their dicks, switching back and forth between the two of them several times until they're both hard as steel.

"Take your shirts off," I instruct, and they both obey as I continue to suck them off. I sneak a glance up and see Xander staring at Cole, and I know in this moment I'm right about what I'm thinking, because shining bright in Xander's eyes isn't just love for a friend—it's lust. I stop sucking him, and he looks down at me, and I swear I almost see a flicker of guilt...or maybe fear.

"Come here," I command softly. His eyes widen, but he does as I say, kneeling next to me. Turning back to Cole, he's standing there, frozen in place. I stroke Cole a few more times before I make my move. Taking the back of Xander's head, I guide him over to Cole's dick. I glance up again at Cole, and when he doesn't say anything, I press my fingers against the back of Xander's neck. His eyes flicker up to Cole's face, but Cole stays silent. I hold my breath, waiting to see if Xander will follow through, and then he does. His lips part, and he takes Cole's dick into his mouth. He stops about an inch in and sucks on the crown before opening his lips more and swallowing Cole's entire length. I can see it when the tip of Cole's dick hits the back of Xander's throat because his Adam's apple bobs slightly.

Then Cole lets out a shaky groan that spurs Xander on. His hand comes up to Cole's scrotum, and he massages his sac while he sucks Cole's dick. All too soon, Cole is warning Xander that he's coming, but Xander doesn't care. If anything, the warning has him sucking harder and faster. Cole's hips buck a couple times, then he completely stills, as Xander takes every drop of cum Cole gives him.

When Cole's dick begins to visibly soften, Xander removes his mouth from around him and backs up slightly. I'm about to say something, address what just happened, but before I can, Cole curses under his breath and says, "That shouldn't have fucking happened." Then he stalks out of the living room and into his bedroom, slamming the door behind him and leaving Xander and me alone.

"Xander," I begin to say, but he stops me.

"Don't. You shouldn't have done that, Delilah." Xander stands, grabbing his boxers and pants and pulling them on, with his back to me. It's not often Xander calls me by my first name, so I know he's really upset.

"I just thought that if I gave you guys a nudge..."

Xander's head whips around to face me. "We're not rabbits, Delilah! You can't stick us in a cage together and force us to mate."

"That's not what I was doing." I shake my head back and forth.

"Fuck!" Xander punches his fist into the wall, and the drywall crumbles. "I need to get out of here." And without another word, Xander grabs his keys and is out the door.

In this moment, a feeling of dread washes over me. What if I just made the worst decision in our relationship? My nudge to get them together could do more damage than any earthquake ever could. What if I just doomed what the three of us have shared for so long? No, I refuse to believe that. I'm going to fix this. The guys will both calm down, we'll sit down and talk, and we'll figure it all out. Everything is going to be okay.

CHAPTER EIGHTEEN

Xander

"PLEASE DON'T DO THIS," DELILAH PLEADS AGAIN, BUT IT'S POINTLESS because it's already been done and there's no going back. And even if I could somehow get out of it, I wouldn't want to. This past month has shown me that I've made the best decision for the three of us. Does it hurt like a bitch? Hell yeah, it does. I'm about to leave the only true family I've ever known. But it needed to be done. After the way things went down between Cole and me the last time the three of us were together, I need to get away. I can't be around someone I'm in love with, only to watch him love somebody else. People look at me and see a six-foot-four, one hundred eighty-five pound basketball player who can deadlift four hundred pounds. They praise my strength and agility on the court, but what they don't realize is that even strong men can be weak, and Cole Andrews is my weakness. I believe in my heart that somewhere deep within him, there's a possibility he feels even a fraction of what I feel, but because he's so bent on making his mom proud, he'll never allow himself to come to terms with his feelings.

"Delilah, we've been through this a dozen times in the last month. It's already done." I tape up the last box of my items and carry it out of my room and to the front door. Taking my keys in my hand, I glance around the condo one last time. I've only lived here for less than a year, but during that time it felt more like a home than anywhere else I've ever lived. My eyes linger on the hallway leading to Cole's room, a small part of me wishing he would come out and tell me not to go, not that it would make a difference. The commitment has already been made.

"I know, but I mean...maybe you could tell them you made a mistake and want to finish college." My eyes leave the hallway and land on Delilah. Her chocolate brown hair is up in a messy bun, her caramel colored eyes are red from crying, and her cheeks are stained pink from the tears that have fallen. I hate that my leaving is why she's so sad, but she had to know when she made the decision to push Cole and me together, there would be some kind of fall out.

"But I didn't make a mistake. I signed a four year contract with the Houston Armadillos."

Tears well up in her eyes, and I open my arms for her to give me a hug. She rushes to me, her body crashing into mine, and she lets out a loud sob that nearly shatters my heart. "I-I'm so sorry, Xander. I'm so, so sorry. Please forgive me." Delilah's tiny arms wrap around my waist, and she hugs me like she's afraid if she lets go, I'll disappear.

"Shh...it's okay. There's nothing to forgive, sweet girl. Your heart was in the right place. Unfortunately, Cole's heart isn't mine for the taking." I pull back slightly so I can look her in the eyes. "I'm always going to be here for you, and I'm only four hours away."

"I know," she cries, fresh tears falling. I wipe them away

with my thumb, but they keep coming.

"I need you to promise me two things."

"Anything," she says through her sobs.

"First, I need you to promise me that you won't say a word to Cole about me: not about what happened the last time we were together, or about how I feel towards him. You can't push him to feel something he either doesn't feel or doesn't want to feel."

"What?" She shakes her head. "No. Please, Xander. We're going to work this out. Cole just needs time."

"No, we're not. Even if Cole reciprocates my feelings for him, he will never act on them."

"Why? I don't get it."

"His mom had a heart-to-heart with him before she died. She made him promise all this shit. About following his dreams and getting married, and none of it involved him falling for his male best friend."

"Oh, Xander." Delilah hugs me again. "We can talk to him together."

"Delilah, no. Promise me."

"I hate this," she cries into my chest.

"I know, but it's the way it needs to be."

"Okay," she agrees. "I don't like it, but I promise." She lifts her face and wipes her tears.

"Thank you." I give her a kiss on her forehead.

"I'm afraid to ask, but what's the second thing?"

"I need you to promise me you'll forget about our pact: all of us or none of us."

"Xander, stop, this is crazy. There's no us without you."

"There is now. Not that you need it, but I'm giving you my blessing."

"Blessing for what?"

"For you and Cole to be together. He loves you, and

you love him. The two of you can be happy together. Now promise."

"Damn it, Xander!" Delilah bites down on her bottom lip as fresh tears race downwards. "Okay, I promise."

After giving her one last hug, I remove the condo key from the ring and hold it out for her. "No, I'm not taking it. This will always be your home. Keep it in case of an emergency, or if you change your mind. I'm not taking it."

Not wanting to upset her any further, I agree. Then I take one last look down the hall, and picking up my final box, I head downstairs to the new car I purchased with my signing bonus—leaving my heart behind as I walk away. I never imagined that the pain from my heart being shattered could bury itself so deep into my soul that it would feel as if I can't even catch my breath—especially over someone I never truly had to begin with. I remind myself that Cole would never be okay with being with me in the way I want to be with him. And I would never be able to settle for less than all of him.

PART TWO

CHAPTER NINETEEN

Cole

TWO YEARS LATER

I'M HOME!" THE DOOR SLAMS CLOSED, AND DELILAH COMES RUNNING TOWARDS me, her smile almost bright enough to light up the darkness I feel perpetually stuck in. She jumps onto the couch and her arms go around my neck, pulling me toward her for a kiss. Her lips crash against mine, and I close my eyes, enjoying the feeling of getting lost in her: in her touch, in her smell, in her beautiful heart.

When she pulls back, she notices the channel the television is turned to, and her smile morphs into a sadder version, but she doesn't say a word. She never does. Since the day Xander walked out the door and out of our life, Delilah has never once said a single word about any of it. Not about Xander sucking my dick. Not about the tension so thick, it about choked the three of us. Not a damn word.

"Who's winning?" she asks, instead. Her way of bringing him up without actually doing so.

"Houston." I grab the controller and turn the TV off. "They're playing incredible. They definitely have a good shot at winning the championship a second year in a row." And by '*they*' we both know I'm referring to Xander. In the two years he's been playing for Houston, he's blown the fuck up, breaking rookie records left and right. It doesn't surprise me, though. He's always been an amazing athlete. "Now tell me...how did your interviews go?"

Delilah's genuine smile returns. "I interviewed at three different schools, but my favorite was Worthshire Elementary. It's actually where I ran into Summer. She was interviewing there as well." Before Delilah left earlier for her interviews, she'd said she would be home for dinner, but then she called and said she ran into her friend, and they were going to grab a cup of coffee.

"Worthshire? Isn't that the elementary school down the street?" I remember seeing the name listed under the schools that are hiring in the area.

"It is...and guess what? I got the job there! Actually, Summer and I both did! The principal called us both while we were having coffee, which is why I'm home so late. We ended up trading in our coffees for martinis to celebrate. We'll both be teaching fourth grade!"

"That's awesome! Congratulations! So, does that mean we're staying here?" We always said after graduation we would go back home to get jobs, but then we graduated almost a month ago and neither of us, so far, has made any decisions. The truth is, while I would go back to Brenton for Delilah, it's not my home. My home has always felt like it was here, in this condo, with my two best friends. Even now that one of them is gone.

"We are. I spoke to my parents and told them I would like to buy this place from them. They laughed at me and said they would allow no such thing…and then they insisted that they would be gifting it to me as a graduation present. We're staying here, Cole."

I feel my shoulders sigh in relief. "Thank you."

"Of course…this is our home." Her words come out soft, and I thank god for giving me this woman. "Now you just need to find a job and we're set."

"I'll look later, but right now, I'd really just like to make love to my beautiful, amazing, newly employed, girlfriend."

Delilah giggles. "That sounds good to me." Her arms snake back around my neck, and I pick her up, her legs wrapping around my torso so I can carry her into our bedroom. I lay her down on the bed and take a second to admire just how fucking beautiful Delilah is. Her long, silky hair is spread out across her pillow, her brown eyes are wide open and twinkling with happiness. Her cheeks are still a bit flushed from the kiss we shared earlier. She looks alive, and I feel like the luckiest fucker in the world that I get to be a part of her life. That I get to witness every moment with this woman. There was a time when we never thought she would make it past her childhood, but here she is. A college graduate and now an elementary school teacher. She's twenty-two years old and still alive.

I crawl over her, my knees parting her thighs as my hands come down on either side of her head. "I love you, Delilah," I whisper into her ear before I press my mouth to hers, my tongue pushing through her perfect lips. Her hands go to my pants. She undoes them quickly, then tries to push them down with her feet. I break our kiss to help her, and in return, she pulls her dress—the one she wore to her interview—up and over her head, leaving her in only a white-laced bra and panties. I can see her erect nipples on display through the fabric, and I bring my lips down to wrap around one of them. I suck on the hardened bud, and Delilah lets out a needy moan.

"Fuck me, Cole, please," she begs as her hands go to my hair, her fingers running through the strands. I back up slightly, so I can pull her panties down her thighs, then I pull my shirt over my head and bring my hands back down onto the mattress, caging her in. She grips my cock and guides me into her warm pussy. The same pussy I've spent the last year and a half getting lost in. As I pump in and out of her, my thoughts go back to the first time we had sex, just the two of us. I try to push them away and focus on Delilah, but I can't. Once the memories surface, there's no pushing them away.

"You've got to get your shit together, Cole!" Delilah yells at me as she turns the television off and throws the controller onto the table, knocking over several empty beer bottles. "You have finals to study for, and you can't afford to fail them. You're barely going to pass this semester as it is." When I don't say anything, she climbs on me and straddles my lap. It's not sexual, though. It's just to get my attention. My hands settles on the globes of her ass, and my head falls backward, hitting the back of the couch.

"Look at me, please," she softly demands. I raise my head slightly, enough that our eyes meet. "You can't keep doing this to yourself. If you want him..." she begins to say but stops. She always stops. For the last six months since Xander walked out of the door, effectively ending our eight year friendship, Delilah will begin to discuss him, but then she'll stop. My guess is it's because she knows how badly I'm hurting, but she's never said so.

"He's dating another model." There are two times I see Xander: when he's playing basketball, and when he's seen on TMZ whoring himself around. The times when I see him

playing ball, my heart swells with pride that he's following his dreams. The times I see him with those random women, my heart hurts like a fucking bitch, that he left me—left us—for some cheap pussy, like we meant nothing to him.

"I'm sorry, Cole." I don't know why Delilah is apologizing. She isn't the one who left.

"It doesn't matter." I shrug. "Fuck him."

"Cole..." Delilah hates when I let my anger out about Xander, but I can't help it. How the fuck did the guy go from being my best friend to walking out the door? You know how, you fool... you pushed him away because you couldn't handle the idea of being in love with someone of the same sex.

"You know what I don't get? How he moved on so quickly. He literally went from being with us to fucking all of them." My head nods toward the black television screen.

"Maybe it's not what it looks like," Delilah says, and I let humorless chuckle.

"Really? You're going to defend him?" I lift her off me and drop her onto the couch so I can grab another beer from the fridge. "He left you too, you know. Has he called or texted you?" Delilah's mouth opens like she's going to say something, but then she closes it, not answering. "That's what I thought!" I grab a beer and slam the fridge door closed. I pop the cap off and watch as it hits the tiled floor with a clink before I guzzle down half the bottle.

"Cole, please stop." Delilah grabs the bottle from my hand, and I let her. She slams it down on the counter. "I've had enough of this. I can't live like this anymore." Tears fill her eyes, and I feel like the biggest piece of shit. "I'm still here. I'm still your best friend, and I love you. I know I'm not Xander, and if I could..."

Before she finishes her sentence, I'm picking her up and placing her on the countertop. Without even bothering to remove either of our clothes, I push her panties to the side and push myself inside her. She's barely even wet, but I don't care, and she doesn't say anything. I thrust into her a few times, and she starts loosening up, her natural juices lubricating my cock. We don't kiss. We don't talk. We just fuck. I'm so lost in my anger over Xander, I don't even get her off. Only once I've come, do I finally look at her. She has tears racing down her face, and I curse myself to hell for using the only friend I have left as an escape.

"Delilah, I'm so sorry."

"Don't. It's okay. I'm here, Cole. I'm here for you. Whatever you need." Fuck, this beautiful, selfless woman. She's been through two bouts of cancer, lost one of her breasts, and lost Xander just like I did, yet she's here for me. I vow in this moment to do better by her. For the rest of our life, or until she chooses to move on, I'll be there for her. I'll love her and cherish her and put her first. I'll focus on making sure at least one of us is happy.

"Cole, are you here with me?" Delilah's hands frame my face. I look down and see my cock is soft. I must've come while I was stuck back in the past. Jesus, did she even get off?

"Yeah, sorry."

"It's okay."

"Did you...umm...did you come?" I ask.

"Yeah." She nods. "I did." She smiles softly before she throws her legs over the side of the bed and heads into the bathroom, closing the door behind her.

I swipe my shirt up from the floor and wipe my cock clean, then push my boxers up. Throwing the soiled shirt into the hamper, I lay down in bed and press the power button on the remote. Scrolling through a few channels, I stop when I see Xander's face on the screen. His hair is wet, most likely from his shower, and he's in a suit, talking to the reporters about the game. A female reporter asks him something about a play, and he smirks cockily, his entire face lighting up. My stomach knots, and my heart feels like it's being choked by a barbwire. I did this...I pushed him away. I knew he had feelings for me, and instead of dealing with them, I ran and hid. My thoughts go to my mom and everything she wanted for me. I just couldn't do it. I couldn't break the promises I made to her just before she died.

CHAPTER TWENTY

Cole

I EXIT THE GYMNASIUM AND THROW MY GYM BAG OVER MY SHOULDER. IT'S been a long day and I'm ready to head home. I'm locking up when my phone dings with a text from Delilah asking if I can please bring home some sour cream.

Today was the first day of school for the both of us, as well as basketball practice for me. After an entire summer of scouring the job listings, I wasn't sure if I was going to be able to find a job. Apparently physical education is one of those positions teachers hold onto, and who could blame them? You get to spend your entire day teaching kids how to play sports. While my dream as a child was always to play ball, I knew once I tore my ACL that dream would need to be replaced with a more reachable one. You know how the saying goes, "Those who can't do, teach." So here I am, the new physical education teacher and head basketball coach at Worthshire High School. Since the head coach had to leave suddenly due to a family illness, I was able to take over all of his classes and the basketball team. But because he was tending to his family over the summer, he didn't get the basketball team set up like he should've. Deciding it will be best to start fresh, I had the front office secretary announce that there will be basketball tryouts starting tomorrow. It's short notice but time is limited before the basketball season begins.

After I stop at the store to pick up sour cream, I head home. As I'm pressing the up button for the elevator, my phone rings. I look to see who's calling, and it's Joanne.

"Hey Joanne. How are you?"

"I'm good! How was your first day of work?"

"It was good, but then again I'm teaching sports. How could it be bad?" I laugh.

"True. Well, I was wondering if you could get our girl home the weekend after next. With both of your birthdays coming up, I would love to make you guys dinner."

"That sounds great. How about we head up Saturday morning?"

"Perfect! We'll see you then."

We hang up, and I enter the elevator. "Wait, please!" A woman's voice yells, and I stick my hand out to hold the door. I look up from my phone and see it's Summer, Delilah's friend.

"Thank you!"

"You coming over for dinner?" I ask as the door closes.

"Yep! Delilah and I thought we'd go over some lessons together." She gives me a warm smile.

***

Dinner is done, and I tell the women I'll do the dishes so they can go work on their lessons. Delilah thanks me, and then a minute later, I hear the patio door close. The woman would live out there if she could. Hell, too many nights we've fallen asleep out there. After I'm done with the dishes, I jump in the shower then go over some work stuff: lessons on safety, rules for the different sports, and an activity on endurance. I come up with a good workout for the kids in my weightlifting class and figure out the drills I'm going to run with the kids trying out for the team.

When I'm done, I check to see if Delilah is still working with Summer, and when I see she is, I make my way to the living room, flipping through random channels while going through my various social media accounts on my cell phone. My finger swipes up as I scroll down briefly eyeing post after post. My finger freezes when I see a photo of Xander. His brown hair is trimmed short, and his eyes are shining bright. He's standing on a huge yacht between two gorgeous females with his arms thrown over both of their shoulders. He's shirtless, and both women are in tiny bikinis. But what catches my attention is the tattoo on his chest. It's been two years since I've seen him without his shirt on, and back then he didn't have a single tattoo. Over the years, I've gotten several. Some in memory of my parents, others to symbolize whatever I was feeling at the moment. I even have a pink ribbon to commemorate Delilah beating her breast cancer. But Xander was never into that sort of thing. Sure, he came with me to get them, but he never got one himself. He used to say he couldn't think of anything worth putting on his body forever.

I click on the photo, and using my thumb and forefinger, I zoom in. *What the fuck!* Drawn on his left pec directly over his heart is a tattoo almost identical to the one I have across my chest, but it's different. Where mine is of a ship wheel and anchor, his is of the same anchor, but instead of a ship wheel, he has a pink breast cancer awareness ribbon wrapped around the anchor with a nautical star compass. My mind goes back to the day I got my tattoo.

"Why the ship wheel and anchor?" Xander asks, checking out the finished tattoo in the center of my chest.

"When I was little, every year my parents and I would take a trip to the Florida Keys. My dad would rent a boat, and we would go out in the ocean every day. While on the trip one year, a fisherman had a similar tattoo. When I asked him what it meant, he told me the wheel symbolized the journey, and the anchor symbolized stability. I guess it just always stuck with me."

"So something to symbolize your yearly trips with your parents," He says, approvingly. "That's cool, man."

While he's right that the tattoo definitely symbolizes my family's yearly trips, the part I don't tell him is that for me, the meaning runs deeper than what the fisherman said. When I lost my parents and grandma, I was scared as fuck. It felt like my ship had gone adrift—stuck in a storm with water coming in over the edges and attempting to take me under. But the moment I met Xander and Delilah, they became my compass. It was as if they guided me out of that storm and into safer waters. And once I was back to where I needed to be, they then became my anchor, keeping me grounded and safe. And I know that no matter how rough and choppy those seas become in the future, we will always face them together.

Why I didn't tell him the entire meaning I'm not sure, but looking back I wonder if maybe it was because even back then I felt something for Xander. Something more. And I was terrified over those feelings.

"Is that Xander?" I jump at Delilah's voice over my shoulder, my phone slipping from my hand and falling to the tiled floor. I pick it up and check it out, thankful it didn't shatter.

"Yeah," I choke out. "It was on his fan page."

"That's a beautiful tattoo," is all she says before she heads down the hall.

"Where's Summer?" I call out.

"She left a few minutes ago. You didn't notice because your eyes were glued to your phone."

"JOANNE, AS ALWAYS DINNER WAS DELICIOUS."

"Thank you, Cole." Joanne stands and picks up a couple dirty dishes. "After we're done cleaning up, we'll do cake."

"Did you make the all-white cake with vanilla frosting?" Delilah asks as if her mom would make anything other than her only child's favorite cake for her birthday.

"You'll just have to wait and find out." Joanne shoots a wink at me and grins.

Despite Joanne's protests, we all help with the dishes, and once everything is cleaned up, her parents insist on singing Happy Birthday before we enjoy some cake.

"Delilah, sweetheart, Dr. Morton called and mentioned you haven't been in for your yearly checkup yet," Joanne mentions, taking a bite of her cake.

"Oh, um..." Delilah glances from her mom to me, nervously. "Yeah, I've just been busy with starting my new job, but I'll make it soon. Promise." Something sounds off with her tone. I can't quite put my finger on it, but something isn't right.

"Hey." I reach around her and pull her chair close to me. "You know everything is going to be okay."

"Yeah, I know. We go through this every year." She smiles but it looks forced. "I've just been busy. I promise I'll make the appointment this week." She leans over and gives me a chaste kiss. "Now, you have to taste this delicious cake." I open my mouth, and she feeds me a bite.

Once we're done eating, we all move to the living room for presents. It doesn't matter how old Delilah gets, her parents buy her birthday presents every year. One year she jokingly asked if this will continue until she's eighty, and her mom said, "If it means you're still alive at eighty, then damn right."

"I'll be right back," Delilah says. "I just need to use the restroom." She heads down the hall, and I follow her, concerned about her behavior. Knowing the skeleton key is kept over the door frame, I reach up and grab it, then unlock the door. When I open the door, Delilah is standing against the sink with her head hanging down, and a bottle of Advil on the counter.

"You okay?" I ask, and she jumps.

"Jesus, Cole! You scared me."

"You're scaring me."

"I'm fine. I just have a bad headache." She holds the bottle up. "It's just pain reliever." She opens the medicine cabinet and places the bottle on the shelf.

"Okay, but please remember to schedule your checkup with Dr. Morton," I insist, and she rolls her eyes.

"Yes, *Dad*."

CHAPTER TWENTY-ONE

Delilah

I'M KNEELING ON THE COLD TILE FLOOR, MY FACE PERCHED OVER THE TOILET as I throw up everything I just ate for breakfast. Something is wrong. The only time I've ever felt this sick was during my chemo treatments, and now I've thrown up several days in a row. I wait a another minute just to make sure I'm not going to throw up again before I stand, wash my face, and brush my teeth. I glance back at the clock in the room and see it's already almost eight o'clock. If I don't leave soon I'm going to be late for work. Luckily, Cole leaves earlier than I do, so he hasn't been here to see me throwing up, because if he had, he would be dragging me to the doctor immediately.

I throw on a skirt and blouse and finish the outfit with a pair of flats. On my way in, I call Dr. Morton to schedule my appointment. I should've scheduled it back in September when my mom reminded me, but I kept putting it off. Now, I'm over a month late scheduling it. I've never thrown up just from having cancer, but I'm not taking any chances. The receptionist schedules me for next week, and

I do my best to push my nervousness away. I have a class of nine-year-olds to teach.

I'M NOT EVEN AN HOUR INTO OUR MORNING, AND I'M RUNNING TO THE bathroom to throw up. Every day I throw up it gets worse, lasting longer than the previous day. I don't know what's going on, but this can't be good. Thankfully, I have a teacher's assistant who is able to take over for me when the principal suggests I take the day off in case it's a bug of some sort. I don't bother telling him a bug wouldn't last this long. Instead, I go home and spend the rest of the day watching TV and ignoring the uneasiness I'm feeling in my gut.

By the afternoon, like the last several days, I'm feeling fine. It's as if I'm not even sick. Not only do I feel okay, but I'm energetic and in the mood to cook. I pick up some groceries, and when Cole gets home, dinner is waiting for us to eat together.

"Damn, babe, I can't remember the last time you cooked," he jokes after clearing his entire plate.

"Very funny." I laugh.

"Why don't I do the dishes and you go take a bath?" he offers, and because a bath sounds perfect, I agree.

"Maybe after you're done, you can join me." I shoot him a flirtatious wink and crack up laughing when he jumps up from his seat to rush the dishes over to the sink.

I fill the tub with hot water and bubbles, then undress completely. I sink down into the warm bath and press play on my playlist, and Sam Hunt's voice croons over the portable speaker. Laying my head back against the plush bath pillow, I close my eyes and enjoy the peacefulness.

I'm not sure how long my eyes are closed, but when I

feel Cole's hands massaging my breasts, I slowly open them. He's naked and leaning over the tub. His mouth goes to my taut nipple and he sucks...hard.

"Ow," I screech, and Cole's mouth leaves my breast.

"Did I hurt you?"

"No, sorry." I shake my head. "I just wasn't expecting it." Ever since my breast augmentation, it takes a lot for me to feel any sensation, so the fact that Cole sucking on my nipple actually hurt me is shocking to me.

"Delilah, have you been to the doctor yet to get your yearly checkup?" Cole asks.

"I've made the appointment. I'm fine. My nipple was just a little sensitive. Now will you please get in this tub with me?" I sit forward, and Cole drops down behind me. His large body wrapping itself around my tiny one. He squirts some body wash onto my loofah and begins soaping up my shoulders and neck, working his way down my arms.

"How was basketball practice?" I ask as he lifts my arms and gently runs the loofah over my breasts and down my belly.

"It was good. I think I have a really good team. The kids are excited for the season to be starting in a few weeks. Oh! And get this, I got them into a really cool camp over winter break. It's run by the NBA. An entire week of them getting to learn from the professionals."

"Wow, that's awesome. Is it local?"

"Unfortunately, it's in Oklahoma, so I'll be gone for a week." Cole trails the loofah lower, spreads my legs, then rubs it up and down my sex.

"Maybe I'll use that week to visit my parents. Mom has been bugging me to visit more."

"Sounds good, babe." Cole reaches around me, and his fingers land on my clit. His lips trail kisses down the side of my neck. Then his fingers enter me, and my head goes back against his chest. He expertly works my pussy and clit over, and less than a minute later, I'm moaning out my orgasm.

"Damn, you came fast," Cole murmurs before pressing a soft kiss against my earlobe.

I might've just came, but I'm still horny as hell. "I need you inside me."

"Gladly."

Cole releases the water from the tub and stands, taking my hand to help me up. Grabbing a towel, he wraps me up, and we step out of the tub. As I'm bending over to wipe the bubbles off my skin, I notice Cole's massive erection. Dropping my towel to the floor, I kneel down on it and take his dick into my mouth, eliciting an appreciative groan from Cole. I suck him for a few minutes, until I can't take it anymore and need him to be inside of me. Not wanting to waste any time, I release his dick from my mouth and turn around. Using the edge of the tub to hold onto, I spread my legs and jut my ass out, then I tilt my head back slightly and say, "I need you to fuck me, now."

Cole smirks and nods, and gripping my hips, he guides his hard cock into my pussy.

CHAPTER TWENTY-TWO

Cole

DELILAH AND I HAVE A HEALTHY SEX LIFE. I WOULD SAY WE HAVE SEX AT least three to four times a week easily. I don't know how it is with other couples, but with us it's always amazing. Maybe it's because we were friends first...I'm not sure. However, in all the times I've gotten Delilah off, I've never seen her come as fast as she did in the tub.

And then the way she sucked my dick before she turned around right there in the bathroom and demanded I fuck her...*Jesus!* Gripping her sides, I push into her, and fuck if she isn't soaking wet.

"Damn, woman, you're dripping."

She doesn't say anything, just pushes her ass into me and moans. I pick up my speed, thrusting in and out of her, and I can feel her tight cunt clenching, but then she moves forward, and my dick slides out of her, immediately missing her warmth.

"Can you fuck my ass?" she asks, but it comes out like a plea, and I freeze in place. Delilah hasn't asked for anal since…I shake myself out of those thoughts. Wordlessly, I reach into the drawer where I know the baby oil is kept, and popping the top open, I drip some down her ass crack. Before I stick my dick in her, I want to make sure she's ready, so I start with my fingers. Pushing one into her asshole, I fingerfuck her until she's writhing in pleasure, then I add another.

"Yes, please, Cole. Fuck my ass," she begs. I can see she has one hand holding onto the tub and the other is massaging her clit. Using my hand that has the baby oil on it, I stroke my dick a few times to get it lubed up. Then spreading her cheeks apart, I shove my dick into her puckered hole. Delilah lets out a groan, and my dick twitches inside of her. I forgot how tight it feels inside her ass. Every time I enter her, it's like she's choking the fuck out of me. She hasn't been taken this way since we were with Xander, and even then it was mostly Xander who would fuck her in the ass. He would always joke he was an ass man.

Trying to get Xander out of my head, I focus on fucking Delilah. I pull out until just the tip of my dick is inside her, then just as slowly I push back in. I watch as my dick enters her, then leaves her. When she lets out another moan I wonder what it would feel like to be fucked in the ass. I've always been on the giving end of sex. What if I was the one being fucked? My thoughts go to Xander. He loved to fuck Delilah's ass. Would he love to fuck mine? Memories of the one and only time he went down on his knees and sucked me off, surface. I'd never come so hard in my life knowing it was his mouth wrapped around my dick. The way he took me all the way in. Would he let me fuck him? Would he take my entire dick in his ass like he did in his mouth? My eyes close as I lose myself to the fantasy of fucking Xander, and before I know it, I'm coming so fucking hard, my legs are shaking.

And before I can stop the words from leaving my lips, I moan out, "Fuuuuck, Xander." My body stills at what I just said...what I just did. Holy shit, I just visualized fucking Xander then called out his name. I pray I said his name in my fantasy, that I didn't say it out loud, but when Delilah moves forward, my softening dick falling out of her, and turns around without saying a word, I know she heard me.

CHAPTER TWENTY-THREE

Delilah

WHEN COLE CAME INSIDE ME WHILE CALLING OUT XANDER'S NAME I KNEW what I needed to do. There was just no coming back from that. The last two years I have watched Cole love Xander from afar. I knew I didn't have his entire heart, but I was okay with that because I love Xander too. I miss him and think about him every single day. The difference is, though, if Cole wasn't so hellbent on making good on whatever promise he made to his mom, if he actually was honest with himself, he would choose Xander over me, and that's just not something I can spend my life being okay with. Not for my sake, and not for Cole's.

Needing to clean up, I take a quick shower, and when I get out, Cole's no longer in the bathroom. I get dressed, then go in search for him. My heart is pounding, and my palms are sweaty. This is the last thing I want to do, but I know it's what needs to be done. I find Cole sitting in the living room. It's dark with only the overheard lighting shining from under the microwave. His head is down, and

I know he hates himself for what happened.

"We need to talk," I say, sitting on the coffee table across from him. He raises his head, and I see the regret and guilt in his eyes. "I know it's not my place to discuss you and Xander..." I begin to say, but Cole cuts me off.

"There is no me and Xander."

"Cole..." I take a deep breath. "I can't do this anymore." I take his hands in mine. "I love you, and I love Xander, but when he walked out the door that day, he left a gaping hole in your heart. I saw you in pain, and I just wanted to make it better. The way you've always made me feel better. But I was wrong for what I did. I stuck a giant band-aid over your heart and allowed you to act like there was no wound there." I cover his heart with my palm. "I can't be your band-aid anymore."

Cole tugs my hands toward him and pulls me onto his lap. "Don't do this, Delilah, please. You know I love you." His head falls against my chest.

"I know you do, but I'll never have your whole heart, and I thought I was okay with that, but I'm not." I don't bother to mention that we both know Xander has it. "Before Xander left, I made a big mistake by pushing you guys together." I stop speaking for a second, knowing I'm about to break my promise to Xander, but also knowing I have to. "All these years I was so incredibly selfish."

"What? How?" Cole asks, his head lifting slightly so he can meet my eyes.

"Some women aren't lucky enough to find one man who loves her unconditionally, but I found two. The problem was I held onto your hearts knowing they belonged to someone else, and for that I'm sorry." I dip my head down and kiss Cole's forehead.

"Delilah...I can't..." he shakes his head.

"I know, Cole, but I can't be the reason why you *can't* any longer."

"So, this is it? We're over. Xander left, and now we're ending?"

"We will always be friends," I promise him. "Always. But yes, we're ending." Tears prick my eyes, and I have to close them so they don't spill over. I need to be strong.

Cole wraps his arms around me and holds me close. "I'm so sorry, Delilah. I love you," he says, his face now nuzzling into the crook of my neck. "I'm sorry it wasn't enough."

Me too, Cole...me too...

CHAPTER TWENTY-FOUR

Delilah

PREGNANT. OH MY GOD. I'M PREGNANT. I WOULD NEVER HAVE BELIEVED IT IF my doctor wouldn't have insisted on doing an ultrasound. After running my bloodwork for my yearly checkup, he called me in. I was terrified the cancer was back, but I never imagined he would tell me I'm pregnant, and not just pregnant. I'm twelve weeks along. Holy shit! I've been on birth control since the first time Cole, Xander, and I made love. I'm on the shot, and I take it on time every three months...except for a few months ago when I was busy getting ready for school to start, and I had to put my appointment off. Dammit! I'm so irresponsible. I know it takes two to make a baby, but Cole trusted that I was taking my shot on time. From being on the shot for so long, I'll go months without getting a period, so it never occurred to me the throwing up was due to morning sickness. But it should've.

And now, here I am, pregnant with my ex-boyfriend's baby. Sure, he's still living in the condo with me, but he's moved back to his old room until he can find a place of his own. And I know exactly how he's going to react when he finds out. He's going to beg me to stay with him. He's going to want to marry me so we can be a family, and I can't do it. I can't do that to him, or to me. We both deserve better.

"And right here is the heart." *Whoosh. Whoosh. Whoosh.* Dr. Morton stills the ultrasound image and points to the tiny little blip on the screen. It's too small to see the actual baby, but it has a heartbeat. I know people have different opinions, but as I stare at this little dot on the screen, to me it's alive. It's a he or she, and there's a heart.

"Obviously I'm not an obstetrician, so I'm going to recommend you pick one." He turns the monitor off and pulls the probe out of me, gently replacing the paper cover over my bottom half.

"Delilah, we're going to need to discuss this further. I can't make the decision for you, but I will make sure you completely understand all your options. Are you sure you don't want Cole or your parents here?"

"I'm sure." I can't tell them about the baby yet. I know what they would say, but this needs to be my decision. It's my body and my baby, and while Cole and my parents would want to put me first, it's my duty as this baby's mom to put him or her first.

"Okay, then go ahead and get dressed, and I'll meet you back in my office. We have a lot to discuss." He gives me a warm smile before he leaves the room, so I can get dressed.

CHAPTER TWENTY-FIVE

Cole

MY EYES OPEN, AND I CHECK THE TIME: 9:00 A.M. I ROLL OVER AND FIND THE spot next to me empty and then remember I'm no longer in the master bedroom. I'm no longer sharing a bed with Delilah. I'm in my old bed because we're over. I hate that this is what we've come to. The three of us now estranged. It tears me apart that Delilah blames herself like she forced us to be with her. We all made our choices, and I don't for a second regret being with her. I love her, and I always will. I'm just not the person for her, and she was right to break things off with me. She deserves a man who isn't fantasizing about someone else while he's having sex with her. She deserves to be the center of someone's world.

Throwing the sheets off me, I pull on a pair of pajama pants then head to the kitchen to make some coffee. Stopping in front of Delilah's room, I see she's still asleep. She's been more tired lately. She hasn't mentioned if she's yet been to see her oncologist for her yearly appointment, and that worries me. I haven't voiced my concern since the day at her parents' place when she got that headache, but I'm going to soon. It's Thanksgiving break which means we have a week of no work. We're planning to visit her parents for Thanksgiving, do some Black Friday shopping—at her request—and just simply relax. While our sexual relationship is over, we're determined to remain friends.

My thoughts go to Xander. I wish I could call him up and invite him to Delilah's parents' house for Thanksgiving. Up until two years ago, we celebrated every holiday together. Delilah is the only family we have. The first year I actually did call him, but it didn't go over well...

"Cole? Is everything okay?" My heart picks up speed at the concern in Xander's voice. It's been six months since he left, and I miss my best friend like fucking crazy.

"Yeah, everything is okay."

"Oh, Good. So...why are you calling?" His tone isn't rude. More curious and guarded.

"Well, it's Thanksgiving next week, and I know you guys are playing, but I wanted to see if maybe you wanted to join Delilah and me for dinner at her parents'."

There's a long moment of silence before Xander says, "I can't. I'm sorry. But uhm...wish Delilah and her parents a Happy Thanksgiving for me. I gotta go."

That was the last time I tried to call him. It was clear he had moved forward with his life and wasn't about to look back. He didn't say it, but I could hear the hurt in his words. I hurt him. I'm the reason he stays away. He doesn't understand, though, what it's like to have your mom pass away right after making you promise things. My parents were amazing. They loved and supported me. They were at every one of my basketball games. Every parent/teacher conference. They always put me first, and on her death bed, after losing her husband, my father, the love of her life, all my mom asked of me was to find a woman and a career I love and create a life like the one she and my father had.

"What's going on in that head of yours?" Delilah's soft voice pushes the past to the side. I was so lost in my own head I didn't hear her come into the kitchen.

"Just wishing Xander was here to celebrate Thanksgiving with us."

"I know. I wish he was here too." She gives me a sad smile. "Want to head to my parents' house around ten?"

"Sure."

"WE HAVE SO MUCH TO BE THANKFUL THIS YEAR," JOANNE SAYS FROM ACROSS the dining room table. "I would like to start. I'm thankful for my daughter, who is healthy and happy. I'm thankful for my husband, who has finally decided to hire some help on the farm, so we can have some time to ourselves."

"Oh, Mom!" Delilah gushes. "Does that mean you and Dad will be traveling?" John groans playfully at the same time Joanne nods happily.

Joanne continues. "I'm also thankful for you, Cole. For being an amazing friend and boyfriend to our daughter. We couldn't have asked for anybody better."

I nod but don't correct her. Obviously Delilah hasn't told her parents about us splitting up yet. "It's my pleasure." I smile at Delilah. "I guess I'll go next. I'm thankful for Delilah. When I was twelve years old and lost from losing my family, it was her friendship that grounded me."

"And Xander's," Delilah adds, and I swallow thickly. It never ceases to amaze me how big of a heart Delilah has. She should be angry at me. I called out another person's name during sex for god sakes. But instead of hating me, she's understanding.

"And Xander's," I add softly. "I'm thankful for the two of you"—I nod to John and Joanne—"for welcoming me into your home, even after all the years of sneaking into Delilah's bedroom." I chuckle, and everyone laughs.

"Yes, well if we believed anything was going on we would've stopped it. But it was obvious from the beginning, the three of you were nothing more than best friends." *Nothing more than best friends...*if they only knew. When Xander left, and several months later Delilah and I started dating, we felt it was best to pretend as if we had only just gotten together. Two best friends that turned into more.

"I'm thankful for every one of you at this table," John says, "And I would like to add I'm thankful to God and modern medicine for making sure my daughter is here today." He smiles at Delilah warmly, and I notice she has fat tears in her eyes that weren't there a minute ago.

"Well, I'm obviously thankful for all of you," Delilah says, "But this year I'm thankful for what God has given us." She turns her gaze to me. "A baby."

A baby? Holy shit! A baby!

"You're pregnant?" My eyes go down to her belly as if it will confirm what she's saying is true.

"I am." She turns in her seat to face me. "And I just want to be upfront about it. I was late getting my shot. I'm sorry for that." I can see the apology and fear in her eyes. She's afraid of how I'm going to react. But fuck that! She's having a baby. I could never be mad at her for that.

"I don't give a fuck!" I stand and pull her into my arms, my heart happy as hell. "You're pregnant." I hug her tightly. "We're having a baby."

"We are," she says, her voice watery. When I pull back, I see she's crying, and I'm immediately worried. I know we're no longer together but surely this changes things. We need to put the baby first, the way my parents always put me first. The way her parents put her first.

"Have you been checked out? Is the baby okay?"

"I have, and he or she is perfect. I'm four months along now, due in April."

"Oh, sweetheart!" Joanne gets up and rushes over to her daughter, pulling her out of my arms and into hers. John comes over and joins. "What a blessing."

As I watch Delilah cry with happiness, I know this is what my mom wanted for me, and I hope she's watching me from above and proud of me. Now I just need to convince Delilah that we're meant to be together.

"WHAT ABOUT THIS?" I HOLD THE YELLOW ONESIE UP FOR DELILAH TO SEE, and she grins.

"We're supposed to be looking for items on sale, not baby clothes. We have a long way to go."

"I know, but I can't help it. I'm so excited. I hope it's a little girl who looks just like you." I smile down at her.

"That's what everyone says." She rolls her eyes playfully. "And I'm supposed to say I hope for a boy who looks like you." She stops walking and stares up at me. "Obviously I just want the baby to be healthy, but I kind of would like a little girl as well. I could see you spoiling her." Tears leak from her eyes.

"We'll both spoil the baby, no matter the sex." I kiss her forehead. "Is there anything else you want to look at?"

"No, I'm exhausted. Let's go home and take a nap."

"You don't have to tell me twice."

"Cole..."

"Yeah?"

"We're going to need to discuss this," she says, and I nod in understanding.

"I know, but we have several months to figure it all out. Right now, let's get you home so you can rest."

We get home, and Delilah immediately falls asleep in her bed. Because I'm not pregnant or tired, and because I have no clue if she'll let me lay in her bed since I'm sleeping in the other room, I don't take a nap. Instead, I head down the hallway toward the other room we don't use. If Delilah insists we can't be together, I'm hoping she'll still let me live here for a while to help with the baby. If that happens, we'll need to use the third bedroom for the nursery.

I open the door to Xander's old room. I haven't been in here since before he left. When I step inside, I inhale deeply, and even after two years of him being gone, I can still smell his scent. My eyes go to the empty mattress and the lone nightstand. He was never big on furniture. He would say all he needs are the necessities to survive. I walk farther into the room and open the closet door. I see a couple of storage tubs Delilah must've stored in here—Christmas decorations and such. I pull the Christmas tub down so she won't try to do it herself. Delilah loves to get a tree the minute Thanksgiving is over. I haul it out to the hallway and set it down. Then I come back inside the room and sit down on the edge of the mattress. After looking around for a few minutes at the empty walls, I open the top drawer of the nightstand to see if Xander left anything here. I'm shocked to see that there's a white envelope in it. I pick it up and see my name scrawled across the front in Xander's handwriting. Running my finger along the flap, I crack it open, and inside is a letter.

Dear Cole,

If you're reading this, you've found my letter. When I made the decision to enter the draft, it wasn't an easy one. I had every intention of staying here until I graduated from college. Every time I pictured myself leaving, my heart hurt at the thought of walking away from you and Delilah. It still does. But then we crossed the line and you couldn't even look at me, and I knew the only solution was for me to leave...to set you free. I was hoping to say all of this face-to-face, but when I realized you weren't going to speak to me, I figured it was best to put it in writing. I love you, Cole. You are the best friend a guy could ever ask for. But I don't just love you. I'm in love with you. When I came to this realization, I wondered if I was gay, and it kind of scared me. At this moment, I'm not really sure what I am. I didn't fake enjoying sex with Delilah, but if I'm honest with myself, many times I imagined it was you instead of her. The problem is that I know you don't feel the same way, or if you do, you have no intention of acting on it, and because of that, I knew I had to leave. You have all these hopes and dreams and plans for the future, and they don't include me, no matter how much I wish they did. And because they don't include me, I felt it was time to find my own future. I'm not sure how quickly you found this letter, but if you and Delilah haven't gotten together yet, I want you to know (not that you need it) you have my blessing. I'm officially bowing out of our pact. And if Delilah isn't the woman you see as your future, I know whoever you find will be damn lucky to be loved by you. I wish you the best. Take care of our girl.

Love,

Xander

I read the letter once more before I stuff it back into the envelope. I refuse to have any feelings about this letter. Delilah is pregnant. She and our baby need to be my entire focus.

It doesn't matter if my heart is breaking every step of the way...

CHAPTER TWENTY-SIX

Cole

"Alright, boys! Listen up! Here are the rules. Cell phones stay on the bus or in the hotel room. Each of you will be separated into a group with a different NBA player. If he's not one of your favorites, don't be rude. These guys are taking time out of their day to spend time with you. You'll spend the morning doing drills. Lunch will be served in the onsite restaurant, and afterwards, everyone will play a few games. We'll meet back at the front of the arena at four o'clock sharp."

It's the first day of winter break and also the first day of basketball camp. I hated to leave Delilah home alone, especially since she's pregnant, but she insisted she's fine and will most likely visit with her parents, hang out with her friends, Summer and Kaelyn, and catch up on her sleep. I'll be gone for a week, and when I return it will be Christmas eve. We haven't spoken at all about our current situation and we're still sleeping in separate rooms, but I'm planning to talk to her once I get back. I'm hoping the holidays will put her in a festive mood, and she'll agree to give us another chance. I hate the idea of us raising our baby separately. That's not what either of us wanted for our futures. But for the next week, my focus needs to be on the fifteen teenage boys I'm responsible for.

We all get off the bus and enter the arena. On the outside I'm cool as a cucumber, but on the inside I'm an idiot who bit into a fucking jalapeño pepper with no water on hand. It's probably over nothing. I mean, what are the chances of *him* being here, right? And even if he is, it's a huge arena with hundreds of people. I probably won't even see him if he is here. But just as I'm convincing myself I have nothing to worry about, I see him. He's dressed head-to-toe in his team's workout gear. His hair is still the same—shaved short with the top slightly longer and gelled neatly to the side. His arms are more muscular from working out, and I spot another tattoo on his bicep. He's dribbling the ball down the court. He stops just before the three-point line, pulls up and shoots the ball, knocking down the shot the same way he's done a million times, with nothing but net. He runs up to some woman who's watching him from the sidelines and gives her his signature smirk. I can't see the face she makes since I'm standing behind her, but I can see her shake her head and hold out a bottle of water for him, which he takes.

It's as if he can feel me watching him, because even with all the people in the arena, his eyes find mine. We stare at each other for a few moments, neither of us wanting to be the first one to look away. But then his name is called, and without another glance, he runs toward the person calling him. And I know it sounds crazy, but it feels like once again, he just ran away with my fucking heart.

CHAPTER TWENTY-SEVEN

Xander

HE'S HERE. OF COURSE HE'S HERE. I KNEW HE WOULD BE WHEN I SAW HIS name on the sign-up form. When I signed up I didn't even think about Cole being here. Why would he be? I knew his plans were to one day teach physical education, but the last time I saw him he was just finishing his sophomore year of college. So when I received the email with the dates I would be volunteering and the schools that would be attending, I didn't think anything of it. Until I received the email detailing which schools I would be working with and their point of contact. Cole Andrews of Worthshire High School. I looked up the school and found out it's in the same area where we went to college, which means he's still living in Dallas. My first thought was if Delilah was still living there as well, but then I stopped myself. It doesn't matter. He made his choice, and I made mine.

Each player is assigned ten students and a coach. Luckily, I'm not assigned Cole, but as fate would have it—while laughing in my face—he's assigned to Dean Marshal, the center on my team, who is located directly next to me on the court. I spend the next four hours trying my best to focus on running drills with these kids, but it's hard knowing Cole is so close. It's like I'm drawn to him. His voice. His laughter. His presence. It doesn't matter how much I try to push my thoughts of him aside, I can't help but gravitate towards him.

I have a couple of his players on my team, and they mention him a few times. It's clear he cares about them by the way they sing his praises. They tell me their season is only halfway through but they're undefeated, and when they played for their old coach, they never won nearly as many games. Then one of the kids says something that has me stopping in my tracks.

"I hope Coach Andrews does basketball camp this summer."

"Me too! But with his girlfriend having a baby, he'll probably want to be home with her," another kid says.

Baby...is Delilah pregnant? Is he dating someone else?

LUNCH IS OVER, AND IT'S TIME FOR THE KIDS TO PRACTICE WHAT THEY'VE learned this morning during a couple games. As luck—or lack of—would have it, Cole's group is paired with mine to play the first game. The NBA players and coaches aren't supposed to be playing, just refereeing the kids, but when Dean comes down the court dribbling the ball and tries to dunk on me, and I block his attempt, the kids all go crazy.

"We want to see you guys play!" Trevor, one of Cole's kids yells.

"Yeah! C'mon, Coach!" James, another one of Cole's kids, exclaims. "You said you used to play in High School!

Show us what you got," he taunts Cole, and I laugh.

"Ehh, I don't know." Cole shrugs. "That was a long time ago."

"And he wasn't even that good," I joke.

"Wait! You knew him?" James asks Cole in awe that his coach actually knows an NBA player. "Is he the friend you used to have, who made it into the NBA?"

Coles eyes go wide. *So, he was talking about me? Interesting...*

"I am," I say answering for Cole who seems to be stunned silent. "Not only did I know your coach, but he *almost* beat my record of most points at our high school," I say to piss off Cole. It used to be an ongoing argument who was better between the two of us. We even kept a running record of our points scored, steals, blocks, and rebounds. He likes to play it off like he never would've had a shot at playing professional ball, but the truth is if he would've rehabbed his knee after the surgery, he could've easily proven himself again. The only reason why he didn't was because he wanted to be there for Delilah.

"Bull crap," Cole says, finally finding his voice. "The only reason you had more points than me was because I got injured in the middle of my senior year. I would've broken your record. I almost did."

"Maybe...but you didn't." I know it's a low blow. Cole tearing his ACL about killed him. He hated not being able to finish his season.

"Maybe not, but I had you beat in steals and blocks."

"And I had you beat in rebounds," I volley back. "And everyone knows rebounds win the game."

Dean laughs. "I think the kids are right. We need to see you guys play. One game, just you two. One-on-one. May the best man win."

"Sounds good to me." I smirk.

"Fine." Cole snatches the ball I'm holding out of my hands and dribbles it over to the three-point line. "First to eleven. Make it, take it."

"Game on," I say with a grin, joining him on the court.

Cole checks the ball to me, anger evident in his actions. I laugh, checking it back to him, which only seems to piss him off further. With the ball in his possession, he immediately drives to the basket and scores his first point before I can even react.

He stalks back over to the three-point line and aggressively throws the ball at me to check it once again. This time when I check it back to him, I'm ready, and when he drives by me, I trail behind him. As he comes up for the lay-up, I block his shot from behind. I get the rebound and go straight back up with the ball, slamming it through the net and making a show of hanging off the rim.

The kids scream and shout as I drop to the ground and make my way back to the three-point line. Cole is fuming, and it only has me grinning harder. *Fuck, I've missed him...*

The game continues back and forth as we both get our points in. Cole is dripping in sweat, having not played at this rigorous of a level in years, while I've yet to break a sweat. I have to give him credit, though. He's actually kept up with me. The game is tied at nine all, and it's Cole's ball. He was never good at shooting from the perimeter, so when we check the ball and he begins to dribble, I'm not expecting him to pull up right there from the three-point line and take the shot. Everybody watches as the ball goes in—nothing but net. The kids all cheer, and Cole's students pile on top of him to congratulate him on his win.

When they're done celebrating, I walk over to Cole and extend my hand, wanting to show the kids what good sportsmanship looks like. He takes it and shakes my hand.

"Good game," I say, squeezing his hand.

"You too." He smiles at me then looks down at our conjoined hands. My gaze follows his, wishing we could stay like this for just a little while longer, knowing that as soon as our hands part, we'll most likely never get this moment again.

All too soon, he does in fact pull his hand away, and with one last small smile, he turns his back to me and calls the kids over to pick teams. I sit down on the bench and watch as he laughs and jokes with everyone, and my heart aches over how much I miss him.

"That guy was pretty damn good," Dean says, sitting down next to me.

"Yeah, he is. Could've made it to the NBA for sure."

"Why didn't he?"

"He chose to take care of our best friend when she was sick." I frown when I think about Delilah. I hate that we've barely spoken since I left two years ago. But the truth is a text here and there is all I can handle. Now, though, I'm wondering if she and Cole still speak. If she's not the one who's pregnant that would mean Cole moved on...or was it Delilah who moved on? And if she's pregnant, it sucks that she didn't feel she could text me to tell the good news. Is she afraid it will hurt me to know they're having a baby together? Or maybe she hasn't texted me recently because she's with someone who doesn't want her talking to Cole and me...I hate that I have no clue what's going on with them. At one time they were my entire world.

"Hey, man, you okay?" Dean asks.

"Yeah, just thinking about the past." I smile the fake smile I've perfected the last couple years while deep down my heart feels like it's shattering all over again.

"My mom used to always say the past is just that. *The past*. It's done. Move on."

Easier said than done…

I'VE JUST FINISHED HAVING DINNER WITH CIARA, MY ASSISTANT-SLASH-publicist. She doesn't usually go everywhere with me, but while I'm here, she has me shooting a couple commercials, so she wanted to be here to make sure everything goes smoothly. She sets up all of my PR and makes sure I know where I need to be and when. I never knew there was so much more to playing professional ball than just simply showing up and playing. When I first got an agent for the draft, I was shocked when he recommended so many different people to me. At first, I ignored his suggestions, but once I was in over my head, I gave in and hired a team of people. It took a couple different tries, but I have finally found a good team who look out for my best interests.

"Are you going up to your room?" Ciara asks.

"I think I'm going to grab a drink at the bar."

"Be careful, X. I don't want to have to do any clean up while I'm here." She shoots me a wink, but it's not flirtatious. Ciara is the only person who knows the truth about me. I wave her off and head to the bar. It's almost midnight and the place is quiet. It's not often I'm able to sit in a public bar and have a drink anymore.

"What can I get you?" the male bartender asks with a smile.

"Jack and Coke, please." The bartender nods, and I watch him as he goes about making my drink. He has dirty blond shaggy hair, bright green eyes, and lips that I imagine if he were into that sort of thing—and I'm almost positive he is—would be perfect for sucking dick.

He sets a napkin down and places my drink on it, then he tells me to let him know if I need anything else, before he moves down the bar to take someone else's order. When I finish my drink, I order another and then another, attempting to drink until my chest is numb from the pain. Playing professional basketball means being on a strict diet, one that doesn't include alcohol, but after seeing Cole today, I'm willing to risk the hangover to just forget for a little while.

"Is it too late to order from the kitchen?" I hear someone ask, and my head snaps toward the voice. Even half drunk, I would recognize that voice from anywhere.

"We have a late night menu you can order from," the bartender says, handing him a menu. Like he can feel me looking at him, Cole glances in my direction.

"That's what room service is for," I point out, my words sounding a tad bit slurred. *Shit...Ciara is going to kill me.*

"They stop room service at ten o'clock," he shoots back before eyeing the menu. "Can I just get a grilled chicken sandwich and a Coke, please?" He hands the menu back to the bartender.

"I heard you're having a baby," I say, getting straight to the point—the alcohol doing nothing to filter my words. Cole stares at me for a moment before he sits down two stools over from me.

"What's wrong? You afraid you might catch the gay?" I laugh, bringing my glass up to my lips to take another sip of my drink.

"Gay? With all the women you're seen with? I'm more afraid I might catch an STD." He scoffs, and I glare his way but don't say a word. I'm well aware of all the women I'm seen with. Ciara makes sure of it.

"So is the baby Delilah's?" I ask.

"Yeah, she's five months pregnant."

"Good for her." I nod. "She deserves to be a mom after everything she's been through."

"Yeah," he agrees.

"And hey, looks like you're on course for making your mom proud," I point out. *Damn, this alcohol.*

"Yeah, well, it was great talking to you, too, Xander," Cole says dryly then waves the bartender over. "On second thought, I'm not all that hungry," he says before he walks away, and I don't do shit to stop him.

CHAPTER TWENTY-EIGHT

Cole

shake my hand then Delilah's.

"Um…where's Dr. Blake?" Delilah asks.

"He had an emergency delivery, and since we work as a team here, I'm seeing his patients this afternoon. Now it says here, you're twenty-two weeks pregnant and scheduled for an ultrasound. Go ahead and lie back and put this against the top of your pants so I don't get any gel on your clothes." She hands Delilah a paper cover-up, and Delilah does as she says, lifting her shirt almost to her bra, and placing the paper along the edge of her jeans.

"Perfect." Dr. Stein squirts some blue gel onto Delilah's belly then places a wand looking thing on it, using it to move the gel all around. She flips a couple switches and the heartbeat comes over the speakers loud and clear. I recognize it from all the times the other doctor does it.

"One hundred and sixty. Good, strong heartbeat." The doctor smiles at us. "I'm just going to take some measurements and then we'll get to the fun stuff." She moves the wand all over while clicking on the computer screen. It looks like she's taking pictures.

"Okay, your baby is measuring at twenty-two weeks and five days, and everything looks perfect." The doctor points to the screen. "These are the hands, the feet, and if you look closely you can see the sex. Do you two want to find out if you're having a boy or girl?"

I look over at Delilah, and she has tears dripping out of her lids and falling down the sides of her face, wetting her ears and hair. One thing I've learned throughout her pregnancy is that pregnant women are emotional.

"Delilah?" I take her hand in mine. "Do we want to know the sex?"

She shakes her head. "No, I don't want to know." She sniffles. "Life only offers us so many surprises. I would like to keep the sex of the baby a surprise." She looks at me. "If that's okay with you."

"Of course it is." I dip my head down to give her a kiss but stop myself, remembering that's not who we are anymore.

The doctor takes some more pictures of the baby then hands some wet wipes to Delilah to wipe the goo off her stomach. Once she's clean, I help her sit up.

"Now, according to your records," the doctor says while looking down at a folder in her hands, "you had decided to put off any drug therapy during the first half of your pregnancy. Are you planning to begin any type of therapy now that you've reached twenty weeks, or will you be waiting until after the baby is born?"

The doctor looks up at Delilah at the same time my head whips around to look at her. Delilah's eyes go wide in what looks like shock, and her hands cover her mouth.

"Delilah...why would you be doing drug therapy?" I ask. Then it hits me. "Drug therapy...like when you had..." I can't even finish my sentence before I'm moving around in front of her. "Delilah...do you have..." I can't say the fucking word. It won't come out of my mouth. It's like Beetlejuice. I'm afraid if I say it, it'll appear.

Delilah's eyes are still wide open as fat tears fill her lids. She blinks slowly and they tumble down her cheeks, but she doesn't answer me.

"Delilah!" I raise my voice, and the doctor's hand comes up to touch my shoulder. Delilah is now full-on crying.

"Cole, please calm down." I can hear the confusion and worry in the doctor's voice, but I shake her off.

"Delilah, I'm assuming the worst here, so you need to give me something," I beg. "Why would the doctor be asking about you doing drug therapy?"

"Because I have cancer," she admits through her tears.

CHAPTER TWENTY-NINE

Delilah

THREE MONTHS AGO

"AS YOU KNOW, WHEN WE RAN YOUR BLOOD, WE FOUND YOUR BLOOD CELL count to be abnormal, which is why I called you in here," Dr. Morton says. "After doing a full examination and meeting with my team we have determined that you have stage three Hodgkin's Lymphoma." He stops talking for a moment then says, "I'm so sorry, Delilah. In all my years I've never seen cancer spread this quickly."

"What are my chances?" I ask.

"If treated immediately, about eighty percent," he admits, and my heart drops into my stomach at the word *immediately* because we both know I'm not going to immediately start treatment.

"You have a couple of options: you're only twelve weeks along, so you can terminate the pregnancy and we can set up an aggressive treatment plan, or we can wait until you're further along and then begin treatment. There are a few treatments that have been used on women who are pregnant and have cancer."

"And those treatments...have they proven that they don't harm the baby?"

"It's all too new. Most studies show they're safe, but there's no guarantee."

"And if I stay pregnant and refuse treatment until after the baby is born?"

Dr. Morton sighs. "If you wait until the baby is born before beginning treatment, the cancer has nine more months to spread. I don't recommend—"

"I'm not aborting my baby." My hand goes to my belly. "This is my third time with cancer, and who's to say if I survive, I will be able to get pregnant again. At least before I die I can bring another life into this world."

"That's if you make it. Without treatment we can't be sure how quick the cancer will spread."

"At how many weeks can a baby survive if taken out?"

"I'm not an obstetrician, but I spoke to a friend of mine before meeting with you. She said ninety percent of babies if born after twenty-seven weeks survive." I do the math in my head. That's only five months away.

"I'm not aborting my baby."

"What if we reassess at twenty weeks along? See how much it's spread and go from there?"

"I'll agree to reassess then, but I doubt I'm going to agree to get treatment until after the baby is born. Once he or she is safe, I will do whatever treatment is necessary."

"By then it may be too late."

"It's a chance I'm willing to take. I believe everything happens for a reason. I'm keeping my baby."

"Okay, we're going to need to monitor you closely. I want to see you every week. I'll send over all your information to the obstetrician you choose, and if you or Cole—"

"I'm not telling Cole...or my parents."

"Delilah..."

"No, this is my decision. I'm over eighteen, and Cole and I aren't married. We aren't even together. I'm choosing not to tell anyone, and I am making it clear to you right now, they are not to be informed on anything regarding my cancer. I'll tell my obstetrician the same thing."

CHAPTER THIRTY

Cole

DELILAH HAS CANCER. MY SWEET AND BEAUTIFUL BEST FRIEND HAS STAGE three Hodgkin's Lymphoma. And because she chose our baby over her health, there's a good chance she won't survive this. I shouldn't have left her, but I had to get out of there. She wanted to talk on our way home, but I needed time to think. So, when we got home, I made sure she was inside and then I left.

She's going to die. She said she'll be treated after the baby is born, but it could be too late. It's spreading too quickly. This is why she's had headaches and has been so tired. I chalked it up to her being pregnant but that's not why. She has cancer.

I don't know how long I'm driving, but when I look at the sign and see I'm in Houston, I realize where I've been heading—to Xander. Only I have no clue where he lives or if he's even in town. He could be out of town for a game. I pull over on the side of the road and lose it. My head hits the steering wheel, and I cry harder than I've ever cried in my life. Harder than I cried when I lost my parents, or when I lost my grandma. My throat and heart and stomach hurt, but I welcome the pain. I can't believe this is happening. She's going to die.

Before I can stop myself, I dial the number I know by heart, not even sure if it's still in service. It rings once, twice, and then he answers.

"Cole."

"She has cancer." And just like that, no more words need to be spoken. I know he's on the other line because I can hear him breathing while I cry. I cry for the woman who over the last ten years has come to mean everything to me. My best friend, my partner, my lover. I cry for the years she will never see. For the baby she won't be around to raise. And when my body feels like it can't possibly shed another single tear, I go silent.

"Where are you?" Xander asks.

"Houston."

"Send me your location. I'm on my way." He hangs up, and I send him my GPS location. While I'm waiting for him, I pull up my text messages. I see several from Delilah. She's worried. It's been five hours since I left. Not wanting her to worry, I send her a text to let her know I'm okay and that I'll be home later. About twenty minutes later, there's a knock on my window. I turn my car off and get out, and before my door is even shut, Xander is pulling me into a hug I didn't realize I needed so damn badly.

"Let's go to my place," he says. I lock up my car and get into his. We don't say anything the entire drive. When we pull up to his condominium complex, I notice it's gated. He drives through and parks underground. When we get out, he leads us over to a set of elevators, but when he types in a code, only one opens. We get in, and he doesn't press a floor, and I notice there are no numbers.

"Is this your private elevator?"

"It's for the penthouse," he says. Both of us are silent as the elevator shoots us up to the top floor. When the door opens, Xander gets out first. I glance down the hall and see this is the only door on this floor. He unlocks his door and pushes it open, waiting for me to go in first. Stopping in the foyer, I take the place in. It's beautiful and clean, but it's bare. There's a single couch and a flat screen TV in the living room. One lone barstool against the island. I spot a door just off the living room, but it's closed, as are the others off the hallway.

"Did you just move in here?" I ask.

"No, I've been living here for almost three years."

"The place is empty," I say, completely baffled. I knew he only needs the necessities but Jesus, this place doesn't even look like it's been lived in.

"I have a couch and a bed, I don't need anything more." He throws his keys onto the counter, and I watch as they slide across the black and grey granite before they finally stop. "Beer?" he offers.

"Sure." He pops the top to two beers and hands me one before he walks over to the couch and sits down. I watch as he takes a long pull at his beer, his Adam's apple bobbing as he swallows.

"You going to come sit down or what?" he asks.

"Ye—" My voice comes out horse, so I clear it before I try again. "Yeah, sorry. Thank you for the beer and for coming to get me."

I sit down on the couch next to Xander, leaving a cushion of space between us.

"Regardless of what's gone down, I'm always going to be here for you, Cole. As long as you want me to be there, that is." His gaze bores into mine, and if I were a stronger man, I would tell him I'll always want him to be there, but I'm not. I'm weak, and I don't deserve him or Delilah in my life.

"Now tell me everything," he says.

"She went in for her yearly checkup and found out she has Hodgkin's Lymphoma, but then she also found out she was pregnant. She apparently was late getting her shot and that's all it took."

"Fuck." Xander shakes his head. "And let me guess...she kept the cancer part from you and her parents."

"Of course she did, because she knew we would beg her to terminate and start treatment. I should've figured it out." My head drops to my hands. "She's been getting these headaches and is always tired. She has to force herself to eat, and she always feels sick. I thought it was the pregnancy, but it's not. Her cancer is growing and spreading every goddamned day, and until she gives birth, she's not getting treated. I don't know what to do." I lift my head up and look at Xander. "What do I do?"

"You do the same thing you've been doing for the last ten years. You be there for her. You love her and spend your days making memories with her. You know that she's going to be okay. She's always okay." The strength in Xander's words almost have me believing it, but this time feels different.

"What if she's not?"

Xander slams his beer down on the small coffee table and edges closer to me. "If you go home and allow doubt to seep through the cracks, you are setting her up to die. You believe she'll be okay. You be her fucking strength."

Tears fill my eyes. "I don't think I can do this without you," I admit, my eyes closing in fear of being rejected. When Xander doesn't say anything, I open them back up and see he's staring at me.

"I'm always here. I might not be in Dallas with you guys, but I'm only a phone call away."

Xander gets up and grabs two fresh beers, and when he sits down, I change the subject. I'm too close to begging him to come home, and I know his life is here now.

"I've been watching your games. You're killing it."

Xander grants me his signature cocky smirk that always has a tad bit of shyness to it. "Yeah." He shrugs. "They're talking about re-signing me next year. I love it, man. I love playing."

"When I watch your games, I can't believe you're out there playing with all of the guys we've spent our life looking up to."

"It's un-fuckin-real. I swear the first time we played Cleveland, and I stepped out onto the court with Lebron, I almost asked him for his autograph."

"I probably would've!" I laugh, and Xander cracks up. "How long are you home for?" I ask.

"I leave first thing in the morning. We have ten days on the road."

We talk sports for I don't know how long, Xander telling me all about his practices and his time on the road. The non-basketball related stuff like fundraisers. He wants to start a charity soon, but he's not sure what kind yet. Eventually the conversation steers toward me. We discuss my job and coaching. I don't know why, but I don't mention that Delilah and I aren't together anymore. I'm not sure if it's because I'm hoping she'll take me back so we can be a family for this baby, or if it's because if I told him I'm single, he might ask why, and then I'd have to tell him the truth, and I just can't bring myself to do it. When my phone pings with a text from Delilah asking if I'm okay, I look at the time and see I've been here for several hours, and it's already almost four in the morning.

"Shit, it's already morning," I say to Xander. "I told Delilah I would be home last night." I stand. "Thank you for this. I know…I know shit is weird between us, but thank you."

Xander stands up and pulls me into a hug. "Delilah will always come first. If either of you need anything at all, please call me. Whatever happened between us doesn't fucking matter."

I know his comment is meant to make it clear that he's here—we can be adults and put our shit aside to be there for Delilah—but fuck if it doesn't hurt when I hear him refer to *us* in the past.

CHAPTER THIRTY-ONE

Cole

"DR. BLAKE, THANK YOU FOR RETURNING MY CALL." I THROW MY GYM BAG into the passenger seat of my car and turn the ignition on.

"Of course, how are you?"

"I'm good." I switch the conversation to Bluetooth and pull out of the high school. "I was calling because I was hoping you could take a look at the ultrasound images and tell me the sex of the baby." He's quiet for a moment, so I explain. "As you know, Delilah has cancer. We don't know what the future holds, so I would like to get things ready for the baby."

"I understand, Cole. I'm pulling her file up now." After several seconds, he tells me the sex of the baby, and I thank him. We hang up just as I'm pulling into the baby store. I've seen Delilah circle tons of shit for both sexes when she's hanging around the house. When I returned home, I insisted she quit her job, and she agreed. She needs to relax and focus on her health. I also insisted I go back to sleeping in her bed with her. We haven't had sex, but I'm not going to spend our days together in a different room. Once the baby comes, and after she's done fighting for her life and survives, she can leave my ass and find her happily ever after, but for now, she's stuck with me.

I grab a shopping cart and start combing the aisles for everything Joanne said we'll need: a crib, a changing table, a dresser, bedding. I pick up some diapers and wipes, bottles because she'll need to formula feed so she can be treated. Joanne is in charge of throwing the shower, so she told me not to pick up too much, since a lot of people will want to buy stuff. I find a lamp and wall décor that matches the bedding, and once I'm done I check out and load it all into my car. The big stuff is being delivered tomorrow. I've already spoken to Summer, and she's agreed to take Delilah out for the morning to breakfast and to do some light shopping while the furniture is delivered and set up.

When I get home, I leave everything in my car so she doesn't see it, and head up to our condo. When I get inside, I find Delilah sleeping on the couch. Her hand is covering her protruding belly in a protective way. I pull my phone out and snap a picture of her and send it to Xander. We've spoken a few times over the last few weeks when he texts or calls to ask about Delilah. He sends a text back, saying she looks beautiful and to let him know when the baby shower is, so he can make sure he's there. He sent me a couple of dates that he will be in town. I want everyone who loves Delilah to be there.

"Hey," Delilah says groggily. She sits up slowly, wincing in pain.

"What hurts?" I ask, going to her.

"My body is just feeling sore, and my headaches are kind of bad," she admits, opening the bottle of Tylenol and popping a couple into her mouth. Her hand goes to her belly, and I see it shift.

"Here, feel!" she whispers in excitement, grabbing my hand and sticking it on her stomach. She's been feeling the baby move for weeks, but any time she tries to show me, I don't feel anything.

"I think he's done." I laugh. Delilah has resorted to calling the baby a 'he' instead of an 'it,' so I do the same thing.

"No, don't move your hand," she demands. We sit like this for a good minute, just staring at each other with my hand on her belly and her hand covering mine. Her hair is up in her signature messy bun, and she's makeup free. Her skin has gotten paler the last several months, and I know it's because she's sick. But she's still Delilah. She's still gorgeous—on the inside and out. Fully aware it's probably a bad idea but needing to feel her soft lips against mine, I lean toward her to kiss her. Only when I do, I feel a bump under my hand and then another one. I jump up in shock, and Delilah throws her head back in a full-on belly laugh, and fuck if it isn't the most beautiful sound in the world.

"You felt it!" She giggles. "Isn't it so cool?" He continues to bump up against my hand a few times before he stops.

"That's unbelievable," I say in awe. "There's a tiny little human inside you."

"I know." She nods her head emphatically. "I know." Tears brim her eyes, and when she blinks, they race down her cheeks. "I know you don't understand why I'm risking my life, but there's a baby in me. He's part you and part me, and he deserves to be brought into this world."

Her crying gets harder, and I pull her into my lap so she's straddling me. I can feel her stomach between us as she wraps her arms around my waist and sobs into the crook of my neck. "I'm so sorry, Cole. I'm so, so sorry. I'm going to fight. I promise."

Holding Delilah close, I rest my chin on top of her head and let her cry. She's been so tough the last couple of months since she admitted she has cancer. She's refused to cry and barely acknowledges she even has cancer, aside from the weekly visits she has to go to so they can monitor her closely. She even told them she doesn't want to know anything unless it affects the baby because she isn't changing her mind.

"Cole, I need you to promise me something," she says through her tears. "Promise me that if I die—"

"No," I say, cutting her off. "Nope, we're not going there. You're not fucking dying. You hear me?" I lift her chin. "You. Are. Not. Dying. You're going to give birth to our baby, and then you're going to fight like hell, and once you're all better, you're going to live out every damn dream you've ever had."

"What dreams?" she asks, confused.

"Meeting the love of your life and getting married," I say, repeating the words she said years ago. "Damn it, Delilah. I hate that you've wasted so many years on me."

"No, Cole. I didn't waste anything on you. I love you." She presses her lips to mine softly. "I was meant to spend my life with you." I open my mouth to argue, but she kisses me again before I can get a word out. When our kiss turns from gentle to rough, I pull back slightly.

"Delilah..."

"Don't say anything, please. Just make love to me," she pleads, her big caramel eyes blinking through her tears, and because I'll always give this woman whatever she wants, I agree. Picking her up, I carry her to our room, lay her down on the bed, and make love to her while I pray to whatever God is above not to take her from me or from our baby.

This isn't a world I want to live in, if it doesn't have Delilah in it.

CHAPTER THIRTY-TWO

Delilah

"SURPRISE!" I WALK INTO THE CONDO WITH COLE AND SEE, STANDING IN MY living room, the small group of people that make up my world: my mom, my dad, Summer, Kaelyn. Some friends I made during my short time at work. My grandparents, aunts, uncles, and cousins are even here! And then I spot him, and if I wasn't eight months pregnant, I would be running over to him and jumping into his arms like I've done so many times before. But I am, so instead, I waddle my ass over to him and throw my arms around his neck. I inhale his scent, and it confirms he's my Xander. I haven't seen him in person in almost three years, but it's as if he never left. His body is a bit firmer, more muscular, but it's still him.

"I missed you so much," I cry into his chest, forgetting about all of the other people standing around. I just need him. I need to feel his protective arms around me.

"I'm here, sweet girl. I'm sorry it took me so long to come back."

Shaking my head, I murmur, "It's okay. I know why you've stayed away." And I do. I know how much he loves Cole. There's so much more I want to say—need to say—but right now isn't the time. So instead, I stand up on my tiptoes and give Xander a kiss on his cheek, then I turn around to face the rest of my friends and family.

"Thank you everyone for being here!" I look around and see dozens of pink and blue balloons with a huge banner that reads "Baby Shower." There's a beautiful three tier cake and tons of cupcakes and other sweets. When Cole insisted on taking me to lunch, I was exhausted and achy but said okay. He's made it a point to keep me positive through my pregnancy. I had no idea we were leaving so we could come home to a surprise baby shower.

"This means so much to me," I tell everyone before I start walking around to say hello to everyone who's here. I give my parents a big hug and catch up with my family. I thank my old colleagues for coming, and I thank my mom for helping Cole to make this day happen.

"Alright!" Cole announces, "First up are the baby shower games. I know usually it's all women at these things, but there was no way any of us were missing this party. So, men, you will just have to endure the games, and women, don't be upset when us guys kick your ass at every one of these games." Everyone laughs.

"First game is called Pee in the Pot." Cole smirks. "Since pregnant women pee a lot..." He gives me a knowing look, and I giggle. "The object of the game is to see who can pee the most into the pot, but don't worry, we aren't using real urine because that would just be unsanitary." He grabs a tray of baby bottles that look like they're filled with apple juice and another one with mason jars.

"One person will hold the mason jar and the other

person will be using the bottle to try to squirt as much of the *pee* into the jar. Whichever team has the most in their jar after all the juice has been squirted out, wins. The catch." Cole smiles wide, clearly proud of himself. "You must be three feet apart." There's a collection of laughter and groans. "Alright! Find your partner."

I could easily pick Cole or Xander, but instead I grab my mom, hoping Cole and Xander will work together since Xander doesn't really know anyone here but my parents and sort of Summer and Kaelyn. When I look over, I see my plan did in fact work. Cole is grinning while he explains something to Xander, showing him the baby bottle, and Xander is smiling softly, that shy smile he always reserves for Cole. And my heart feels once again completely full.

For the next couple of hours, we play game after game: Pin the sperm on the egg—a baby shower version of pin the tail on the donkey. Baby food tasting—we all have to guess which baby food is which. Belly measuring—everyone has to guess the size of my belly in inches. Cole even has a chart drawn up for everyone to guess the sex of the baby, as well as the date and time he will be born. There is a baby book for everyone to fill out with wishes for the baby, and a box where people can write down a name they love. Cole and my mom have literally thought of everything to make this day perfect.

After we have cake and open all of the presents, everyone starts trickling out. When it's only my parents, Cole, and Xander left, I give my mom a huge hug and thank her.

"Oh, sweetheart, it was my pleasure. I can't wait to meet my grandbaby." Mom kisses my cheek. "I love you, Delilah."

"I love you too." I hug her again before moving to my dad. "Thank you for everything," I tell him.

"It was all Cole and your mom."

"Not for the party. For being my dad." I hug him tighter. "I love you."

"I love you too."

They say goodbye to Cole and make Xander promise not to be a stranger, and then they're gone.

"And then there were three…" I joke.

"Actually, I have an errand I need to run," Cole says.

"On a Sunday?" I ask.

"Yeah, you planning to hang out for a little bit?" he asks Xander.

"Yeah, I booked a hotel for the night."

"Perfect, I'll be back in a little while." Cole pulls me into his arms and gives me a kiss to my temple. "Did you have a good day?"

"It was absolutely perfect. Thank you."

Cole grabs his keys, leaving Xander and me alone, and I have a sneaking suspicion he's leaving to give Xander and me some time together.

"I could use some air," I say to Xander. "Want to join me on the roof?"

"I would love to."

"Sorry about Cole leaving," I tell him once we're sitting across from each other in the lounge chairs.

"I think he wanted to give us some time together," Xander says.

"That's what I was thinking. So, how's basketball?" I ask, and Xander barks out a loud laugh. "What?"

"How's basketball? Other than a few texts when I first moved out of you asking how I'm doing, one conversation where you confirmed you have cancer, and a few texts of me asking if you're okay and you telling me you're fine, we haven't spoken in three years, and your first question is 'How's basketball?'"

"Well, I was starting off small." I laugh. "Fine, how's your sex life?" I grin, and Xander chuckles.

"Now that's more like the Delilah I know." Xander winks.

"I haven't spoken about you," I tell him. "I kept my promise. It hasn't been easy." Xander smiles but it's sad, and I hate that talking about his feelings for Cole makes him sad.

"I appreciate that, sweet girl."

"Look, Xander, I need to say something. There's a chance I'm going to die, and—"

"Nope! Not happening." He shakes his head. Damn, these guys! Of course he has the same response as Cole to my wanting to talk about the future.

"Xander, please," I beg. "For so long, the three of us have ignored the future. I don't want to die and then—"

"I said no, Delilah. You're not dying, so fucking stop, please. You want to talk about anything else, I'm down, but I'm not going to sit here and discuss you dying because it's not happening."

"Fine." I huff. "Let's discuss you and Cole."

"There is no me and Cole."

"There could be!"

"Are you trying to pawn your boyfriend off on me?" Xander smirks, trying to lighten the mood, and I realize he doesn't know.

"Cole and I aren't together." Xander's eyes widen before he schools his shocked expression. "We broke up before I found out I was pregnant. Want to know why?" When Xander doesn't answer, I continue. "Because while he was having sex with me from behind, he called out your name while coming. Now, it's time we talk. And before you say a word, what I mean is, I'm going to talk, and you're going to listen."

♡ ♡ ♡

I'M LAYING OUTSIDE ON MY LOUNGE CHAIR, ENJOYING THE COOLNESS OF THE evening and looking up at the dark clear sky, when I hear the patio door creak open and then close, telling me Cole is home. "Xander left?" he asks.

"Yep."

"Did you have a good visit with him?" Cole sits down next to me.

"I did. I miss him." I'm staring at all of the twinkling stars when I see it, a shooting star.

"Cole, look!" I point at it. "Make a wish." I close my eyes and make a wish, the same wish I've been making since I was a little girl." When I open my eyes, I see Cole is staring at me. "Did you make one?" I ask.

"Of course." He eyes me for a long beat before he says, "I put everything away from the baby shower."

"I would've helped but you won't let me in the room." I shoot him a playful glare. A few months ago I came home from lunch with Summer to find a sign on the door to Xander's old room telling me to keep out. Cole said it's a surprise, and I can't see it until after the baby is born. I was looking forward to picking out everything for the baby after he or she is born once I know the sex, but knowing Cole did this out of love and excitement for our baby, I didn't have the heart to argue. I'm sure whatever he picks out will be beautiful and perfect.

"Nope, I got it. I saw on the calendar you added a hospital tour. Are you getting excited? It's surreal to think about the fact that in the next eight weeks our baby will be here."

My heart pangs at the thought. I want to be excited,

but I'm also scared. I can feel it in my bones. I'm sick. The cancer is spreading, and I'm terrified every day that I'm not going to make it to see my baby being born. But I don't tell Cole that. I made this decision, and I won't for a second regret it.

"I'm really excited," I say. "I can't wait to meet him or her."

"Have you spoken to Dr. Morton about starting your treatment as soon as the baby's born?"

"I have. They're monitoring me closely, and they have a game plan in order."

"Good, because Delilah..." Cole looks over at me. "I can't do this without you."

CHAPTER THIRTY-THREE

Cole

nurse, points to the hallway where several other nurses and doctors are bustling about. "Let's take a look in an empty room so you know what you can expect." She guides us to the first empty room, and we all congregate inside. There's about ten of us here for the hospital tour. Paula has taken us by the registrar's office to make sure we're all situated and the paperwork is filled out, then to the labor and delivery ward.

Now we're in the hospital wing where the women are taken to recover after they've had the baby. Being here makes it all feel so real. Like holy shit, we're going to have an actual baby. One we're responsible for loving and taking care of. And while all these couples are ecstatic, I'm freaking the hell out because Delilah's situation isn't like any of these other couples. She has abnormal cells that like to multiply in her body and slowly—or not so slowly—kill her. Every time I think about Delilah and how her body keeps working against her, I want to curse God. How could he make someone so beautiful on the inside and out and then make it to where she has to fear and fight for her life every goddamned day. She's one of the good ones. Give cancer to the rapist or the pedophile! Not to Delilah. I mean, come the fuck on. My grandma used to say God only gives you what you can handle, but fuck, so because Delilah is strong, he's going to just keep throwing this at her?

I take a deep breath, so I don't get myself worked up. I just hate that while everyone is smiling and planning for the future, Delilah and I are silently praying for her to just simply live. I try every day to remain positive and strong, but it's getting harder and harder.

"Hey Cole," Delilah says softly, taking me out of my thoughts. "I'm not feeling too well. I think I need to..." She doesn't finish her sentence because her eyes roll in the back of her head, and she goes limp. Luckily, I'm standing next to her and catch her before she falls. It takes me about a second before I realize Delilah has just passed out.

"I need a doctor!" I yell, and everyone looks at me as I lay her gently on the ground. "Now! She has cancer. I need Dr. Blake and Dr. Morton, now!"

Paula immediately jumps into action, and less than a minute later, everybody is removed from the room and several doctors are scurrying in. Using a gurney, they move her into a hospital bed and start checking her out.

"What's her name?" one of the nurses asks.

"Her name is Delilah Cross. She has Hodgkin's Lymphoma, and she's thirty-five weeks pregnant," I tell her.

"We're going to need you to wait outside until we get her situated," the nurse says as she walks me outside and into the waiting room.

"I'm the dad. Can you please let me know when you

know anything?" I beg.

"I will." She scurries away, and I drop to the chair, my head falling into my hands as I say a prayer for Delilah and our baby to be okay. Then I start calling everyone. I first call Delilah's parents who tell me they're on their way. Next, I call Xander and leave him a voicemail. I call Delilah's obstetrician's office and her oncologist just to be sure. I text Summer and let her know, and she texts back that she will let Delilah's other friends know.

"Are you the father of Delilah Cross's baby?" a nurse asks. Her nametag reads Lucy.

"I am," I say, standing. "Is she okay?"

"Dr. Blake was on call and notified. He's prepping her for an emergency cesarean. Her blood pressure was too high, so he wants to take the baby out now, so as not to risk infection to the mom due to her condition. They have her stable and gave her anesthesia for the surgery. Would you like to be in the room?"

"Yes, please."

"Follow me." Nurse Lucy hands me a set of scrubs, booties, and a cap. "Wash your hands twice, and I will be back to get you as soon as the doctor is ready."

A few minutes later, she returns, and I follow her to a freezing cold surgical room. I walk around the corner and see Delilah laying on a medical bed. There's a rectangular drape covering her entire lower half, but because I'm tall, I can see her pregnant belly on the other side.

The doctor is throwing out orders, and everyone is preparing for this birth, and me, I'm freaking the fuck out. The nurse moves a stool next to Delilah and tells me I can sit down, so I do. Delilah isn't awake, so I take a moment to move a stray hair from out of her eyes, pushing it under the surgical cap.

"Alright, sweet girl," I say, using Xander's nickname for her. "It's time. I need you to be strong, please. They're going to take our baby out of you, and then you're going to start getting better." Bending over, I give her a kiss on her forehead.

"Dad," I hear the doctor say, and I look up. "Do you have a camera?"

Oh shit! "No, I left my phone with my clothes."

"I have one," the nurse says with a smile. "I'll take some pictures for you."

"Thank you."

"Okay, here we go," Dr. Blake says. "Unless you have a strong stomach, don't look over the sheet until I tell you to." He gives me a wink, and out of morbid curiosity I look over the sheet. Delilah's stomach is being cut open. The doctor presses on her stomach slightly and liquid gushes everywhere.

"And...it's a..." The doctor pulls the balled up baby from inside Delilah. "...girl!" The nurses scramble to clean up the baby, and a few seconds later, our baby girl is screaming her head off. They do whatever they do while Dr. Blake starts to clean up Delilah.

"Here you are, Dad." One of the nurses comes around and hands me my daughter, and for a brief second all is right in the world. The nurse with the camera takes a couple pictures as I look down at her. She has a tiny patch of brown hair, and her eyes are black. She's squinting, trying to keep her eyes open, but it's too hard. Her nose is scrunched up in a cute button shape that is identical to Delilah's nose. Dipping my head, I kiss her nose.

"We have to take her to run some tests. Once we're done, we'll bring her to you." And just like that, they whisk our baby girl away. I want to tell them to give her back, but I don't. I know they need to do their job.

"Follow me," Nurse Lucy says, "Dr. Blake needs to finish stitching up Delilah and then they'll meet you in her room."

After changing out of my scrubs and back into my clothes, I head back to the recovery ward where I spot Delilah's parents and Summer.

"Is she okay?" Joanne cries. "Is my baby okay?"

"She's okay. She had high blood pressure so they had to deliver the baby early, but she's perfect. They both are."

"It's a girl?" She smiles through her tears.

"It's a girl, and she looks just like Delilah."

I give Summer a hug and thank her for coming, promising that once Delilah is awake and up for visitors, I will text her and let her know. Then Delilah's parents and I head to her room to wait for her.

CHAPTER THIRTY-FOUR

Delilah

MY HEAD FEELS GROGGY LIKE EVERYTHING IS IN A HAZE. I ATTEMPT TO OPEN my eyes, but I'm so tired. I just need a small nap and then I'll wake up rejuvenated. Then I remember why my eyes are closed. Cole and I were taking a tour of the hospital, and I started to feel light headed. Oh no! The baby. My eyes fly open, and I look down at my belly. It's deflated. It's not flat but there's no longer a baby bump there. *Where the hell is my baby?*

"Cole," I yell out, and he comes to my side. That's when I look around and see my mom, dad, and Cole are all in the room with me. *I'm still alive...*

"Is the...is the baby okay?" I ask.

"She's perfect," Cole says. *She? The baby is a girl?* "How are you feeling?"

"Tired...kind of out of it," I admit.

"You gave us a scare." Cole half-smiles. "Here, take a sip of water and then I'll introduce you to our little girl." He presses a button that slowly raises my bed so I'm sitting up, then he hands me a cup of water. I take a sip, wetting my mouth and throat, before I hand it back to him.

"Oh, sweetheart," my mom coos. "I'm so glad you're okay." She kisses my forehead then backs up so my dad can do the same.

"Alright, Delilah," Cole says, "I would like for you to formally meet your daughter." He places the most angelic, bundled up baby girl into my arms and the tears instantly fall.

"She's perfect," I cry, and then because I have to make sure everything is perfect, I undo her blanket, ignoring the fact that she's sleeping. I lay her on my lap, and she starts whimpering. I count her ten fingers and ten toes. Then I undo her diaper and check that she has all her parts. Her belly button still has the brown looking stump I remember reading about. It will dry up and fall off in the next week or two. I close her diaper back up and run my fingers down the side of her face. It startles her awake, and she starts crying, and my heart picks up speed at the beautiful sound.

"Most moms try to let their babies sleep," the nurse chides, walking into the room. She smiles at me and hands me a tiny bottle.

"I know. I just wanted to make sure she's okay." I look down at my daughter's coal eyes and wonder what color they will end up being. Light brown like mine or black like Cole's?

"Understandable. Her Apgar scores came back perfect. She weighed in at six pounds two ounces which is a great weight, especially for being a little over four weeks early. Why don't you feed her and if you have any questions, Cole can come get me so I can help."

"I need to go pee," I say.

"You're on a catheter. I'll remove it once you're done

feeding her."

"Thank you."

I swaddle my baby girl back up and, settling her into my arms, feed her for the first time.

"So, now that you know it's a girl, what are you going to name her?" my mom asks.

"I was thinking about Zoey for her first name, and for her middle name Amelia." I look to Cole for his approval.

"You want to give her my mom's name as her middle name?" His eyes are glossy with unshed tears.

"Well, Zoey is my mom's, grandma's, and my middle name so I thought it would be perfect. She could have a piece of both of us."

"Oh, sweetheart," my mom murmurs, coming over to me for a hug. "I think it's beautiful."

"I agree," Cole says. "Zoey Amelia."

"Zoey Amelia Andrews," I say, and he smiles.

I watch Zoey drink her bottle, and for a few minutes everything feels simply perfect.

"OH MY GOD! COLE!" MY HANDS COVER MY MOUTH IN SHOCK AND AWE AS I take in the amazing nursery Cole created for our daughter. "It's perfect! It's everything I wanted." I turn to face him. "You did all of this yourself?" My eyes follow along the light pink wall in front of me to the golden moon and array of stars. Underneath them is a comfy-looking white rocking chair. On another wall, directly above a white washed wooden changing table, there's a cluster of stars, and in the middle is the quote: *We wished upon a shooting star and twinkle twinkle here you are.*

"Well, except for setting up the furniture. I left that to

the experts."

"Cole," I say his name again because I'm in shock. "I can't believe you did this." My gaze goes to another wall. There's a beautiful matching crib and directly above it, another quote: *We love you more than a thousand shooting stars.*

I step into the middle of the room and try to take it all in. It's everything I circled in the baby books: the bedding, the lamp, the rug. Cole took everything I circled and ran with it, turning it into the most gorgeous nursery.

"Wait a second!" I exclaim. "How did you know she was a girl?"

Cole chuckles. "I might've cheated and asked Dr. Blake."

"Thank you." I cut across the room and pull him into a hug. "Thank you for making my dreams come true."

We're standing in the room hugging when I hear the front door open. We separate, and a second later, Xander enters the nursery, dressed head-to-toe in his basketball gear. "Where is she? Where's the princess?"

"I'm right here," I joke, wiping my tears, and he grins.

"As good as it is to see you, I'm looking for a tinier, cuter princess."

While I was in the hospital, Xander must've texted me a million times apologizing for not being able to make it when Zoey was born. He said too many times to count that he hated not being able to meet her in the hospital, and I told him just as many times that I understood. He's in the middle of his season.

Xander is about to give me a hug when Cole stops him. "Wash your hands and use the hand sanitizer first," he says. He's been like this since Dr. Morton visited me in the hospital after Zoey was born. All it took was Dr. Morton saying he's concerned about my white blood cell count being low to send Cole into overprotective mode.

"Yes sir." Xander gives Cole a two-finger salute and leaves the room to wash his hands. I make my way back out to the living room and place Zoey into the portable bassinet before sitting down on the couch. Cole, of course, excuses himself to the other room.

"How are you feeling, sweet girl?" Xander asks, pulling me into a hug.

"Like they cut me open and took a baby out of me." I wink, and Xander laughs.

He looks into the bassinet, and I see the huge smile on his face. "Jesus, woman, if I knew you made such pretty babies, I would've knocked you up first."

"Oh my god!" I laugh. "Shut up!" I slap Xander's chest, and he grunts. "But she is beautiful, isn't she?"

"She's the perfect mix of both of you," Xander says softly, staring down at my sleeping daughter.

"Xander," I say to get his attention. "Would you maybe want to be her Godfather? I know I'm supposed to have a Godmother and father, but well...I just want you."

"Oh, sweet girl," Xander murmurs. "It would be my honor."

CHAPTER THIRTY-FIVE

Delilah

"THERE YOU GO. BURP FOR MOMMY," I COO TO MY DAUGHTER, AND JUST LIKE the perfect little princess she is, she burps like a trucker. I laugh as I wipe her mouth. Who knew something as insignificant as my baby burping could make my heart feel so full. Well, I guess it's not really the burping itself, but getting to experience the moment. Getting to feed her and change her diaper and give her baths. Getting to hold her and kiss her. It's like a dream come true.

"Is she done?" Cole walks into the nursery holding his arms out, but I don't want to give her up just yet. I know he's just trying to help, but right now I'm feeling good. Since I've started my treatments, most days are rough, and that's putting it mildly. There were a few moments when I felt so sick and weak I almost wished for death to take me. But right now I'm feeling okay, and I'm going to soak up every second I can with my daughter, knowing at any moment I can go back to feeling sick. My treatments are every three weeks, leaving me two weeks in between to recoup. They're monitoring my blood cell count. It's the reason I passed out and had to deliver Zoey early. My white cell count was too low. If it drops like that again, they'll be forced to hold off any further treatment.

"She is, but I think I'm going to hold her a little longer," I tell Cole, and he grants me a soft smile. I know he wants to tell me not to overdo it, but he doesn't say anything. Instead he dips his head and gives me a kiss on my forehead, then dipping lower, he gives Zoey one. He's been amazing since we came home. He took a few weeks off of work and has been doting on Zoey and me every second of every day.

"I'm going to do some laundry. If you need anything just let me know." He leaves the nursery, and my gaze goes back to my little girl. Her eyes are fluttering open, somewhere in between being awake and falling asleep, satisfied and content with a full belly. Raising her body to my nose, I sniff her, attempting to memorize her baby smell. If I could, I would bottle it up so I could have it with me when I'm stuck in the hospital for hours getting treatment. I hate any moment away from Zoey.

After rocking my baby girl to sleep, I bring her with me into my room and lay her down in her bassinet so we can take a nap together. "Sweet dreams," I whisper. "Mommy loves you."

"GOOD MORNING, SUNSHINE. DID YOU SLEEP GOOD?" I OPEN MY EYES TO FIND the best view in the world. Cole is sitting up in our bed, holding our daughter and talking to her like she understands everything he's saying. I love that he calls her sunshine. The first time he called her that, I asked why, and he said she's the brightest part of everything. I happen to agree.

"Morning." Cole smiles at me. "How are you feeling?"

I stretch my body out, and although I feel sore for so many reasons, I say, "I feel good." He frowns slightly but doesn't call me out on it. "How long was I asleep for?"

"Twelve hours. It's five in the morning."

"Geez, I guess I was tired. I can't believe I slept through her waking up." I frown. Scooting closer to Cole and our daughter, I give her a kiss. "What if she needed me and you weren't here?"

"I moved the bassinet out to the living room, so don't go there. You're an amazing mom. You just gave birth a couple weeks ago, via C-section no less, and you're going through chemo. Give yourself a break, please."

"I know. I just feel bad that you're doing everything."

"Don't feel bad about anything. Your job is to love our daughter and get better. Leave everything else to me. Now, how about you go pee, then you can hold Zoey while I make us breakfast?"

"Sounds perfect."

CHAPTER THIRTY-SIX

Cole

 since I need to go back to work to finish out the year," I tell Delilah. I've been home with her since Zoey was born, but I need to go back so I don't lose my job as well as my insurance for the baby.

"That would be good," she says. She's laying across the couch with her eyes closed. She's not feeling well today. Some days it's as if she isn't fighting a life threatening disease, but other days such as today, we're reminded she is indeed fighting for her life.

"I hate that you have to bring her to the doctor for her checkup without me," Delilah pouts, noncommittally. It's been six weeks since Zoey was born and Delilah started her chemotherapy. Her body is fighting it, and she's weak, which means she can't be in public, especially a doctor's office with a million kid germs. It's a small sacrifice to make so that she can get better for our daughter, but I know she's struggling. Even if she could go, she's not up for it today.

She spent yesterday at the hospital having poison injected into her veins, and it's hitting her hard. This is the third round of chemo and she's struggling, but she's trying to stay positive. She just feels like she's missing a lot.

"We'll be home in a couple hours, I promise." I give her a kiss on her forehead, then I hand Zoey over to her so she can say goodbye to her before we go. She opens her eyes and love shines through as she says bye to our daughter.

"Be good for daddy, precious," Delilah coos. "I love you."

ZOEY AND I GET TO THE DOCTOR'S OFFICE AND WE'RE SEEN ALMOST immediately. The nurse weighs her in at eight and a half pounds and says she's grown another half inch since birth. I undress her down to her diaper, which pisses her off, and the pediatrician comes in a few minutes later. She checks her out and tells me all the shots she'll be getting. The nurse comes back in, pricks the hell out of my daughter, making her scream, then smiles and tells me I can schedule the next appointment in the front. I refrain from telling her to go fuck herself as I imagine shoving a needle up her ass.

On our way home, I text Delilah to ask her if she needs or wants anything, but she doesn't respond, so she's probably sleeping. I hate what she's going through. I hate the way the chemo drags her down, making her feel sick and exhausted for days at a time, and I really fucking hate that it's ruining her experience as a first time mom. Wanting to cheer her up, I see a floral stand and stop to get her some flowers.

"Delilah, we're home," I call out as I place Zoey's car seat on the coffee table. Not seeing Delilah on the couch, I figure she's taking a nap in our room, but when I walk inside, she's not there either. I check the bathroom and the nursery, trying not to panic, but she's not anywhere. Then I head outside onto the roof patio and find her laying on the lounge chair. Her eyes are closed, and I take in a deep breath of relief. She must've come out here for some fresh air and fell asleep.

But as I get closer, I notice her face is pale, and her lips are blue. "Delilah!" I yell, running over to her. I shake her several times but she doesn't wake. "Delilah! Wake up!" I scream, but her lids stay closed. Pulling her lifeless body into my arms, I fall onto the cement and check for a pulse. There isn't one.

"No. No. No! Wake up!" I yell, but she doesn't move. Her body is still. With shaky hands, I pull out my cell phone and call 911. "I need an ambulance." I rattle off our address and quickly explain she has cancer and isn't breathing. The emergency operator walks me through how to do CPR, but I know it's too late, so instead I just hold her in my arms. She's warm from the sun beating on her for god knows how long, but the longer I hold her, the colder she gets. "Dammit, Delilah," I cry. "Please don't leave me. Please," I beg. My face rests into the crook of her neck, my eyes squeezed shut as I inhale her scent, wishing for this to be a nightmare. I'm going to open my eyes, and she's going to be awake. Only when I reopen them, she's still lifeless.

Several minutes later, the EMTs show up. They ask me questions I have no patience to answer, and then they tell me they're taking her to Texas General Hospital. Robotically, I call Summer and ask her if she can watch Zoey. She tells me she'll meet me at the hospital. On the way, I call Delilah's parents. Her mom cries and eventually her dad gets on the phone and says they're on their way. Just as I'm pulling in, I call Xander.

"Cole, how are you?" he answers, and I choke up. I can't

get the words out. Why is it so much harder telling Xander? "Cole? You there?"

"She's gone." My voice is nothing more than a whisper, the gigantic lump in my throat preventing me from speaking louder.

"What do you mean she's gone?" He asks, his words coming out slow.

"I came home, and she wasn't breathing. I'm at the hospital now."

"I'm on my way," is all he says before he hangs up.

Grabbing Zoey's car seat from the back, I make my way through the front doors. Summer comes running over and pulls me into a hug. "Are you sure, Cole? Are you sure she's gone?"

"Yeah, I'm sure," I choke out. I hand the car seat over to her and walk up to the front desk. "The ambulance brought in Delilah Cross. She wasn't breathing."

The woman types in something on the computer then says, "I will have a doctor come out to see you as soon as we know anything." And while I know it's not her fault—she's just saying what she's supposed to say—right there in front of her desk, I lose it.

"As soon as you know anything? What do you need to find out? I just told you she wasn't breathing! She's dead! Delilah is dead!" I scream. "Are they going to bring her back to life? Do they have some magical fucking powers in the back? Because if they do, why the hell didn't they use them on her before? Huh? You know, when she spent the last twelve years fighting the cancer!"

"Sir, I'm so sorry. I didn't know." The elderly woman shakes her head. "I'm so sorry."

"Cole." I hear my name being called, and when I turn around, I see Dr. Morton standing in the doorway. His face says it all. He's seen her, and she really is gone. No magical powers in the back, no nightmare to wake up from. She's fucking gone.

"What happened?" I demand.

"We're looking into it now to determine the cause of death," he says. "I'm so sorry, son." He pulls me into a hug. "I know it won't make a difference, but I'll get answers for you."

"Cole!" I turn around, and Joanne and John are running through the front doors. "No, please no," Joanne cries. "I need to see my baby," she yells at Dr. Morton.

"Joanne, I just came from back there. She's gone. Are you sure you want to see her like this?"

"I-I need to. I talked to her today! She was alive and laughing. I swear she was." She nods her head like she's trying to convince herself and everyone around her that Delilah is still alive. Her gaze goes to me, and with devastation pouring down her face, she says, "Cole, I don't understand. She was alive." And suddenly I'm just so fucking pissed that I left her at home.

"Dammit!" My fist goes through the concrete wall. "I shouldn't have left her! I took Zoey to the doctor. Fuck!" I punch the closest thing to me—a vending machine—and the glass shatters everywhere.

"Cole, Joanne, let's move this out of the waiting room." Dr. Morton guides us to a private room. "If you would like to wait here, I'm having the medical examiner examine Delilah right now to determine what happened. Give me a little while, and I'll be back." He turns to Joanne. "And if you still want to see her, I'll bring you back."

He leaves the room, and Joanne asks, "Where's Zoey?" Suddenly realizing she's not here.

"Summer took her."

The three of us wait in the tiny room for I don't know how long. None of us cry or speak. We just sit and wait. My mind replays this morning over and over again. *Was there any signs of this coming? What if I wouldn't have left her? Did she know she was going to die?* Eventually Dr. Morton returns and the look on his face tells us Delilah is in fact dead.

"We've determined she died of a heart attack."

"A heart attack?" Joanne cries. "But she's so young."

"She's had cancer several times and has been on so many medications. Everybody's body reacts differently. According to the examiner, Delilah's arteries had severe blockage. It's common in patients with recurring cancer. I'm so sorry. Her heart just couldn't handle it."

*Her heart couldn't handle it...*how ironic is that. The woman with the biggest, most selfless heart dies because her heart was too weak.

CHAPTER THIRTY-SEVEN

Cole

I'M SITTING IN THE FRONT ROW OF THE FUNERAL HOME WHERE JOANNE insisted I sit. Next to me, she's holding my daughter. Zoey is crying, and everyone is staring, but I don't have it in me to do anything about it. The truth is she sounds how I feel: a mixture of pissed off and devastated. The pastor is speaking, but Zoey's cries are getting louder, and soon nobody will be able to hear what he's saying. She shouldn't even be here. It's not like she knows why we're all here. She doesn't know her mother is dead and never coming back. Or maybe she does know. Maybe she senses her mother is gone, and that's why she's crying.

"Do you want me to bring her outside?" Xander leans over me and asks Joanne, but she shakes her head no. She's been staying at the condo the last few days while they plan the funeral. They're sleeping in my old room while I sleep on the couch since I refuse to sleep in Delilah's room.

"Are you sure?" Xander asks again.

"Are her cries disturbing your service?" I ask way too

loudly, and everyone's gaze hits us. "I don't even know why you're sitting over here. It's not like you came around at all the last few years."

"Cole, don't go there," Xander whispers. "I can smell the alcohol on your breath. Don't ruin this service."

"Don't ruin this service? Really?" I scoff. "What's going to happen if I do? Newsflash! Delilah is dead! She's been cremated, and she's now nothing more than ashes in a fucking can. The only reason we're all here right now is for ourselves. She's already gone!" I stand and look around me. I see the sympathy and pity in everyone's eyes, and it makes me sick. I don't deserve it.

"C'mon, man, let's go." Xander grabs me by my arm and pulls me out of my seat and down the aisle until we're outside. It's dark out now. The moon is huge, and the stars are shining. Just like Delilah loved. I fall onto the bench, and Xander sits down next to me.

After a few minutes of us sitting in silence, and me realizing I was an asshole to say the shit I said in there, I say to Xander, "Fuck, I shouldn't have lost it in there."

"It's to be expected." He gives me a sad smile.

"I'm sorry. I shouldn't have said what I did."

"It's all good. Say whatever you need to. You were right. I was gone for three years. That's on me."

"I don't think I can do this," I admit.

"Do what?" Xander asks.

"Live without her."

THE REST OF THE FUNERAL GOES SMOOTHLY. JOANNE GETS UP AND READS A poem, and John says a few words about his daughter. When it's over, we move to another room where food is served and everyone socializes. After the third person comes up to me and says they're sorry for my loss, I've had enough. Since I came in the same vehicle as Joanne and John, I call for a Lyft.

"Where you heading?" the driver asks.

"Pick a bar, any bar."

He drops me off at some hole-in-the-wall shady looking place, but I don't give a fuck. As long as it has booze, I'm good. When I walk in, country music is pumping through the speakers. It's a Monday evening, so the place isn't busy. I grab an empty stool and order a double shot of Johnnie Walker. The bartender delivers it, and I down the shot and order another one. After the third one, she brings the bottle over.

"You driving?"

"Nah, just keep 'em coming." I throw my credit card down onto the bar top.

"Want to talk about it?" she asks, pouring me another shot. She places the glass in front of me and shoots me a flirtatious wink.

"Talk about what? How the mother of my daughter died a few days ago from a heart attack after having cancer for more years than not? Or how about we discuss how she was my best friend who turned into my girlfriend, yet I spent the majority of my time fantasizing about someone else? You sure you want me to talk?"

The bartender leans her forearms against the bar top. "And let me guess, you feel guilty?"

"Fuck yes, I do!" I throw a shot back. "But it's pointless. She died before she could even be loved properly. She wasted the little bit of life she had on loving me." The bartender pours me another drink, and I down it, attempting to numb my mind and heart with the alcohol.

"This other woman you fantasized about...did you cheat on your girlfriend with her?"

I laugh and shake my head. "Him," I say, correcting her. "I Fantasized about our best friend who is a guy...and ready for the punchline?" I ask. "The three of us slept together for several years." Then I laugh even louder when her eyes go wide in shock.

"I think you might need something stronger."

"Tell me about it. Like I said, keep 'em coming."

Part Three

CHAPTER THIRTY-EIGHT

Xander

"I DON'T KNOW WHAT TO DO," JOANNE SAYS SOFTLY. "I'VE LOST DELILAH, AND now it feels like I'm losing Cole. He's drinking a lot and won't take care of Zoey. He rarely ever comes home. I have no clue where he's going, but I can't keep doing this. John wants me back home. If something doesn't change soon I'm going to have to petition the court for temporary custody."

I should've known Cole was going to spiral. When I called him the night of the funeral, after he left, the bartender answered his phone and said he was passed out drunk. I picked him up and brought him home. He refused to go to the room they shared, though, passing out on the couch instead. I wanted to stay with him, but with our team in the playoffs, I had to get back. I had already missed two of the semi-final games, and I'm contractually bound to play. Joanne told me she was going to stay with Cole and Zoey at the condo until he gets his shit together, so I assumed she would have things under control. We're all devastated that Delilah passed away, but the truth is, nobody loved that girl as much as Cole did. She was his entire world. Every decision he ever made was for her and because of her. If you'd asked her, though, she'd have told you something different. My thoughts go back to the evening of her baby shower. The night I found out Cole and Delilah were no longer a couple. We sat outside on the roof patio and, even though I didn't want to hear it, she gave me a piece of her mind.

"Cole and I aren't together," Delilah admitted. *"We broke up before I found out I was pregnant. Want to know why?"* Before I could answer, she continued. *"Because while he was having sex with me from behind, he called out your name. Now, it's time we talk. And before you say a word, what I mean is, I'm going to talk, and you're going to listen."* I was in such fucking shock from what she just said I couldn't have interrupted her if I wanted to. Cole called out my name while having sex with Delilah? It didn't make any sense.

"I saw it the first time we were together," Delilah admitted. *"I was watching the two of you, and you were watching each other. I don't know when or how your feelings grew to be more than friendship, but I know when I realized it. That very first time."* I knew back then my feelings for Cole, but I never imagined in a million years he felt the same way. I'd seen him slowly developing what I thought were feelings for me over the years, but he'd never admit to them and he sure as fuck would never act on them.

"I've sat by and watched you two dance around each other for years, and if I'm honest, at first I didn't point it out because I didn't want to lose either of you." She shrugged. *"I'm sorry for that. If I could go back and do things over again, I wouldn't have been so selfish. It's just that you and Cole were all I knew. I couldn't remember a time when I didn't have you both protecting and loving me, and I was scared to lose that feeling*

of security when, for the majority of my life, I felt like I was stuck in a tornado, and everything was out of my control."

"Cancer or not, you were never a burden or an obligation. We were with you by choice. We love you and always will."

"I know, but it's a different kind of love. When I pushed you guys together, I thought you guys would finally admit your feelings, but I didn't know Cole made some stupid promise to his mom." She rolled her eyes. "And then you made me promise not to say anything to him. When you left, he lost it, Xander. He turned to drinking and sank into depression. I shouldn't have let him use me to get over you, but I didn't know what else to do. He was hurting and, just like all the times you two made me feel better, I wanted to make him feel better. I allowed us to live in denial for too long, but when he called out your name, I knew I needed to do something." She sighed. "But then I found out my cancer was back and that I was pregnant."

"It wouldn't have mattered. Cole will never see me in his future as anything but a friend he's attracted to. He won't allow himself to go there."

"Well, then you need to fight for him, Xander. Promise me. Promise me that once I'm out of the picture you will fight for him." I couldn't imagine Delilah ever being out of the picture, especially with them expecting a baby, so I did what I always did when it came to Delilah...I gave her what she wanted.

"I promise."

"Xander." Joanne's voice brings me back to the present. "If Cole doesn't get it together soon I'm leaving, and I'm taking Zoey with me. I don't want to do this. I know Delilah would want Cole raising her, but not like this."

"Game five is this weekend. Can you please just stay until the championships are over. Hopefully we win this game, but if we don't, I'll just need a little more time."

"Of course," Joanne says. "I shouldn't have called you.

I'm sorry."

"No, I'm glad you did, and as soon as I get everything wrapped up here, I'll be there."

"And what are you going to do? He's in a really bad way, Xander."

"I don't know, but taking his daughter away can't be the answer. Let me just get through this game and then I'll figure something out."

We hang up, and I head out to practice. With already three wins on our side to Cleveland's one, if we win this upcoming game, we'll be the champions. The game is taking place on Saturday, and we've got homecourt advantage. My first year playing we made it to the playoffs but lost in the first round. Last year we won the championship in the seventh game. Not many players can say they not only got a championship ring their second year in the NBA but played in every damn game. As my rookie contract stipulates, Houston can offer me a player extension this coming year, which is something I really fucking want. I love playing for Houston. I love my teammates and my coach. Unfortunately, nothing is set in stone, and if I'm not offered an extension this summer, next summer I will go into free agency. I know I'll be picked up. I'm one of the highest paid rookies in the industry right now, plus I was picked first and have already broken several rookie records on top of helping to win a championship. But what I want is to stay here in Houston. Maybe it's knowing I'm only a few hours away from Cole, I don't know.

"X! WHAT THE HELL IS GOING ON WITH YOU?" MY TEAMMATE, LANCE WILLIAMS, shouts at me during halftime. "Your body is clearly here."

He throws a towel at me. "But are *you* here?"

I don't even bother to respond, knowing he's right. While I'm physically here, my head isn't in the game at all. I've been racking my brain with what to do about Cole, and I'm stumped. I was up way too late last night, tossing and turning. I tried to call him a couple times when Joanne said he didn't come home again, but he wouldn't answer my calls. She said his boss called the house looking for him and mentioned they're not renewing his teaching or coaching contract. He was supposed to go back to work the week Delilah died. He obviously didn't, and now he's out of a job. That's all the more reason why I need to get my head in the game, because if I don't, I'm going to lose my shot at renewing my contract, and no contract means no money, and I can't do anything to help Cole without an income.

"I'm sorry, you're right," I say, "I have a lot of shit going on, but I'm here. We got this. We're only down by fifteen with an entire half to go. Let's go get that fucking ring!" I yell, pumping myself up in an attempt to block everything but this game out.

And for the next twenty-four minutes, that's exactly what I do. We win the championship: 115-93. The confetti rains down on us, and hats and shirts are passed out. Reporters interview me and ask about my future, but I go through it all without any emotion. As I watch everyone cheer and hug each other, I've never felt so lost in my life. Every time I imagined being here, it was with Cole and Delilah watching in the stands, yet neither one of them have ever been to one of my professional games, and now Delilah never will. That thought has me needing to get the fuck out of here. Cole is all I have left, and I'm all he has. Delilah was right. I need to fight for him.

I'm making my way off the court to shower so I can

head to the aftergame conference when a reporter stops me and asks, "So what are your plans for offseason? Are you planning any trips?" And that's when it hits me what I need to do.

"Umm...yeah. I'm not sure where, though. Any recommendations?"

She smiles and thinks for a moment. "Hmm...I would probably go to the beach, like to Florida or maybe Martha's Vineyard. Oh! Or California. Sand, sun, and relaxation."

"Good choices. Maybe I'll hit up one of those places." I shoot her a wink and head back to the locker room.

CHAPTER THIRTY-NINE

Xander

 JOANNE SAYS WITH A FROWN WHEN SHE OPENS THE DOOR to let me in. "And I don't know where he is." She rocks Zoey in her arms as she walks back inside, then lays her down in her portable bed thing. "He came home last night...or I should say this morning, took a shower and changed his clothes, and was back out the door before I could even confront or stop him. Not that it would do any good." She sits down on the couch.

"Alright, I'm going to see if I can find him. He was at that one bar the night I found him after the funeral. Can you do me a favor? I need you to pack a couple weeks' worth of clothes for Zoey and Cole. Also, I've put a call into a nanny service that comes highly recommended by one of my teammates. There are three women willing to travel on short notice. They're going to be here to interview. Can you please pick the one you think is best if I'm not back?" I check my watch. "They're scheduled thirty minutes apart, and the first one should be here soon."

"I don't understand. You want to leave with Zoey?" Joanne grimaces. "I don't think that's a good idea."

"I want to take her away with Cole. He needs to get away from this condo and from this environment. He's grieving over the loss of Delilah, and until he's ready to be a dad again, I'm going to need help with Zoey. You said it yourself, you need to get back to your husband. So, hiring a nanny is the perfect solution."

"I know. It's just that I'm going to miss this sweet girl," Joanne says, looking over at Zoey.

"We're only going to be gone for a few weeks. I found a private rental on Martha's Vineyard with a guest house. If you want to visit anytime, just let me know."

Joanne sighs then nods her head. "Okay. You go find Cole, and I'll make sure to pick someone perfect for you." Joanne stands up and gives me a hug. "Please take care of my granddaughter."

I PULL UP TO THE BAR I FOUND COLE AT A FEW WEEKS AGO AND PARK. I walk inside, and the place is dark, especially for it only being three in the afternoon. I glance around and notice the windows are all blacked out. Some loud as fuck country music is playing, and there's maybe a handful of people hanging out. I walk farther inside, past the pool tables, and head straight for the bar. If Cole isn't here, I'm planning to ask the bartender what other bars are in the area.

At first, I don't spot anyone manning the bar. There's one guy sitting on a stool nursing a beer, but other than him, I don't see anyone else. Then out of the corner of my eye, I spot a couple practically fucking against the jukebox. The woman has her legs around the guy, and he's dry humping her. *Real classy...*I'm about to turn around and head out since Cole clearly isn't here, when the guy lifts his face from out of the woman's neck. His glossy eyes lock with mine, and I freeze in my place as he drops her to the ground. *Fucking Cole...*

"Real fucking nice!" I yell, pissed as hell, and if I'm honest, also jealous. "The mother of your daughter hasn't even been dead for two months and you've already moved on?" I walk up to Cole, and even though it's obvious he's drunk, I push him backwards. "You're here, sucking face with someone while your daughter is at home! What the fuck, man!" I push him one more time, and his back hits the wall.

"Hey! You need to leave," the woman yells, and when I look at her, I recognize her from the night I picked up Cole. She's the bartender.

"You need to go back behind the bar where you belong." I point my finger in her face. "Now." Then I turn my attention back to Cole. "Let's go. It's time to go home."

I turn my back on him and start walking toward the front entrance when he shouts, "Fuck you! You have no idea what it's like to live somewhere where the person you loved took her last breath." I turn around and see tears running down his face. "I just want to fucking feel something, anything, that isn't fucking pain."

I step towards him until I'm less than a foot away. "You have a daughter at home that needs you. You aren't the only one who lost Delilah. You want to feel something? Go love that little girl who will never know her mother! You're searching for the wrong goddamned feelings. And you know what? You're going to lose your daughter if you keep this shit up."

"I can't go back there. I can't sleep where she slept. I can't make coffee where she made her last cup." Cole drops to the ground in defeat. "Every time I'm there all I can see is her lifeless body in my arms. I thought she was napping. I thought she fell asleep. She wasn't sleeping. She was fucking dead." He drops his head into his hands, and my heart breaks for my best friend. He's right, I have no idea what he's going through, but I'm going to get him through this.

I kneel down in front of him and lift his chin with my thumb and forefinger. He looks at me for a brief moment before he closes his eyes and shakes his head, several more tears racing down his cheeks. "Hey," I say to get his attention, and he opens his eyes back up. "We're going to get through this. I promise." I stand and extend my hand, and Cole takes it, rising up onto his feet. "Let's go."

Wordlessly, he follows me out of the bar and to my car, neither of us saying anything the entire drive to the condo. When we arrive, I tell him to stay in the car and I'll be back in a few minutes. I go upstairs and find Joanne and an elderly woman conversing on the couch. When Joanne makes eye contact, she nods and stands. The woman stands as well, and they both walk toward me.

"Xander, this is Mallory Arno; Mallory, this is Xander Thompson. He's the one who is in need of your services."

"Nice to meet you," Mallory says.

"Likewise," I say to her and shake her hand. "Joanne, can I speak to you for a minute in the kitchen?"

"Sure." She follows me into the kitchen.

"Did you meet with all three women?" I ask.

"I actually only met with two. But I love this woman. I called the number you gave me and told them to cancel the last interview. Mallory is great. She is a grandmother and usually watches her grandkids for her daughter and son-in-law, but they are out of the country on business for a year, so she's been nannying to keep busy. She's a retired nurse, so she's more than capable of caring for Zoey, and as you know, she's willing to travel."

"Thank you." I give Joanne a hug. "I found Cole, and he's downstairs. He can't come up here. I'm going to bring him and Zoey to my hotel tonight, and we're flying out in the morning."

"Please video chat and send me pictures."

"Of course." I'm about to head back into the living room when Joanne says my name.

"Delilah left letters for you and Cole. I'm allowed to give you yours now, but I can't give Cole his yet."

I turn around, stunned. "She knew she was going to die?"

"Oh no! She didn't know, sweetheart, but when she started her treatment, she wrote them just in case. She actually wrote one for both of you every time she went through chemo." Tears pool her eyes. "And then when she was told she was one year in remission, she would take them back from me. Did you know to be considered officially in remission, you have to be cancer free for five years?"

I shake my head. I didn't know that.

"She never once made it five years. Since she turned eleven years old and was diagnosed, my little girl never went more than four years without having cancer. She was just so tired, Xander."

"I know she was."

"Here's your letter." She pulls a light pink envelope out of her purse and hands it to me. "She loved you boys so much."

I take the envelope from her, and even though it's only paper, it feels like a hundred pound weight in my hand. "What determined you being allowed to give me this?" I ask curiously, since she said she's not allowed to give Cole his yet.

"She said that if she died, Cole would need you, and the day you showed up to be there for him, to give it to you. And she asked that you please not tell Cole until he gets his letter."

"When are you allowed to give Cole his?"

"Oh, you know I can't tell you that." She winks and wipes her tears.

We head back into the living room, and I let Mallory know that she's been hired and we'll pick her up to leave tomorrow morning. We're going to be on the beach, and since she'll have plenty of time off to do as she wants, she should bring a bathing suit or whatever it is she needs for warm beach weather. After she thanks me and leaves, Joanne helps me get Zoey ready and walks downstairs with me. I throw Zoey's stroller into the trunk along with their two suitcases. Joanne shows me how to buckle Zoey's car seat into the car while Cole sits in the front seat, not saying a word. He's either passed out or too embarrassed to say anything. Joanne gives Zoey a kiss goodbye and makes me promise for a second time to send daily pictures and video chat often. And then we're on our way. Cole stays quiet the entire drive, but opens his eyes once we pull into the hotel parking garage, which tells me he wasn't really asleep.

"We're only staying here for tonight, but you'll need your luggage to change your clothes. How drunk are you? Can you carry the luggage, or do I need to get someone to help?"

Cole eyes me, warily. "Where are we going tomorrow?"

"Away. Now, can you help with the luggage or not?"

"Yeah," is all he says before he gets out of the car. While he grabs the bags, I grab Zoey. She's sleeping like a little angel, but I imagine it won't last for long. I probably should've asked Mallory to start tonight, but she needed to go home and pack.

We take the elevator up to my room and once we're up there, Cole heads right for the shower while I stay in the main room, watching Zoey sleep and praying I'm not in over my head here. When I stand to get a drink, I feel the crinkle of the letter Joanne gave me. Hoping Delilah will have some final words of encouragement for me, I bring Zoey—still sleeping in her car seat—outside with me on the balcony, so I can read Delilah's letter.

Xander,

If you're reading this letter, my luck ran out and I'm no longer with you guys (but I'll always be with you in spirit). It also means Cole needs you, and you've come home to be there for him. I've had cancer three times, and every time I've written you and Cole a letter, but this time it feels so different. Maybe it's because as I write this letter I'm sitting next to my sleeping newborn daughter, or maybe it's because unlike the other two times when I would classify you, Cole, and me as best friends, this time I know better. You and me, we're best friends. Cole and me, we're best friends (don't let the baby fool you). But you and Cole, you two are destined to be so much more than best friends. The fact that you're reading this tells me you haven't given up on him, and that makes me so happy.

If I know Cole like I think I do, he's probably feeling

lost right now. He's probably sunk into depression and is regretting every decision that led up to the moment of my death. Please don't let him do that because I don't regret a single day of my life with you two. For one thing, it gave me Zoey, and I could never regret anything that led me to be a mother to my precious little girl. My only regret is that I didn't break my promise to you. The one where I agreed not to talk to Cole about you. But that's okay, because I would like to think everything happens for a reason. As much as we would like to be in control of our lives and futures, sometimes we can't be. Sometimes we just have to sit back and hold on tight while we see where life takes us. I know it sounds cliché, but I think you needed to leave so Cole could realize how much he loves you, and don't for a second think he doesn't. He loves you, and he needs you.

I don't know how old Zoey is right now, but I know she needs you as well. Remember when I asked you to be her Godfather? Well, now I'm asking you to be her father alongside Cole, which means you need to fight. Fight for Cole. Fight for your best friend, the man you love. Fight for your happily-ever-after. And I know what you're thinking: how do you fight for someone who doesn't want to be fought for? Well, he does. You just have to make him see that. Show him that loving you would make his mom just as proud as if he was with a woman, because as a new mother, I can tell you, the only thing we want for our children is for them to be happy. And not that you need it, but please know that you both have my blessing.

Life is too short to not be with the person you love. I was lucky. I loved two men in my life, and I got to be with both of them. My life might have been short-lived, but it was filled with so much love. Thank you for being part of the reason I felt loved and cherished every day of my life.

Please give my daughter a kiss for me and tell her I love her. Tell her I'm looking down and watching over her, and that there isn't a moment that goes by that I'm not wishing I was still there with her. Please make sure she spends plenty of time outside under the starry sky. Teach her how important it is to wish upon the shooting stars. Every child should have hopes and dreams, and I hate that I'm not going to be there to watch hers come true. Please, Xander, make sure every one of my daughter's hopes and dreams come true.

Until we meet again.
All my love,
Delilah

"Oh, sweet girl, I can promise you your daughter will know all about her amazing mother." I fold the letter up, stuff it back into the envelope, then stand and push it down into my back pocket. As I turn around to bring Zoey back inside, I see Cole standing in the doorway, his face devoid of all emotion.

"Was that..." He nods toward my back pocket. "Was that a letter from Delilah?" I promised Joanne I wouldn't tell Cole, but right now I can't bring myself to lie to him.

"It was," I admit.

"She wrote you a letter?" he asks, hurt evident in his tone.

"She wrote you one as well, but Joanne was given strict instructions by Delilah when she can give you yours, and before you ask, I don't know when that is. You weren't supposed to know I received mine. I'm sorry."

"What...what did she say?" he asks softly. I'm not sure how much to tell him, but before I can answer, Zoey starts crying.

"Can you help me with her?" I ask. "I have no idea what I'm doing here." Cole looks down at Zoey, whose cries are now getting louder, and frowns.

"Maybe you should have thought about that before you showed up and decided to be a part of our lives. Why are you even here? Because Delilah is dead? Because your basketball season is over? Are you here to play hero? I don't need or want you. We were doing just fine the last three years since you walked out the door and left us. You want to play hero...you figure it out your damn self." Cole turns his back on me and his now screaming daughter and heads toward the door.

"Cole!" I shout out his name. "Don't do this. Don't walk out that door, please." I see his feet falter slightly, and

I pray he comes back, but instead he walks out the door. "Dammit!"

I bring Zoey inside and call Joanne. She walks me through how to make a bottle and explains to me about burping her and changing her diaper. Once I have Zoey situated, drinking her bottle, Joanne asks me where Cole is.

"My guess...probably at the bar."

"Xander...maybe this wasn't a good idea."

"Tomorrow morning we're leaving. Cole will be two thousand miles away from here, with no booze or anywhere to run to. I have to believe he just needs time and he'll come around."

"And if he doesn't?" Joanne asks.

"Then I'll raise Zoey myself with your help, just like Delilah asked."

Joanne is silent for a moment before she says, "You read the letter."

"I did."

"I'm rooting for you, Xander," she says, and I know she isn't just referring to helping Cole get through this. Knowing Delilah's mom—a woman who is the closest thing to a mother I've ever had—is in my corner, for some reason gives me the renewed confidence to fight for Cole.

CHAPTER FORTY

Cole

I'VE TAKEN A HANDFUL OF PAIN RELIEVERS AND DOWNED PROBABLY A DOZEN glasses of water, but even after several hours, my skull still feels like it's being eaten from the inside out by a pack of savage hyenas. It probably doesn't help that when I staggered in this morning, Xander was up and ready to go, which meant I've gotten zero sleep. Where we're headed...I have no fucking clue. But anywhere is better than being in that fucking condo where Delilah died, so I'm not arguing. Plus, even in my hungover state, I must admit it's nice to have Xander around again, even if he's only here because Joanne called him.

The first flight was out of Dallas to Logan airport in Boston. I slept most of the way, so I didn't bother to ask questions. When we arrived, I realized Xander picked up some old lady on the way. From what I heard, she's tagging along to help with Zoey. My initial thought was to tell Xander to fuck off. Zoey already has a mother, but then I remembered that her mother is dead, and her father has turned into a fucking drunk, so I kept my mouth shut.

Now we're on our second flight on a much smaller plane, and I probably should've paid attention to where it said we were heading, but it doesn't really matter. After ordering a Jack and Coke—figuring the best way to cure a hangover is to just stay drunk—I down the drink and close my eyes. All too soon I'm being shaken awake, and when I open my eyes Xander is glaring at me. I just shrug and enter into the center aisle to deplane.

After getting our luggage, Xander rents an SUV, and we're on our way. With the nanny sitting in the back with Zoey, I'm forced to sit in the front with Xander. He doesn't say a word to me the entire drive, but I do finally notice a sign on the side of the road that says we're on Martha's Vineyard. *Hmm...apparently we're taking a vacation.* When we pull up to a massive house that's situated on the water, Xander turns around to face the nanny.

"Mallory, if you can please help me get Zoey situated, that would be great, then I'll show you to your room. You actually have an entire guesthouse to yourself, so during the times you aren't watching Zoey you'll have your own space. From what I've seen in the pictures, you have a bedroom, bathroom, kitchen, and living area."

"Great, thank you. Zoey is due to be fed, so how about we get her in, I'll feed her, and after I lay her down, I'll check it all out. I was also hoping maybe we can go over a schedule."

Xander smiles. "Sounds good. Thank you again for taking this job last minute." I feel him glance my way, but I ignore him and get out of the vehicle. I don't need his shit. What I need is a drink. I consider going straight to the house but instead go around to the trunk and help grab some luggage.

Mallory grabs Zoey, and Xander grabs the pieces of luggage I didn't. He unlocks the front door, and when we step inside, I'm taken aback by my surroundings. The home is one story and probably a good five thousand square feet, but unlike the elegance it exudes from the outside with the perfect cut shrubs and flowing fountain, inside it's as Delilah would've described as homey. Dark wood floors and high rise wooden beams. The furniture looks lived in and comfy but you know it's meant to look that way. Nothing in this home is cheap.

I walk past the kitchen and living room and open the curtain that leads to the back patio. There's a huge outdoor grilling area, a large pool and jacuzzi, and just past that is the view of the bay. This place more than likely costs more a night than most people pay for their monthly mortgage. It's the ideal vacation spot. Private and luxurious, yet it makes you feel like you're still at home. My thoughts go to how much Delilah would've loved this place and that has me thinking about the fact that she'll never see it. She'll never vacation again. I think back to the last couple years. We were so caught up in school and work, then she found out she was pregnant and that her cancer returned, we didn't take the time to travel. Not since...well since the three of us traveled during spring break our sophomore year, right before Xander entered the draft and left us. And that depressing thought has me needing a drink.

I drop my luggage on the ground and head into the kitchen. I start opening cabinet after cabinet. Somebody has clearly been by to stock the place. There are fresh fruits and vegetables in the fridge, meat in the freezer, but there's not a drop of fucking liquor anywhere. *Motherfuckingsonuvabitch!*

"I need the keys to the vehicle," I say to Xander, putting my hand out. I paid attention on our drive here. Nothing is in walking distance.

"Sorry, man. I didn't add you to the rental insurance. Need to go somewhere? I'll have to take you." He shrugs, and it takes everything in me not to knock him the fuck out. I should've seen this coming.

"That's fine, I'll call for a Lyft." I pull up the app but nothing comes up. Of course it doesn't. We're on a goddamned island! "Xander!" I bark. "I'm not playing. Give me the fucking keys." Before he can answer, Zoey starts crying, and Mallory lifts her out of her seat and scurries out of the room. Great! Now I'm making my daughter cry. *My daughter...fuck!* A woman I don't know just took my daughter out of the room, so I wouldn't upset her.

Needing a breather, I shove my phone back into my pocket and head out back. I walk past the covered patio and pool and down to the dock. When I sit down at the end, I stare down at my hands and see they're shaking. It's because I need a drink. *Fuck!*

"You're not an alcoholic yet, but you must realize that's where you're heading," Xander says, sitting down next to me. "I want to say this isn't what Delilah would want for you, but I know it's just going to set you off."

"You're damn right it will," I say, feeling myself getting worked up. "What the fuck are we even doing here? Vacationing like we're still friends?" I regret the words as soon as they leave my mouth, but I don't verbally acknowledge it to Xander.

He glances my way and frowns. "Joanne threatened to take Zoey away from you. She said you stopped coming home, and I get it, because it's where Delilah died, but what about the fact that you lost your job? And you haven't even so much as looked your daughter's way since before the funeral. This isn't you, man. And you're right. We aren't friends. Not the person you've become anyway. But the old you, we're still friends, and we always will be."

"Says the guy who ran away like his ass was on fire." I let out a huff and stand. "You didn't see me running." I look down at Xander, and he stands. He only has maybe an inch or two on me, so we're standing head-to-head.

"I didn't run. I entered the draft and had to move to where I was picked up, which happened to be in Houston. My dream was to play professional ball and that's what I'm doing."

I can't help but chuckle because we both know that's not how it went down. "You were supposed to stay for another year, but you entered it to run."

I shrug and am about to walk away when Xander says, "You ran first. I sucked your dick, and you ran like a little bitch because you couldn't handle it." I know he's right but fuck him for pointing that shit out.

"Maybe it just wasn't good, and I didn't want to embarrass you by pointing it out," I shoot back.

Xander steps toward me, so close our bodies are almost touching. His eyes dart to my mouth, and instinctively I lick my dry lips.

His eyes come back up to meet mine. "That's not what your hard-as-fuck dick was conveying, or the moans of pleasure you let out while coming down my throat." My traitor dick twitches at the memory of Xander sucking me off. His hot mouth gripping me like a vice.

"It wasn't personal. I'm a guy...anything warm and willing gets me hard."

"Real fucking mature," Xander murmurs as he backs up and starts to walk away. I'm about to make a comment back when his palm hits the center of my chest, and I'm pushed off the fucking dock. I try to catch myself but there's nothing to hold onto, and I fall backwards, hitting the salty water and sinking down a few feet, stunned that this asshole just pushed me into the bay. Paddling my arms, I rise to the surface and shake the water out of face, then swim over to the side and pull myself up.

"Looks like you're just as mature!" I shout, needing to have the last word.

Xander cackles as he walks away with his middle finger raised in the air. I stand and remove my drenched shirt to squeeze the water out, no longer watching him, when I hear his voice ring out. "I figured the water would help with your hangover, plus you kind of stink." I glare at him and see he's laughing, his grin big and wide, and my heart thumps just fast enough to remind me what this guy does to me. *Sonuvabitch.*

Figuring it's best if I give us some space, I strip down to my boxers and lay my shirt and shorts out to dry. The sun is still beaming even though it's probably close to 6 p.m., so I stretch myself out to take a nap. Closing my eyes, I will myself not to think about everything Xander said or the fact that when he stood that close to me, a part of me was hoping he would kiss me, and as I fall asleep, my last thoughts are of him standing on the dock with his lips crashing against mine.

CHAPTER FORTY-ONE

Xander

"MALLORY, WOULD YOU LIKE TO STAY FOR DINNER?" I ASK AS I PULL THE baked chicken out of the oven. In the city, I don't cook. Because I need to eat healthy, I have someone who cooks my meals for me, and when I'm hungry all I have to do is heat them up. Being on this island, I don't have that, and since there isn't a whole lot to do, I've been cooking every day. We've been here for close to two weeks and Cole still won't talk to me. Well, aside from our one conversation where I proceeded to almost kiss him, only for him to tell me my mouth was nothing more than a warm hole to stick his dick into, which ended with me pushing his ass off the dock and into the water. Since then Cole comes out to eat or to go for a swim. I'd like to say the fact that he's not drinking anymore is a step in the right direction, but at the same time he's still refusing to even acknowledge his daughter.

"Thank you, but if it's okay with you, I'm going to go call my grandbabies," she says. Some nights she will eat with me, but other nights she excuses herself to call her family. With the time difference, our night is their morning.

"Absolutely, I've got Zoey for the night. Thank you." I look over at the little angel who is sprawled out on her cushion of blankets and kicking her piano toy. Every time her tiny foot connects, it makes a noise, and she babbles in excitement. I'm making myself a plate of food just as Cole walks inside from the pool with only a white towel wrapped tightly around his torso, beads of water dripping down his muscular chest and toned front.

"There's chicken, rice, and vegetables," I offer like I always do. I'm prepared for him to tell me no thanks like he always does, so I'm shocked when I hear his wet feet pad into the kitchen and stop next to me. He's so close, I can smell the chlorine on him. He picks up a piece of chicken from my plate and drops it into his mouth.

"Damn, that shit's good," he says.

"I can make you a plate," I say, stunned.

"Alright, let me just change into something dry." He walks away, and I'm frozen in place. What the fuck just happened? I turn to watch him go just in time to see him pause in front of Zoey. She kicks the piano and babbles, and Cole's eyes widen. I hold my breath, waiting to see how he's going to react. She was only six weeks old when Delilah died, which is the last time Cole really looked at her. Eight weeks doesn't seem like a long time, but in baby time, a lot happens. Just these last couple weeks with Zoey, I've witnessed her change so much. She tries to hold her bottle when I feed her. She doesn't smile yet, but she does look at me like she recognizes me now. She's kicking her feet and babbling now, and when she wakes up in the morning, I've spotted her trying to roll over. She hasn't done it yet, but it's only a matter of time. I've googled her age, and she appears to be on track. She's eating more and lasting longer between feedings. Her naps are getting longer and less frequent. Mallory has been a godsend. She assumed she was simply here to babysit, but once I explained I wanted to learn how to care for Zoey, she started helping me instead of just doing it for me.

I watch Cole watch Zoey for a few long beats. I don't say a word, waiting to see what he's going to do, praying he doesn't walk away from her. And when he bends down and picks her up, I feel myself let out a breath of relief I didn't even realize I was holding. He holds her close, closing his eyes and inhaling her scent. When he opens them, his gaze finds mine—tears visible in his eyes.

"What did I do?" he whispers, and I'm almost positive it's just hit him that he's been ignoring his daughter for the past eight weeks. I can see the guilt in his features.

"Don't do that," I say. "Delilah died, and you needed to grieve." I set the plates down then cut across the room to him.

"She's making noises. She's kicking shit. What the hell did I do?" he repeats, and it's clear he's in shock.

"Cole, you were grieving," I say again. "Joanne took care of her, then Mallory and I took over. She's being cared for."

"Not by her parents," he points out. "Her mother is dead, and her father abandoned her." He looks up at me. "What kind of father doesn't even notice his daughter is months older?"

"The kind who needed some time to get over her mother's death. No, what you did wasn't ideal. But look, we've been here for two weeks and you haven't drank."

"Oh great!" He chuckles humorlessly. "Your expectations of me go as high as my simply being sober." He situates Zoey, who is squirming in his arms, and starts talking to her.

"Daddy's here, sunshine. I'm so sorry." He brings her to his chest, and she lets out a soft coo. "I need to go change." He kisses her forehead and lays her back down. "I'll be right back," he tells her before he hurries down the hall. Once I hear his door shut, I kneel down in front of Zoey, who is back to kicking her feet out.

"Everything's going to be okay, sweet girl."

The first time I called her the same nickname I gave Delilah, I felt guilty. It had just slipped out. But as I watched her, I knew it fit. She looks just like her mother, and she's just as sweet as her. I've read in several baby books that some babies cry all the time and wake up all through the night. Not Zoey, she's as sweet as it gets, just like her mom. She sleeps almost all night and wakes up happy every morning. It's clear she's her mother's daughter, so I've decided the name is being passed down. Delilah might not be with us any longer, but her daughter is alive and will know who her mother was and just how damn loved she was.

Seeing that her eyes are getting heavy, I move her to her swing and give her a pacifier. I chuckle when her eyes almost instantly roll in the back of her head.

"What's so funny?" Cole walks out dressed in a pair of khaki shorts and a plain black tee. His hair is messy from just having showered. His eyes lock with mine for a moment, and I'm almost positive he knows I was checking him out, but he doesn't call me out on it. He never does. Cole is the master at pretending shit doesn't happen.

"She loves her pacifier." I point to Zoey who is already asleep. "Stick her in the swing and stick a pacifier in her mouth, and it's like she's been given a sleeping drug."

Cole smiles but doesn't say anything, instead sitting down at the table in front of a plate of food. I pour us a glass of water and sit down across from him. Unsure of where we stand, I begin eating, hoping he will speak up, and he does.

"Look man, I just want to apologize and thank you," Cole says, putting his fork down and looking at me. "She wasn't supposed to die." He shakes his head like he still can't believe it, and I completely understand because too many days I wake up and forget she's gone. "I just...I lost it, and since I don't remember much, anything shitty I said, please know I didn't mean it. I appreciate you stepping in. The truth is if it weren't for you, I would be halfway to becoming an alcoholic by now."

"If the roles were reversed, you would've done the same for me." I shrug. "I can't even imagine having been the one to find her. I miss her every day and hate that I stayed away for so long," I admit.

Cole nods in understanding. "How long are we staying here for?"

"As long as you want. I don't need to get back for training camp until September."

Cole nods again. We eat the rest of our meal in silence, and when we're done, Cole grabs both of our plates and washes the dishes while I get Zoey's diaper bag ready for our nightly walk.

"Where are you going?" Cole asks, walking into the foyer. Has he really been so out of it he didn't notice that I leave every night with Zoey for a walk?

"I've been taking Zoey for a walk every night when the sun goes down." I pop the stroller open and, plucking Zoey out of her swing, place her into the stroller and buckle her in. "Do you want to go?"

"Umm...yeah, sure. Let me grab my shoes."

We head in the direction of the beach. I figured out it's only a little over a mile walk, so I've been making the trek to and from with Zoey every evening. When we get to the beach, Cole heads to the picnic table I usually sit at and sits on top of it. It's an awesome view, looking out at the Atlantic Ocean.

"Do you want to feed her?" I ask Cole when Zoey starts fussing.

"Sure." I hand him the pre-made bottle, and he takes Zoey out of her stroller. "Do you think she remembers who I am?" he asks.

"I think at her age she just knows what it feels like to be loved."

"I hope you're right." He gives Zoey the bottle, and she starts sucking it down. "So, the note..." Cole starts but doesn't finish his sentence.

"She wrote them when she started her treatment. According to Joanne, she wrote them every time she started her treatment, and once she was done, she would take them back and throw them away."

"I won't ask you what your note says. I know it's between you and Delilah. But do you know why you got yours?"

I glance over at Cole. What he really wants to know is how he can get his. "Joanne said it was my coming to help you after Delilah died." Cole nods. "You weren't supposed to know about the note, and Joanne wouldn't tell me how you get yours. I did ask."

Cole finishes feeding Zoey, and we lay a blanket out on the grass for the three of us. It's a beautiful night on the Vineyard. The ocean giving us a decent breeze to keep it from being too humid.

"Do you see those stars?" Cole says to Zoey, laying down next to her. "They were your mom's favorite part of this world. She could look up at them for hours, patiently waiting for a shooting star to come along." Cole looks over at me. "The world will never be the same with her gone. I don't even think I know how to live in this world without her." This isn't the first time he's said this to me, and it breaks my heart every time he says it.

"You just take it one day at a time, man, and I'll be here every step of the way."

"Until you go back to Houston," he points out.

"You could always come back with me," I say before I consider what I'm suggesting.

"Like move in with you?" he clarifies.

"Yeah, you said it yourself. You don't want to live in the condo where she died. And I'm not sure if you've thought about this, but you're jobless, so you can move anywhere you want."

"So, we would what...live together as roommates?" Cole asks, and while I want to tell him I would like for us to be more than that, I know that's not what he wants or needs, especially right now.

"Why not? I have three bedrooms. Mallory doesn't live in the area, but we can hire another nanny to help out. You can get another teaching job, or just focus on Zoey."

Cole laughs. "You gonna be my sugar daddy, Xander?" *Hell yes, I would be...*

"Funny," I say dryly. I'm about to say something else when my phone rings. Pulling it out of my pocket, I see it's my agent. "Sorry, it's my agent. I need to take this."

"No problem."

CHAPTER FORTY-TWO

Cole

MY EYES ARE STUCK ON XANDER WHILE HE TALKS TO HIS AGENT. I'M NOT trying to overhear his conversation but I'm sitting right next to him, so it can't be helped. But what has me staring at him, isn't what he's talking about but how he's talking. He's smiling and laughing and joking with the person on the other end of the phone call. I can't remember the last time Xander and I joked and laughed together. I miss him and our friendship.

"So, if I sign the player extension that will make me contractually bound to Houston for the next five years?" he asks, a grin splayed across his face. "Ha! You know I can't do that math, that's why I have you." He laughs. I don't know what his agent is saying on the other end, but they're obviously comfortable with each other, and it hits me that I want that comfort back with Xander.

"I know, but five years at twenty-five million a year is still amazing, and it means I can stay in Houston, which is where I want to be." *Holy shit! I knew Xander got paid well, but damn!* While my parents left me a decent trust fund when they passed away that I received when I turned eighteen, it doesn't even come anywhere near what Zander makes in a fucking month.

Feeling like I shouldn't be overhearing this conversation, even though he hasn't made an attempt to walk away himself, I stand and pick up Zoey, walking closer to the water to give Xander some space. There is a huge cluster of rocks along the shore, so I climb up onto the lowest one and sit down with her in my lap. The sky is now pitch-black with only the moon and stars providing any light.

Looking back, I see Xander is still sitting on the blanket talking to his agent, so I take this moment to have my first conversation with Delilah. It seems fitting with us being under the stars. "I'm sorry it's taken me so long to acknowledge your death," I say, looking up to the sky, and while it should be weird that I'm technically not talking to anyone, it's not. I've never, in all the years that my parents and grandma have been dead, tried to talk to them. But for some reason, being under the stars where Delilah always felt at home, it just feels right, like she's looking down and listening.

"I'm sorry for being a shitty dad these past several weeks and not putting our little girl first. I promise that's going to change, though. We're going to move in with Xander, and I'm going to do everything in my power to raise our daughter to be as good of a person as you were." I look back, and Xander is still on the phone. "I also need to apologize for something else, Delilah." I take a deep breath and exhale. "I'm sorry for not loving you the way you deserved. You deserved so much more than I ever gave you. You deserved for someone to put you first, but instead you chose to be with me and accepted me as I was...as I am, even knowing a large part of my heart was with someone else."

"Who was your heart with?" I turn around to find Xander standing behind me. "I didn't know you were talking to anyone," he says.

"I was talking to Delilah," I admit.

"I figured. I've been coming here every night and doing the same thing. With the clear view of the stars, it feels like she's here with us." Xander climbs onto the rock next to me and sits down.

"Yeah, it does."

"So, who has your heart?" Xander asks, not letting me off the hook.

"You," I say before I can talk myself out of it. "You have a piece of my heart, and I have no fucking clue what to do about it. Delilah knew it, and yet she wouldn't call me out on it. Even when I..." I pause, shocked I'm about to admit this, knowing once I do, I can never take back the words. "I called out your name while Delilah and I were having sex." I sneak a glance over to Xander, but his face isn't giving anything away, so I continue. "She finally had enough and broke up with me. She said she couldn't be the reason anymore that I continued to lie to myself." I shake my head, pissed off at how much time I let her waste being with me.

"I know what you're thinking," Xander says. "You think you're a bad person because she was with you all of these years instead of with her soulmate or some shit."

"Can you blame me? Her dreams were to get married and have a family...fall in love. Instead, she settled for me because I couldn't handle it when you walked away."

"She didn't settle, Cole. She loved you. Don't you think maybe it was supposed to happen this way? What other guy would've been there for her like you were? You've been there through all three of her cancer diagnoses. Nobody else would've understood what she needed. Her time was limited, but she was loved and cherished, and she even had the opportunity to give birth to this amazing little girl, and was given time with her."

"Not fucking enough."

"No, it's never enough, but we don't get to decide how long we're here for. I don't believe for a second Delilah broke up with you because she didn't feel loved. She broke up with you because like the selfless woman she was, she wanted you to be with the person you gave your heart to."

"So, now we're pretending to know what she was thinking?" I ask more harshly than Xander deserves.

"No." Xander shakes his head. "I don't need to pretend. She told me."

My head whips around to look at him. "What did she say?"

"I made her promise not to bring me up. I wanted you to admit on your own how you felt about me. She hated it, but she agreed." Now it all makes sense...her refusing to talk about Xander but saying she couldn't be the reason I denied what I felt any longer.

"So, this whole time...she knew how I felt?"

"How we both felt," Xander says. "How I still feel. I've been in love with you since...fuck, I don't even know how long. Sometimes it feels like it's been my entire life."

"Then why did you leave?" I don't get it. If he loved me so much, why the fuck would he leave for the NBA a year earlier?

"Because I knew you wouldn't ever be with me," he admits. "I saw how torn you were after we were together... how much guilt you felt. You wouldn't even talk to me." He's right. I did feel torn and guilty. I never imagined myself being attracted to another guy, let alone falling in love with him. I was able to live in denial for years, until he wrapped his lips around my cock and sucked me dry, making me come harder than I ever had my entire life. At that point, I knew there was no denying it, so instead I ran away.

"I'm sorry," I tell him.

"It's alright, Cole. I'm a big boy." Xander laughs. "I've accepted that we'll never be anything more than friends." He smiles softly. "I'm not asking you to move in as anything other than my friend and roommate. Let me help you raise Zoey like Delilah wanted. And when the day comes that you meet the woman who will help you create that dream your mom wanted for you, I'll be right here as your friend. I shouldn't have run three years ago, and Delilah's death has helped me put shit into perspective. I would rather have you as a friend than not at all."

My mom and her final words to me. Everything she wanted for me. I haven't thought about what she said in years. Xander's words come back to me from the night I ran into him in the hotel bar. *Looks like you're on course for making your mom proud.* I didn't think about it at the time when he made that comment to me.

"Xander, I..." Xander's phone rings, halting my words.

"Shit, it's Ciara, my publicist. Hold that thought, please," he says, answering the call. "Hey, how's it going?" Pause. "Yeah, enjoying the quiet, for sure." Pause. "I'm going to be flying in next week to sign the contract, so it shouldn't be a problem." Another pause. "Okay, sounds good."

Xander hangs up and says to me, "Sorry about that. There's a charity function Ciara wants me to attend while I'm in town to sign my extension contract. I'll only be gone for a couple days, and you can stay here. What were you about to say?" With his words, it hits me that I'm in love with an NBA player. I've seen him out at several functions. The gossip magazines and social media posts it all. He's been seen out with several female models and actresses, but never once a guy. And he didn't ask me if I wanted to go. He said I could stay here while he goes.

"Hey," he says, breaking me out of my thoughts. "What are you thinking?"

"Those functions you go to...I always see you with women. Are you bisexual?"

Xander's eyes go wide. "I don't know what I am to be honest," he admits. "I was attracted to Delilah, and being with her turned me on, but I'm also really fucking attracted to you."

"Have you been with anyone besides us?"

"No." He shakes his head. "Don't get me wrong, I've had the opportunity, but I just couldn't do it."

"Yeah, that makes sense. I don't think there are even any players in the NBA who have openly come out."

"A couple in the past, but that's not why," Xander says. "I would try to imagine being with another guy. A bartender I knew was gay and flirting with me, or some stranger I met in a club when out with some teammates, but I just wasn't attracted to any of them. I don't know if I'm gay or straight or bi, and I don't see why I have to assign a label anyway. I considered being with another woman to see if I could move on, but I just couldn't bring myself to do it." He shrugs. "I know I should've moved on, but I just couldn't stop wanting to be with you."

"Xander..." I'm not even sure what to say to him. He was right with what he said earlier. For my entire life, I always imagined getting married to a woman and having a family just like my parents did. Nowhere in that dream was I with another man. I don't know what to think or feel. While I know Delilah would be okay with me being with Xander, would my mom be? And what about Zoey? It's bad enough she's lost her mom, but what would it do to her to be raised by two men? One of which is in the NBA, in the spotlight for all the world to judge.

"Hey," Xander says, "It's okay. Like I said, I've accepted we can't be anything more than friends. I wasn't trying to make you uncomfortable. I just needed you to know the truth." Xander stands. "You ready to head back?"

I want to stop him. I want to tell him I want more. I want to see what it's like to be with him, see where things go, but I don't say a word because I'm scared as hell. Delilah is gone, and Xander is all I have left. I can't lose him. What if we try for more and it doesn't work out? Then I'll have lost them both, and I just can't take that chance.

"Yeah, I'm ready."

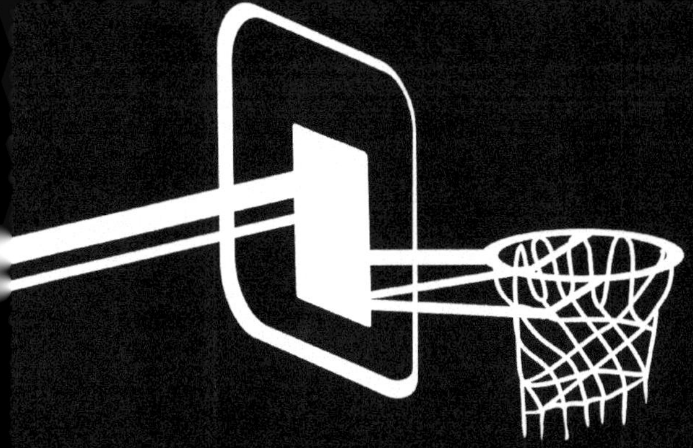

CHAPTER FORTY-THREE

Xander

 his swimsuit that's hanging low on his hips. I try my best not to stare, but fuck, can't he wear a shirt? His biceps are rock solid, and his abs are ripped. He's always been fit but these last three weeks of him swimming has toned his body in a way that has my dick twitching.

"Mallory is laying her down," I choke out. "She thinks she might be teething because she's a tad cranky."

"Oh, okay. I'm going to go for a swim. Want to join?" Cole asks.

"Umm…" Holy shit, this being friends thing is going to be harder than I thought.

"C'mon, I haven't seen you work out once since we've been here. Don't want to lose that multi-million dollar contract, do you? Who's going to pay for these trips?" Cole jokes.

"Funny. Sure, let me throw on my board shorts. I'll be right out there." Walking down the hall, I stop to check on

Zoey and find Mallory sitting in the rocking chair reading one of her novels. "Is she okay?" I ask.

"Yep, she's asleep. I was just reading." She holds up her book.

"I'm going to go for a swim with Cole. Let me know if you need anything."

"Will do." She grins, and I'm almost positive she knows how I feel about Cole, but she doesn't say anything. It's been nice having her around these last few weeks. I hope whoever we hire once we're back in Houston is as nice and caring as she is. I'm tempted to offer to pay for her housing, so she can follow us back and continue to help care for Zoey, but she's mentioned a couple times that she's looking forward to her grandchildren coming home in a few months, which means we'll have to hire someone new anyway.

I throw on my suit, grab a towel from the hall closet, and head out back. Cole is already in the water, swimming laps. I pull my shirt off and throw it onto the lounge chair then join him in the water. Cole stops mid lap and swims over to me.

"Want to race?" he suggests, waggling his eyebrows.

"What are we, ten?" I laugh.

"Afraid I'm going to beat you?" he mocks.

"Are you serious? You might've been swimming the last few weeks, but I've been working out the last several years. Have you not seen me running up and down the court during games?"

Cole rolls his eyes. "Then you should have no problem beating me."

"Fine, what are we racing for?" I step closer to him.

"Whoever loses has to cook dinner."

"Then I lose either way because your ass can't cook," I point out.

"Ha ha! What do you want to bet on?"

I think for a moment. I meant what I said about accepting we're just friends. I know Cole has feelings for me, but I also know he's grieving over Delilah and wants to make his mom proud. I don't know what that means for my future, but for now, I'm respecting it. However, I would like to spend some time with him, getting to know each other again, outside of us taking care of Zoey.

"Loser pays for dinner when we go out tonight."

"Go out where?" he asks.

"I found a cool wing place. I thought we could go out for some wings and catch the Astros/Rangers game."

"All right, deal, but don't think for a fucking second just because I'm moving to Houston that I'm going to turn my back on my Rangers. It figures you would end up in Houston. You were always a traitor, liking them over the Rangers."

"They're both in Texas!" I laugh. This has been an ongoing argument between us since we were kids.

"Rangers are in Arlington! You like the team near you! Everybody knows that." Cole huffs, shaking his head.

"So, does that mean you're sticking with Dallas instead of rooting for the team I play on?"

"I can't help you got drafted to Houston. I'm staying loyal to my teams, even if I'm moving to Houston."

"Whatever." I laugh. "Remember that when you want to use one of my friends and family tickets to come to a game. You ready to race so I can beat you?" I swim toward the wall.

"Yeah, okay." Cole chuckles. "I'll take it easy on you. One time, there and back."

We line up, and when Cole counts to three, we take off. We're head-to-head the entire way there, and I see when Cole hits the wall under the water at the same time as me and heads back. I push myself harder, determined to beat him. I focus on getting there first, and when I hit the wall and come up for air, I see him come up at nearly the same time.

"I won!" I yell.

"No fucking way!" he yells back. "If anything, it was a tie!"

"Says the guy who lost! Everyone knows the loser cries tie!" I laugh, shaking my head, and before I can say another word, Cole cuts across the pool and jumps onto my shoulders, pushing me under the water.

Mother fucking sore loser!

Grabbing his thighs, I pull him under the water with me, and he has no choice but to let go of me. We both come up for air, and before he can tackle me again, I shove him under the water. I feel him trying to grab a hold of me, and then his hand glides across my dick. I jump back in shock, and he comes up for air.

"Shit," he hisses. "Sorry, I didn't mean to..."

"Xander, Cole," Mallory calls out, and we both turn toward her. "Zoey has a slight fever. It's probably from teething, but I'm going to need someone to pick up Tylenol to bring it down."

"I got it," I yell a little too loud, swimming to the edge of the pool and jumping out. "I'll be back," I say without looking back.

I go to the store, grab some baby pain reliever then head back. I try not to think about Cole's hand touching my dick, but I can't help it. It was accidental, I know that, but fuck if my body didn't get the message. I don't know how the hell I'm going to do this. How I'm going to live with Cole while wanting him, especially knowing he wants me as well, and the only thing preventing him from taking action is some promise he made to his mom when he was a fucking kid. I think back to the letter Delilah wrote me.

Fight for Cole. Fight for your best friend, the man you love. Show him that loving you would make his mom just as proud as if he was with a woman...

And that's exactly what I need to do. Fuck accepting we're just friends. He said it himself. He has feelings for me that he doesn't know what to do with. I have a piece of his heart. Sure, there's a chance Cole will push me away again, but I owe it to Delilah and to myself to fight for Cole...for us.

CHAPTER FORTY-FOUR

Cole

"GO! ZOEY IS ASLEEP, AND HER FEVER IS DOWN. I'LL BE HERE WATCHING HER, and if I need you, I'll call. Neither of you have even experienced any of this beautiful island," Mallory says. When Xander and I don't make any move to leave, she adds, "I've seen more of this place than you two."

"She's right," I point out. "I wasted two weeks of our time here. It's only eight o'clock. We can still catch a few innings of the game."

"Alright, fine," Xander agrees. "I've really been wanting to try the wings there, and I bet they'll taste even better since you'll be picking up the bill." He winks, and I bark out a laugh.

"It was a fucking tie!"

"Negative." Xander grabs the keys. "We'll be back in a couple of hours. Text me if you need anything while we're out."

"Will do. Have fun, boys." Mallory smiles and waves before she goes back to reading her book.

"HELL YES!" XANDER PUMPS HIS FIST IN THE AIR. "FREE WINGS, AND MY TEAM is kicking your team's ass." He takes a bite of his food, and after he swallows, he licks the sauce off his lips, and suddenly I'm imagining him using his tongue and lips to do other things. Things I shouldn't be imagining. "It doesn't get much better than this." He grins my way, and my stomach clenches. How the fuck am I supposed to live with this man? I can't even have a meal with him without having sexual thoughts. I'm supposed to be mourning the loss of Delilah, yet I'm fantasizing about Xander. Jesus, I'm all kinds of fucked up.

"You okay?" Xander asks. "You've barely touched your food." He nods toward my half eaten wings.

"Yeah, they're good." I take a bite and smile. We continue to watch the game, but the entire time my thoughts are on Xander. What it would be like to be with him again. The truth is I don't really know what it's like to be with him in the first place. Sure, he gave me head a few years ago, but other than that, our focus was always on Delilah. What if we got together and Xander realized I'm not what he wants? That would fuck up our friendship, and then where would that leave us? But what if he's the one? What if I'm wasting all this time pushing him away when we could be together? Maybe if we figure out what we are to each other before we go back to Houston then we'll know where we stand, and we won't be dancing around each other. Fuck, this is so hard.

"You ready to go?" Xander asks, breaking me out of my thoughts.

"Yeah." I go to grab the bill, but when I look, I see that

he's already paid it. "I was supposed to pay."

"It was a tie, remember?" Xander winks and laughs. "You seemed a little preoccupied when she brought the bill. You can buy next time."

We drive back to the house, but when we pull up, I'm not ready to say goodnight to Xander yet. "Want to go for a walk?" I suggest.

"Sure," he agrees. We get out, and Xander looks around. "Want to walk around back?"

I nod in agreement, and we walk around the side of the house, making our way to the back where the pool is. The area is completely black until Xander flips a switch and the pool light comes on, illuminating the water.

"I'm going to miss this place," Xander says, walking over to the pool. "It's so quiet here...and calm. I forgot what it's like." He takes his shoes and socks off then sits down on the edge, and I do the same.

"Has it been crazy being in the NBA?"

"Yes and no. During the season, traveling can get hectic, but Ciara makes sure not to schedule me too many things. She's been working on rescheduling everything I had planned for the offseason. I kind of sprung this trip on her." Xander laughs. "She hates the unknown."

"Ciara's your publicist, right?" I ask, remembering that he mentioned her at the beach the other night.

"Yeah, but she's also my assistant. I have to do certain interviews and photoshoots, and she keeps it all together for me. She's fucking awesome. Some days I swear she schedules when I can take a leak." Xander shakes his head. "Because I don't date or anything, I'm not really videoed much, which is nice. She says I make her job easy because she doesn't have to do too much damage control."

I laugh. "Are you serious? You're videoed all the time! I

could tell you where you are and what you're doing more days than not."

"What?" Xander looks over at me, confused. "You've been watching my career?"

I pull out my phone and pull up the fan site dedicated to him. "We might've went three years without talking, but that doesn't mean I'm not proud of everything you've accomplished." I hand him my phone, and he starts scrolling through the newsfeed.

"Holy shit! I had no clue. I guess I wasn't paying attention." He scrolls down to the bottom. "Well, I guess leaving last minute without telling anyone where we were going was a good idea. The pictures and videos stopped after the championship."

He hands me back my phone. "So you were keeping tabs on me, huh?" Xander smirks, and I groan.

"Shut up."

"Stalking me..."

"Shut. Up."

"You're probably the president of the Xander Thompson Fan Club."

"You're going to get pushed into this pool."

"Maybe you should just admit the truth now and save me the trouble of having to show you what we both already know."

"And what's that?" I ask, turning my head to look at Xander. His gaze locks with mine, all the playfulness gone. His tongue darts out to wet his lips, and I know what's about to happen. I can see it in his eyes. He's about to kiss me. I should say something. Back up or stop him. But I don't. I can't. This is what I wanted, right? To see what could be between us before we head to Houston.

My heart picks up speed as I sit here, frozen in place, as

Xander leans over and presses his mouth to mine. He waits a beat to see if I'm going to push him away, and when I don't, he edges closer. His tongue presses against my lips, and I open them for him, allowing him access. Xander's fingers find my hair, and he pulls me closer, our kiss deepening. My tongue joins his as we explore each other's mouths. Kissing Xander isn't sweet or soft like it was with Delilah. It's rough and demanding. His lips are harder and stronger. His teeth nip my bottom lip, and I let out a groan, wanting more, but before I can figure out what more is, Xander ends the kiss.

"The truth is you want me," he says with a shrug, answering my earlier question, the playfulness back in his voice. *Cocky motherfucker.*

Pressing my hands onto the pool deck, I pretend like I'm going to stand, and just like I knew Xander would do, he starts to stand as well. I wait until I know he's slightly off balanced and then, with a good shove, I push his ass into the pool, just like he did to me on the dock. Only, he must see it coming because he reaches out and grabs hold of my shirt, pulling me into the water with him.

"Nice try, asshole!" He laughs. "Maybe you need to watch some more of my game footage. I have the reflexes of a cheetah."

I chuckle at how full of himself he is. "I don't even know how we're fitting in this pool together..." I cup my hands and splash water at him. "What with your ego taking up so much of the space."

"Ha! You got jokes." He nods his head, then swims toward me. Out of instinct I back up, only I don't realize the direction I'm going in is a dead end. My back hits the sidewall, and Xander cages me in, his hands gripping the edge of the pool on either side of me.

"In all seriousness," he murmurs, his mouth so close to

mine that all it would take is one of us leaning in just a hair and our mouths would be touching. "That kiss was not a one-time thing. I'm willing to take things slow because I know you need some time to make peace with Delilah's death, but I'm not letting this go. You kissing me back told me what I needed to know. You want to see where things go just as much as I do, regardless of what your mom wished for you."

His eyes dart to my mouth, and he bites down on his bottom lip like he's trying to stop himself from kissing me again. I'm not sure what comes over me, but I lean in, and using my teeth, I tug on his bottom lip until it's pulled out from his teeth. Then I suck on it for a few seconds, savoring the taste that is all Xander before I release it.

"You're right, I do want to see where things go, regardless of what my mom said, but I have two conditions."

His eyes widen in shock. "Okay."

"One, we don't tell anybody. This stays between us."

Xander's brows furrow. "Just until we figure out where we stand," I add.

"And two?" he asks.

"If it doesn't work out, we stay friends this time. Neither of us running."

He bites down on his bottom lip again in contemplation, and I have to force myself to leave him alone. "Okay," he finally says, "I'll agree to your conditions."

CHAPTER FORTY-FIVE

Xander

"ARE YOU SURE YOU'RE READY TO GO BACK? I CAN GO SIGN THE CONTRACT, GO to that charity crap, and come right back," I tell Cole.

"I'm sure. We've been here for three weeks, and as much as I'd love to stay here forever, there's a lot we have to do, like moving all our shit to your place. Fuck! And I'm going to need to go through Delilah's stuff. I also need to meet with Joanne because my apology to her can't be given over the phone, and I'd like to start looking for a new job."

Listening to Cole talk has me grinning on the inside. The last week has been like hanging out with my best friend again. Aside from our kiss by the pool, I haven't pushed him towards anything sexual. I meant what I said about taking things slow. Cole is still grieving for Delilah, and I don't want to rush anything. But hearing him talk about moving in with me and looking for a job gives me hope that we're moving in the right direction and he meant what he said about wanting to see where things go between us.

"You don't have to do any of that alone. I can hire

someone to move all of your stuff. We'll ask Joanne to come over, and we'll go through Delilah's things, figuring out what each of us wants to keep or give to charity. You can apologize when she comes over, but she knows you, Cole, and she knows you weren't in your right mind. I've been sending her pictures of Zoey every day, and we've video chatted a few times. As far as you getting a job, I think that's awesome, but just know if you want to take the year off or however long, that's okay as well."

He gives me a look of appreciation. "Thanks, man. I'm going to finish packing."

"No rush, the flight doesn't leave for a few hours."

IT'S A LONG ASS DAY, AND WE DON'T ARRIVE IN DALLAS UNTIL ALMOST midnight. Zoey is cranky, and we're all exhausted. We drop Mallory off at her house and thank her for everything, then we check into a hotel. Cole mentions he's okay with staying at the condo to save money, but it's not happening. He's come too far to slide back now. We get situated, and Zoey is out like the little angel she is in a matter of seconds, her body sprawled out in her portable crib like a tiny starfish. Cole excuses himself to go unpack and take a shower in his room, and I do the same.

After I've rinsed off the filth from traveling, I throw on a pair of boxers and t-shirt and head out to the kitchen to grab a drink. I'm looking down at my phone and checking my emails, so I don't see Cole. When I bump into him, my phone hits the ground, but I don't bother to look at it, because standing in the kitchen is Cole in nothing but a pair of briefs.

"Shit, sorry," I choke out, even though I'm not the

slightest bit sorry. He's leaning against the counter with a bottle of water in his hand, apparently having had the same idea as me. Starting at his face, my eyes rake down his fit body, eyeing the tattoos he has covering his chest, over his six pack of abs, and ending at the dark patch of hair that trails down, disappearing under his briefs. When I look a little farther, I can see the outline of his dick. It's not hard, but it's not soft either.

Closing the distance between us, my hand comes around and clasps the back of Cole's neck, pulling his face into mine. Our lips crash against each other, and he moans into my mouth. Our tongues both dart out and meet, dueling with each other. My hand finds its way down the front of his briefs as we continue to kiss. He lets out a low groan into my mouth as my thumb brushes across his engorged head, the sticky feeling of precum dripping from the tip. I glide my fingers down the underside of his smooth shaft and wrap my fist around his cock. Cole breaks our kiss, his head going back in pleasure, his eyes remaining shut. I can see his chest heaving as I begin to stroke him slowly under his briefs.

When he's so hard, there's no room left, I push his briefs down, and his dick springs free. It reminds me of the last time we were together like this. The one and only time I had my mouth wrapped around his hard cock. Just the thought has my mouth watering. Not able to take it any longer, I kneel down and wrap my lips around the crown of his cock, my tongue swirling around the tip. The salty taste of precum tells me Cole is turned on by my touch. His entire body stiffens, and I worry he's going to stop me— this definitely wasn't what I had in mind by taking shit slow. But when I feel his fingers entwine in my hair, I breathe a sigh of relief. With one hand stroking the bottom of his shaft, I take him all the way down my throat until my lips meet my fist.

"Fuck!" he groans, which spurs me on. Moving my hand out of the way, I take him all the way into my mouth until the tip of his cock hits the back of my throat. My mouth fucks him while my hand massages his ball sac. His moans have me hard as steel, but I focus on him. Making him feel good. I've dreamt of this for years. Cole letting me be the one to give him pleasure. I wondered if when the day came, if I would be let down. Did I just dream of how much I wanted him? Was the one time I sucked him off a fluke and all these years I've built the experience up to mean more than it really did? But right now as he thrusts his hips and fucks my mouth, I know my feelings weren't just in my head. I want this man. I want his mind, his body, and more than anything, I want his fucking heart.

"Xander," he groans, and my dick twitches at my name being released from his lips. "I'm going to come." It's a warning, but one I don't heed. I need to taste him, all of him. He lets go, and the saltiness hits my tongue as I swallow every drop of him until his cock grows soft in my mouth. His hips still, and I back up slightly. I look up at Cole and hate the look I see. Lust. Confusion. Regret.

"I need to go." He pulls his briefs up while I stand.

"Wait! Don't do this," I beg. "Talk to me."

He lets out a loud sigh. "I don't know if I can…" He nods toward me.

"Don't know if you can what?" I ask, confused. "You said you wanted to see where things go. Did you change your mind?"

"No." He shakes his head. "I do…I just don't know if I can reciprocate." He flinches.

"I didn't expect you to. This wasn't a tit for tat sort of

thing. I know this is all new to you and you're still trying to figure out how you feel. Hell, it's new to me. The only difference is I've had a few years to think about how I feel."

"I've thought about it too," he admits. "I just…everything I learned when we were with Delilah was from you."

"Cole." I frame his face with my hands. "You're my best friend. This isn't about who's better. It's about being with each other. We're both new to all of this, so I'm hoping we can learn together."

I'm shocked when Cole doesn't simply agree but instead leans in and kisses me. Our lips move against each other as we suck on each other's tongues, and then Cole is backing me up against the stove and pulling my boxers down. He breaks our kiss as he drops to the ground in front of me. I'm about to tell him he doesn't have to do this, but then I feel his hot, wet mouth wrap around my dick, and I'm a fucking goner. Delilah gave me head a few times, but this…this is like nothing I've ever felt. Whereas Delilah was gentle, Cole's mouth is rough. I look down and the sight of Cole's lips wrapped around my cock has me losing it. My fingers go to his hair, and I grip the strands as I start to thrust. I quickly stop when I realize what I'm doing, but then Cole glances up at me, his mouth no longer on my dick, and says, "Go ahead. Fuck my mouth." His lips go back around the head of my cock, and his eyes stay trained on mine as he takes me all the way back in. And he sure as fuck doesn't have to tell me twice. My hips start to buck as my cock fucks his mouth. I can feel the saliva from him dripping down my dick and balls, and I know I'm never going to last.

Slurp. Slurp. Slurp. Slurp.

The sound alone has me losing my resolve, and before I can even warn Cole, I'm coming. He doesn't stop sucking until I'm completely soft, and when he backs up, I can see the drool dripping down his chin. Fuck! It's the hottest thing I've ever seen. Pulling him up, my mouth crashes against his. I can taste myself on his tongue. Salty, the same way he tastes. We kiss for a few minutes before we break apart.

"If that's you not knowing what you're doing, I can't wait to see what you do when you're an expert." I chuckle, and Cole laughs.

"You're lucky there's no pool near us or you'd be in it."

"I'm pretty sure you've been in the water more times than I've been." I wink and, pulling my boxers back up, grab a water from the fridge and head into the living room.

"Want to watch something?" I ask Cole.

"Sure." He sits down next to me on the couch. We spend the next couple hours switching from a baseball game that's on and some police show, and I can't help but feel like I've gone from feeling alone to feeling like my heart is completely fucking full. I hate that Delilah isn't here to see this, but I believe she's watching over us and smiling brightly over her two best friends finally finding their way back to each other.

CHAPTER FORTY-SIX

Cole

"XANDER," I SAY WITH A GROAN. "WE SHOULD STOP. JOANNE IS GOING TO BE here soon." Xander ignores my words, which if I'm honest aren't all that convincing, and continues to suck on my neck, his hand fisting my cock as he jacks me off on the couch. We were supposed to meet Joanne at the condo when we returned from our trip, but instead we ended up spending the last four days locked in the hotel room together. When Zoey is awake, we're at her beck and call, but when she's asleep, I swear Xander and I go at it like we're two horny teenagers. With Joanne missing her granddaughter, she offered to meet us here for lunch before we head over to the condo together to get it situated.

"Shut up," Xander murmurs against my neck as his lips move downward over my collarbone. "I can feel it, you're close." His lips wrap around my nipple, and he bites down hard. My cock jerks, and I come all over his hand. "See, told you, you were close." He lifts up and gives me a chaste kiss before he goes to the bathroom to clean up. I follow behind him, stopping at my own bathroom to clean myself off and get dressed. Just as we're both walking out of our rooms, fully clothed, there's a knock on the door.

Xander grabs Zoey while I answer the door. I don't even have it pulled open all the way when Joanne pulls me into her arms and hugs me tightly. It reminds me of the hugs my mom used to give me whenever I would visit my grandma for the weekend and return.

"It's so good to have you back," she murmurs into my ear, still hugging me.

"I'm so sorry," I tell her, then pull back so I can look her in the eyes. "I'm so sorry for the way I acted, for the way I treated you, and for neglecting my daughter."

"Thank you," she says. "But your daughter wasn't neglected. I was here and then Xander was, and you got through it."

"I miss her so much," I admit, tears stinging my eyes. "I just keep thinking if I would've come home earlier, or if I hadn't left to take Zoey to the doctor."

"No, don't you dare do that to yourself. Do you hear me?" Her tiny hands frame my face as she looks up at me. "You loved my daughter until the day she died. You gave her a great life. Her body just couldn't handle it anymore. It wasn't your fault. Say it."

"Joanne..."

"No, I want you to say the words."

"It...wasn't my fault." My words come out choked as my chest heaves with silent sobs.

"Every time you even think about blaming yourself, you say those words, Cole. Promise me."

"Yeah, okay." I wipe the tears from my eyes and let her in the door. She immediately spots Xander and Zoey and runs over to them. She takes Zoey from Xander and hugs her tight, raining kisses all over her granddaughter.

"Oh, sweetheart, I missed you so much," she coos, rocking her gently. "I swear you've grown six inches since I last saw you."

"She has her four month checkup next week, so we'll let you know how many inches she actually grew," I say with a laugh.

After we have lunch downstairs in the hotel restaurant, Joanne follows us in her vehicle over to the condo. When we get inside, I see everything is gone from the apartment except for Delilah's stuff. Even Zoey's nursery furniture is gone.

"I had the mover's pack up everything that's yours and Zoey's and bring it to my place. Your furniture is in my garage, so we can go through it all later and decide what we want to use or get rid of. I also have an interior decorator recreating an exact replica of Zoey's nursery at my place." *Damn it, this man.*

"Thank you." I lean in about to kiss him when I remember we aren't alone. Xander must notice my hesitation because he gives me a confused look but doesn't say anything.

"You're welcome. All that's left to do is to go through Delilah's stuff. Whatever you want to give away, they will be by tomorrow to pick it all up, and everything we're taking, we can load up in my trunk."

"Where's my car?" I ask, realizing I didn't see it outside in my parking spot.

"I had it delivered to Houston."

"Thank you."

I enter the master bedroom, and I'm immediately hit with the overwhelming scent of Delilah. I force myself to choke back a sob as I walk farther inside the room, looking around and seeing everything is the same way she left it before she died. Her cell phone and iPad are still sitting on her nightstand reminding me of every time she falls asleep while reading, and I have to remove the device from her hands to charge it. Her robe is laid out across her bed, where she always leaves it after she changes from her shower—then complains when the bed is damp. I walk into the bathroom and find her toothbrush in the shower, where she insists on leaving it. She swears it's easier and cleaner to just brush her teeth while showering. As I think about all of Delilah's adorable quirks, I realize I'm referring to them in the present tense, like she's going to do any of this again. Delilah is gone, which means everything she does is now in the past. She will never read her iPad again or leave her robe laying out. She'll never brush her teeth or hug her daughter.

Suddenly overcome with more grief than I can handle at the moment, I feel myself dropping to the ground in the middle of her room, only I don't hit the floor because Xander is there next to me, catching me. We both drop to the floor, and he holds me as I cry for Delilah. For the mother she'll never get to be, the marriage she'll never have, the life she's done living. I don't even know how long I cry for, but when my body aches and my heart feels like it can't take the abuse any longer, Xander lifts my chin and kisses me. It's not rough like his kisses usually are. This one is gentle, reminding me of how it was with Delilah, and in this moment I'm one hundred percent certain I'm in love with my best friend.

"I love you," I tell him, not able to hold the words back because fuck if life is too damn short as it is.

"I love you too, Cole."

We sit like this for a few more minutes, and once I've calmed down enough to speak again, I say, "I don't know what to keep or get rid of. I don't even know where to start."

"We'll do it together. I called Mallory, and she's agreed to come and watch Zoey for a few hours, so Joanne can help. We'll take it one drawer at a time and figure it out."

And that's exactly what we do. The three of us go through each of her drawers, separating the items we each would like to keep—whether for us or for Zoey—then we move on to her closet. We agree to donate all of her clothes, shoes, and purses to charity. As I'm grabbing a couple boxes down from the top shelf, several envelopes float to the ground. I set the boxes down and pick up the envelopes. In her handwriting are Xander's and my name scrawled across the front of them.

"Those were the letters," Joanne says. "The ones she wrote every time she went through chemo."

"She kept them." I count them. Two for me and two for Xander. I don't bother to acknowledge that I know Joanne has my third letter. I know when the time is right, she'll give it to me.

"I feel like we shouldn't open these," I say. "She beat the cancer each time which is why we never received them." I hand Xander his two.

"I agree," he says, "but let's not throw them out yet. I don't want you to change your mind and not have them." He takes mine from me and hands them all to Joanne. "Can you hold onto these, please?"

"Absolutely."

We finish going through everything, and by the time we're done it's late into the evening and everyone is exhausted. Xander offers a room in our hotel suite to Joanne, but she insists on driving home tonight. After we thank Mallory for watching Zoey, we say goodbye to Joanne with the promise of visiting soon. With us moving to Houston, we'll only be about a two and a half hour drive away.

We get back to the hotel room and Xander orders room service for dinner while I give Zoey her bath and bottle. Sometimes when I look at her, the ache in my chest feels almost unbearable. I hate that she'll never get to experience the brightness that was Delilah, but that just means I'm going to have to do everything in my power to ensure she knows all about her. Once she's asleep in her crib and Xander and I have eaten dinner, I'm ready for bed. The day was just so fucking mentally draining.

"Do you think it'd be okay if we slept in your room tonight?" I ask Xander, and he grins, telling me he's all for it.

"Yeah, that would definitely be okay."

We shower, get dressed, and finally lay down in bed when we hear Zoey cry. We glance over at each other and chuckle.

"I'll get her," Xander insists, getting back up.

"Bring her in here," I call out, and I vaguely hear him agree before my eyes close and I pass the hell out.

CHAPTER FORTY-SEVEN

Xander

"ARE YOU SURE YOU DON'T WANT TO COME WITH ME?" I CALL OUT TO COLE for the third time, who is in the living room with Zoey. We've spent the last few weeks together, getting all their stuff moved in and situated. I signed my player extension contract, which makes me extremely happy to know I'll be with Houston another few years at least—plus there's the increase in pay which is definitely an added bonus. I missed the charity function Ciara wanted to me attend because we were too busy dealing with everything else— and if I'm honest, I didn't want to be away from Cole—but when I explained to her about him and Zoey moving in, she understood. Of course that also meant I would have to attend another function that I originally wasn't planning to attend.

Zoey had her four-month-old doctor appointment last week. The shots sucked, but she's healthy and perfect. We've found a nanny, who will be coming to work for us, although we haven't figured out the hours yet. The truth is Cole and I enjoy our privacy, and we enjoy taking care of Zoey ourselves. We've gotten used to being in our own little bubble, but we know it can't stay like that forever. The nanny's name is Kacey, and once we hired her, she was required to sign an NDA. We told her we would be in touch with her hours once we've figured it out.

Tonight is the charity gala I've agreed to attend in place of the one I missed. Several players from my team attend it every year along with dozens of other players from different teams, as well as a variety of models and celebrities. I've asked Cole to join me, and while he won't come out and say it, I know he's not ready for anybody to know about us yet, which is why he keeps saying he'd rather stay home with Zoey.

"I'm sure," he yells back for the third time. I finish tying my tie and walk out to the living room. He's sitting on the floor with Zoey, who is shifting her body from side to side. "She's going to roll over," he says with a grin as she pushes up on her arm, but after only rolling halfway, falls back onto her belly, babbling like crazy.

"Come here, sweet girl." I pick her up and lift her into the air, making her babble some more. I give her a kiss on her cheek and then her nose, before I hand her back to Cole.

"It's not too—"

"Xander," Cole says, cutting me off. "Go, donate some money and see your teammates. I'm going to spend the evening applying to the schools in the area. There are tons of high schools, and school is starting back up in the next month. I'll be here when you get home."

"Alright." I kneel down and give him—what I planned to be—a quick kiss, however, it quickly turns into more, both of us groaning as I pull away, knowing I don't have the time to finish what we're about to start. "I won't be too late."

"Bye!"

I step outside my condominium complex and into the awaiting limo to take me to the charity function. It's about a thirty minute drive, so I use the time to go through my emails and confirm any upcoming appointments. When I'm done, I check my various social media accounts. Ever since Cole told me about that fan site, I find myself wondering how often I'm really photographed and have no clue.

I'm not sure how long we're driving for, but when we stop, I assume we're at the gala, only before I can get out, Larissa Cofield steps in. She's a country singer who resides here in Houston when she's not in LA recording an album or on tour. Ciara hooked us up a couple years back for a function after Larissa's boyfriend cheated on her and she needed a date to a function. We've become close friends and often times attend functions together when we're both in the area. She's also the only other person aside from Ciara that knows how I feel about Cole. One drunken night and my turning her down led to her thinking there's something wrong with her, so I ended up telling her my secret to make her feel better.

"I didn't know you were coming," I say as I move over so she can sit down.

"It was last minute. I hope you don't mind. Ciara said it wouldn't be a problem."

"Of course not." I give her a kiss on her cheek. "It's been awhile."

"I know! I'm actually seeing someone, but he's out of town and I didn't want to go alone."

"Good for you, and you know I got your back." I shoot her a playful wink, and she grins.

"I saw your picture the other day," she mentions, giving me a side-eye.

"Oh yeah?" I try to recall what I might've been doing in this photo. Cole and I have barely left the condo.

"Yeah, you were coming out of the doctor's office with your friend and a baby." She grins. "Caption wants to know whose baby it is and where the mom is."

Oh shit! I pull my phone out and dial Ciara. "Hey, did you know someone took a picture of Cole and me coming out of Zoey's doctor's appointment?"

"Well, hello to you too. Yes, I put a call in to the magazine who bought the image and paid them to take it down. I was actually planning to speak to you about this tomorrow during our lunch." Shit! I completely forgot we have a lunch scheduled to go over everything.

"Alright, thanks."

"Xander, you're going to have to decide what you want to tell the media. You are living with another man who has a baby. We can spin it any way you want, but if you say you're only friends and you're seen out acting like more than friends, you're going to get chewed up and spit out alive."

"I know. I'll talk to Cole when I get home."

"Okay, we'll discuss this further tomorrow. Have fun at the charity gala tonight."

"Yeah, yeah." I hang up with Ciara and look over at Larissa whose grin is even wider than a minute ago.

"Are you finally together?" She bounces in her seat, excitedly. "C'mon! I need to know."

"Yes, we are. But it was a shitty situation. Remember I told you about our best friend, Delilah? Well, she died. She had cancer for the third time and her body couldn't handle it."

"Oh no! I'm so sorry, and that poor baby. At least she has you and Cole."

"Yeah, but Cole wants us to stay...how do they word it? In the closet." I shrug. "We're taking it slow."

The door to the limo opens, ending our conversation. Larissa steps out first, and I follow. The camera lights flash like they always do as we smile our perfect smiles and wave to everyone standing on the sidelines as we walk down the walkway and into the function. We spend the next few hours mingling with people, having dinner, and participating in a silent auction. This charity is to help raise money for underfunded youth programs such as sports organizations and other after school activities. It funds several mobile health clinics that visit lower income areas. When the function is over, the driver drops Larissa off first and then me.

It's after one in the morning, and the only thing I want to do is get out of this monkey suit and get into bed with Cole. When basketball season starts and I'm away for two weeks out of the month it's going to suck, so I need to get in as much time as possible while I'm in my offseason. Entering the foyer, it's dark throughout the house aside from a single light in the kitchen. Toeing off my shoes, I throw my keys onto the counter and head straight for my room. When I open my door, I find my bed is empty. While Cole technically has his own room, he's slept in my room every night since he's moved in.

My first thought is that something is wrong with Zoey. I head straight over to her room and find her fast asleep. I chuckle at how adorable she sleeps with her legs and arms flailing out every which way. Not wanting to wake her up, I blow her a kiss and head out of her room. I stop at Cole's door and find it's shut. I knock softly, not wanting to wake Zoey up, but when he doesn't answer, I turn the knob, worried. His room is dark, and he's sleeping in his bed. I'm not sure why he's in here, but I'm not having it. I strip out of my clothes and toss them into the corner of the room then pad over to Cole's bed.

Turning the sheet down, I get into the bed and face him. I know he's asleep because I can hear him softly snoring. I take a few minutes to study him. He's a beautiful man on the inside and out, and I feel so fucking lucky that he's willing to give us a chance. I know how much his mom means to him, so for him to still be willing to see where this goes speaks volumes of how much he cares about me. His eyes are closed, and his hair is a gorgeous mess.

My eyes drag down his face to his exposed chest. I was there for every one of his tattoos, then one day when I was missing him and Delilah, I decided to get a matching one of my own on my chest. Cole will always be the person who anchors me, and Delilah was the glue who held us all together.

"Is there a reason you're watching me like a fucking creeper?" Cole asks, his eyes not opening.

"Is there a reason why you're sleeping in here instead of in our bed?"

He opens his eyes and stares at me for a few moments. "I saw you tonight at the charity function with that country singer."

"I asked you to go with me, and you said no."

"So, it's either I go or you take someone else?"

"It sucks to go to those functions alone. I didn't know she was joining me, but her company was welcome. She's a good friend. I asked you to go. It's not my fault you aren't ready to make our relationship public."

Cole sits up and glares. "Nice, so I'm going to be punished until I agree to go public?"

I sit up next to him. "That's not what I said, and that's

not what I meant. I'm sorry for not telling you she was going once I knew, and I'm sorry if you felt I was in the wrong for going with her. If you don't want me to go with someone, I'll go alone."

Cole curses under his breath. "No, I'm sorry. I'm acting like a jealous boyfriend." I grin at his choice of words, and he raises a brow in question. Edging closer to him, I bridge the gap between us, only leaving a couple inches of space between our bodies.

"You called yourself my boyfriend. Is that what you are? Are you my boyfriend?" I smirk, and he rolls his eyes but grins.

"I'm not sure." He moves closer, and those couple inches of space are gone. "We make out like couples do..."

"And you give amazing head," I add, and he chuckles.

"I learned from the best." His hand makes its way into my boxers, and his fingers grip my shaft. "But I'm pretty sure most couples do more than just make out and give each other oral." His eyes lock with mine, and I look for an ounce of unsureness but don't find any.

"I thought we were taking it slow," I choke out. Cole's now stroking my cock, which is making it hard to converse.

"I think I'm ready to kick it up a notch," he says.

"You think?"

"I'm sure."

"I've never done this before. The extent of my knowledge is from watching porn." I laugh, and Cole grins.

"Aren't you the one who said we'll learn together?" He lets go of my dick and leans back, opening his nightstand drawer. He closes it back up and tosses something at me. When I grab it, I see it's a bottle of lube. "I'm ready to learn."

He pushes my boxers down and then his own, then goes back to stroking my cock. My hand finds his dick, and it's hard as steel. I stroke him a couple of times before I pull him into a hard kiss. Our mouths collide and our tongues move frantically over each other. We kiss for a few minutes, neither of us sure of who should make the first move. Finally, I'm so worked up, I say fuck it and make a move.

Dragging my body down the bed, I move the sheets out of the way, and with Cole lying flat on his back, I situate myself between his legs. Lifting his dick up against his stomach, I press my tongue against the sensitive underside of his shaft and lick upwards until I get to the engorged head. I suck gently on the tip and can taste the precum. Squirting some lube into my fingers, I spread open his ass cheeks, just like all the times I'd done to Delilah. I insert one finger into him, and he lets out a low groan.

"If it hurts, you have to tell me," I say, and he nods. I move my finger in and out of him a few times before I add another and then another. "How does it feel?" I ask him.

"Fucking good. Go harder." I do as he says and push my three fingers into him as far as I can go then pull them out almost all the way. "Holy shit," he moans out, and my dick twitches.

"Stroke your cock," I demand, wanting to see him touch himself. His hand moves down to his hard cock, and he starts to fuck his fist while I continue to fingerfuck him.

"Xander, man, I'm going to come soon. If you're going to fuck me, you need to do it soon." Squirting some more lube into my fingers, I come up onto my knees and stroke my dick. The last thing I want to do is hurt Cole. It took several times of preparing Delilah before she could fuck us both at the same time.

I spread his legs wide enough so I can get between them and slowly guide my dick into his ass. Once I'm all the way in, I grip the underside of his knees and start fucking him with slow and steady thrusts. He's so fucking tight there's no way I'm going to last long. This feels too damn good. My eyes rake down his body until they land on his cock. He's jerking his fist frantically. Our chests are heaving and it's obvious we're both close. Needing to feel his body against mine, I drop my hands onto the mattress, caging him in, and dip my head to kiss him, our mouths as frantic as our bodies are. I can feel Cole still stroking his dick between us as my thrusts get harder and deeper.

Cole breaks our kiss, throwing his head back in pleasure. "Fuck, I'm coming," he screams out, and I feel his warm seed hit both of our stomachs. Unsure if he's okay with me coming in his ass, I sit up and pull my dick out just before I follow him with my own orgasm, my cum shooting onto his stomach. Seeing our seeds mixed together does something inside of me. We both stay where we are for several long beats, our chests rising and falling as we attempt to catch our breath.

Cole opens his mouth to speak, and I'd be lying if I said I wasn't scared of what he might say after having been with him like I just was. After having my dick inside of him, feeling his ass grip and accept me. I don't know what I'll do if he tells me he doesn't want this. "How long do you think it will take for us to get hard again? Because holy fuck, do I want in your ass next go-round."

I drop down onto my back next to Cole and laugh until tears of happiness are dripping out of my eyes and down the sides of my face. I never, in a million years, imagined this is where my life would take me. Sure, I fantasized, but I never dared to hope. Yet, here I am, in bed with the man I've been in love with for most of my life.

When I open my eyes, I see Cole hovering above me. He bends down and presses his lips to mine before he says,

"In all seriousness, that was the best fucking thing I've ever felt. I'm totally digging this whole boyfriend thing." He winks playfully, and I chuckle as he rolls off the bed, and I watch his tight ass saunter into the bathroom to clean up. Then I take a moment to say a silent thank you to Delilah for pushing me to fight for Cole. Even in her death, she's bringing happiness to those she loved.

CHAPTER FORTY-EIGHT

Cole

 so you can hear her in case she wakes up and needs something. The bottles are in the kitchen..."

"Xander, we've explained this to her a dozen times," I point out, doing my best to stifle my laugh. He glares my way but ignores me, continuing to explain things to Kacey, our new nanny, who listens with far more patience than I ever would. It's the first time we're using her, and it's because we're meeting Xander's friends for a night out. One of his teammates and his wife have opened up a new club in Downtown Houston, and he wants to go to show his support.

"We both have our cell phones on us, if you need anything. No reason is stupid, okay?" Xander says.

She smiles and verbally agrees, promising everything will be okay. We jump into one of the vehicles Xander rarely uses these days, mostly because when we usually leave, it's to bring Zoey somewhere, and sports cars and babies don't exactly mix. It's a black-on-black Acura NSX, and while I'm positive he could afford a way more expensive car, I love that he bought the vehicle he used to say he wanted when being in the NBA was nothing more than a dream for him.

"It's weird to be going somewhere without Zoey," Xander says a few minutes into our drive to downtown.

"Yeah, but we had to leave eventually. This is good practice for when your season starts. When does training camp begin anyway?"

Xander glances over at me before his eyes go back to the road. "Another eight weeks, but shouldn't you be starting your job sooner? From what I remember, school starts at the end of August. Have you found a job yet?"

I found a few job openings actually, but I don't tell him that. "I'm looking."

"You know you don't have to work," he points out for the millionth fucking time.

"And you know I'm a man, right?" I shoot back. "If you could quit trying to cut my balls off, that would be great."

His eyes swing over to me, and he shoots me a *what the fuck is going on with you* look, but I ignore it. "I'm well aware you're a man," he smarts. "Your dick in me last night kind of gave that away."

"Then how about you don't treat me like I'm some chick you can throw money at to keep at home. I'm well aware you'll always make more money than me, but I still need to work. I need my own money."

Xander pulls around to the valet and turns to face me. "I don't know what's going on with you, but I've never thrown my money at you. We have a four-month-old daughter at home. Growing up, I had no fucking mother. I had a dead beat dad who left me alone more often than not. You used to tell me how much you loved your time with your mom.

How she used to pick you up from school and go to all your activities, and you said she did all that because she was a stay-at-home-mom. All I was trying to do was give you that option. I might not be able to give you the man and woman life your mom wanted for you, but I can give you that. Stability, a nice home, and the option for you to be home with our daughter."

Xander sighs then adds, "I'm sorry. I didn't even think about the fact that you would feel the need to work as well. If you would've been with a woman, you would've been the one working. Fuck." He shakes his head, and I feel like the biggest asshole. He's just trying to give me the life my mom wanted for me.

"I could stay home," he says. "I have thirty days to void my player extension."

"Stop!" I say. "You're not quitting the fucking NBA. There's nothing wrong with two parents working. Who knows? Maybe I won't even find a job and then I'll have no choice but to stay home." I open my door and get out of the car without waiting for Xander to catch up. There's a huge line of photographers for the grand opening, and he's going to need to put on his NBA player face. I watch as he walks down the walkway, smiling and taking a couple of selfies with his fans, and I feel like shit for how I'm acting. He doesn't deserve to be treated like this. I'm dealing with my own issues, and I shouldn't be taking my frustrations out on him.

"Let's just have a good time tonight, okay?" he says when he joins me at the entrance and tells the bouncer his name to get us in. We make our way over to the VIP section that's roped off, and I spot a bunch of his teammates. They're all laughing and drinking, and they all have a hot woman on their arm. *Great...*

"X!" one of the guys calls out, and Xander walks over to him.

"Fields! What's happening?" He extends his fist out to fist bump the guy I recognize as Antoine Fields. "This is my friend, Cole."

"What's up?" Antoine extends his hand to shake mine while keeping his other arm around the leggy blonde he has tucked into his side, and it takes every ounce of strength I have not to gush like a teenage girl who's just met her favorite boyband. Antoine Fields is one of my favorite players right now in the NBA. "I've heard a lot about you, man." My eyes quickly dart to Xander who doesn't give anything away. "I'm sorry for your loss." I sigh a breath of relief. Xander must've told him about Delilah's passing. He mentioned that he needed to make a statement because someone photographed us coming out of Zoey's doctor's appointment, and he wanted to make sure to be the one to set the facts straight before any speculation could arise.

"Thanks."

"Excuse me!" Antoine lifts his finger, calling the waitress over to us. "What do you guys want to drink?"

"I'll just take a coke, please," I say.

"Same," Xander adds.

"No way! We're celebrating the grand opening of Benji and Tate's new club. You have to have a real drink."

"He doesn't drink," Xander jumps in, and I shoot him a glare. *What the fuck...*

"*He* can speak for himself," I point out harshly. Ignoring the hurt and confused look Xander's giving me, I excuse myself saying that I need to use the restroom. I don't find the restroom, but I do find an emergency exit down the hallway. It beeps indicating a door has been opened, but stops once I shut the door behind me. I'm going to have to walk back around the front to get back in, but right now I just need to take a deep breath. I find a bench on the side of the building and sit down, taking a moment to stare up at the clear sky. I feel Xander's presence before he makes himself known. He sits down next to me and neither of us say a word for several minutes.

"Sometimes I think the clear skies in Texas are a curse," I say. I feel him glance over at me, but my eyes stay trained on the little gold dots in the sky. "For the rest of our lives, every time we stare up at those stars, we'll think of her."

"Do you want to forget her?" he asks, his voice free of all judgment.

"No, never. I just don't want it to hurt so much. Maybe let the pain of her loss take a little break. But every night those stars come out without fail, and it's as if I'm feeling her loss all over again."

"I've never lost anyone before Delilah," Xander says, "so I have nothing to compare this to, but I would like to think that one day we'll look up at the stars and instead of feeling loss or pain, we'll feel her love and light. She was the brightest star in the fucking sky, and she wouldn't want her memory to be dimmed with tears."

I think about what he just said, and I know he's right. Delilah would never want us to mourn her loss, but instead to celebrate her life.

"So, you want to tell me what had you snapping at me in there? Because I feel like I can't do or say anything right tonight when it comes to you, but I have no clue why."

"All those guys are in there, drinking and partying with hot women."

"And what is it you want? The drink or the hot woman? Or is it both?" he questions, and I chuckle. Xander never has and never will beat around the bush. "C'mon, tell me.

Because I know you wouldn't be upset thinking I want either one."

"You can drink if you want to," I point out.

"Thanks." It comes out sarcastic, and when I eye him, he's smirking. "Oh, Cole." He leans forward, his elbows going to his knees. "I love you so goddamned much."

"But?"

"But nothing. I love you. That's it." He stands and kneels in front of me. "I don't know what's going on with you, but I'm here. All I need in this world are you and that little girl at home. If I want to have a drink, I will. But I won't want a hot woman on my arm. I want you by my side. I told you I would give you time and I am, but we can't live like this forever. Every conversation we have with people is a lie. It's not good for us, not as individuals or as a couple. The sooner you figure out what you want and own up to it, the better it will be for the both of us."

CHAPTER FORTY-NINE

Cole

I LAY ZOEY IN HER CRIB AND COVER HER WITH HER BLANKET, GIVING HER A light kiss to her forehead so as not to wake her up. If the same pattern continues that's been taking place this last week, she's just had her last bottle of the night, which means she won't wake up again until 5 a.m. when she's ready for her morning bottle. After switching on Zoey's night light and closing her door almost all the way, I swing by my bedroom to grab a change of clothes, then head to Xander's room. Xander hates that I'm still keeping my clothes in the closet in my bedroom, especially since I've never actually slept in there, but I don't want to take the chance that if someone comes over, they'll see my stuff in his room.

After changing into my sweats, I throw my dirty clothes into the hamper, take a leak and brush my teeth, then lay down to watch some television. It's the first time since Zoey and I have moved in here that Xander is spending the night away from us. He had to head out of town for a photoshoot for some commercial, and of course he offered to take us along, but I told him it would be best if we stay here so he can focus on what he needs to do. It's only an overnight trip, so it's a waste to pack up Zoey and drag her along just to come back the next day. Right now, however, I'm kind of regretting not going. He's only been gone for eighteen hours, and I'm already missing him. Guess I better get used to it, though. Once basketball season starts, he'll be gone for weeks at a time, and we won't have the option of tagging along. Just as I'm about to plug my phone into the charger, it dings with an incoming text.

Xander: Are you awake?

Me: No

Xander: Fucking smartass

I chuckle and begin to type a reply, when the phone lights up indicating that Xander is video calling me. I hit accept, and a few seconds later, his sexy mug comes across the screen. I can tell right off the bat, he's shirtless and lying in bed.

"Hey." His voice is gravelly, and his eyes look tired, but there's a hint of a smile.

"Hey," I say back. "How was the shoot?"

"Long and boring." He sighs, losing that bit of a smile he had a moment ago. "I miss you and Zoey."

"We miss you too."

"Has she already had her last bottle of the night?"

"Yeah, she's out for the count."

"Damn." He frowns. "I was hoping to say goodnight." The sad look he's sporting has me feeling all kinds of guilty for not going with him when he asked. Our time is limited until the season starts. I just couldn't bring myself to go.

"I'm sure she'll be up bright and early. You can call back then and talk to her while I sleep in," I joke, trying to lighten the mood, but Xander doesn't even crack a smile.

"Hey," I say. "You're going to be home tomorrow."

"I know." He nods solemnly. "I just don't like this."

"Well, I don't either, but it's something we're going to have to get used to, Mr. NBA." When his frown deepens, an idea pops into my head. "But there are things we can do to make the days you're away not feel so...long and painful."

He raises his brows in curiosity. "And what is that?"

To answer his question, I ask one of my own. "What are you wearing?" At first, his brows furrow in confusion, but I can tell the moment he catches on, because he lets out a soft chuckle followed by a small knowing grin.

"I'm in my boxers," he answers. "You?"

"Sweats."

We're both quiet for a moment, before Xander says, "It always seems way hotter in the movies when someone initiates phone sex." We both laugh.

"That's probably because it's always a woman describing her tiny bra and panties," I joke, and Xander nods in agreement. "You could always take off your boxers," I add. Xander's eyes widen, then he shuffles around, the phone going blurry for a second before he's back on the screen. Only it's not his face I'm looking at, but his semi-hard cock that he's now slowly stroking.

"Jesus," I groan. "Have I mentioned that I really fucking miss you?"

"Yeah," Xander murmurs, "and what would you do if I was there?" I grin at the cliché phone sex question but love that he's going along with it.

"Well, for one, you wouldn't be stroking your own dick; I would be doing it for you with my mouth." Xander lets out a low groan, and I continue. "First, I'd lick my tongue across the crown of your cock so I could have a taste of your precum." Xander's thumb swipes across the head and it glistens with the same precum I was just talking about.

"Cole, I want to see you," Xander says. Too fixated on his hard dick, I forgot he's still looking at my face. I push my sweatpants down, and my dick springs free. Then I press the button on the phone to flip the camera, and on the screen there's now two hard cocks. My hand comes down to stroke my own, and Xander's hand fists his tighter.

"What would you do next?" Xander asks, his voice husky and turned on.

"I would move down to your balls, licking and sucking on them, taking them into my mouth. I would lick up the underside of your dick until I hit the top again, and then take you all the way into my mouth until your big fucking dick hits the back of my throat."

"Fuck, Cole," Xander groans. His fist tightens around his cock, and his jerks get faster. "I want your mouth on me so bad."

"Once your dick hits the back of my throat," I say, continuing where I left off, "your hands would come down to the back of my head, and you would take control. Pushing my head up and down over your cock, fucking my mouth until you come down my throat." The vision of Xander forcing me to take him in and out of my mouth has my dick twitching. My fist clenches around my hard as steel dick, and my stroking picks up.

"Fuck yes, I love to watch you suck me off," Xander murmurs. "But there's no way I would be coming in your mouth. I would pull out, and turn you around, lubing the fuck out of your ass and sticking my dick right into it."

"Oh fuck." It's my turn to moan out loud at the thought of Xander ramming his dick into my ass. "Fuck my ass hard, man," I groan, needing more, needing him here with me.

My strokes are getting more frantic and so are Xander's. It's not the same thing as him being here, but the fact that we're doing it together, watching each other, is a fucking turn on.

"I am. Stroke your cock. Come all over the bed while I come in your tight fucking hole." Xander's words turn breathy as he strokes himself harder and faster, and then he's coming all over his hand and stomach. The sight of his milky white seed alone has my orgasm following right behind his—warm liquid hitting my stomach.

We both sit here for a good minute, our dicks softening and our breathing labored like we actually had sex, before Xander turns the camera around to his face. He waits a second for me to do the same before he speaks. "When I get home, I'm going to fuck the ever loving shit out of you. My fist has nothing on your ass." I chuckle at the seriousness in his voice.

"You better get used to that fist, because you're going to be gone for weeks at a time." My words are meant as a joke, but Xander frowns.

"You don't think I would ever cheat on you, do you?"

"No, I didn't say anything about you cheating. I said you better get used to doing it yourself." But now that he's mentioned it, the reality of our situation is front and center in my head. Xander is a professional athlete. During basketball season, he'll be gone more than he's home. We barely lasted eighteen hours before resorting to phone sex.

"Cole, I see those wheels in your head turning. Pull the fucking brakes right now," Xander demands. "I went three fucking years without having sex. Unless..." His brows furrow. "Are you thinking about yourself?" he questions.

"What? No, I wasn't. I was thinking about you, but you're right. We both can't be thinking like this. This is your job, and you love it. We can't let a few weeks of you being away during the season fuck with us."

Xander nods in agreement. "It just means once I am home, we double up on the sex." He grins wide, and I laugh.

"I better go get cleaned up."

"Yeah, same. Give Zoey a kiss for me in the morning, and I'll be home tomorrow night."

"Will do, good night."

"Good night."

THE SOUND OF ZOEY'S SOFT CRIES THROUGH THE BABY MONITOR HAS ME opening my eyes. When I press the button on the phone to see the time, I notice there's a text from Xander. He must have sent it after I fell asleep.

> **Xander: Be ready for 8 p.m. I'm taking an earlier flight and taking you out. Kacey will be there at 7:45 to watch Zoey. And before you freak out, we won't be in public. See you tonight.**

I grin at his text and type back that I'll see him later and to have a safe flight. Then I get up, throw on a t-shirt, and begin my day with my beautiful daughter who is more than ready for her morning bottle.

We spend the day mostly inside, aside from our daily jog around the trail that runs behind the complex. Zoey eats, naps, and plays like she does every day. She's growing way too quickly for my liking. It's crazy to think about the fact that in a couple weeks my daughter will be five months old. I give her a bath, which she loves, giggling when I splash the bubbles and squeak the bath toys.

When 7:00 rolls around, I shower, shave, and get dressed. I feed Zoey, and I'm putting her in her swing when

Kacey's voice comes over the intercom letting me know she's downstairs. I buzz her in and open the door, grabbing my cell phone and keys and giving Zoey one last kiss. I haven't heard from Xander, and I'd assumed I'm meeting him downstairs at 8 o'clock, so when I hear a masculine voice as opposed to Kacey's feminine one, I startle and turn around.

And standing in the doorway next to Kacey is none other than Xander, looking sexy as fuck in his black polo shirt and denim jeans. He has an Astros ball cap covering his head, and he's sporting some serious scruff that only adds to his sex appeal. He smirks knowingly, and I clear my throat in an attempt to compose myself. If I had it my way, we would send Kacey home and spend the evening in bed.

"Not happening." Xander laughs, knowing exactly what I'm thinking. "Let's go." He turns to Kacey. "We'll be home by midnight. Thank you."

"She just ate," I tell Kacey, and she smiles.

"Sounds good. Have a good evening. We'll be here when you get home."

We take the elevator down to the underground parking garage, and waiting for us is a town car.

"You're not driving?" I ask, sliding into the backseat.

"No, I didn't want to take a chance of anyone spotting us." Xander leans over and gives me a kiss. I glance toward the driver and see the privacy partition is up. "The windows are blacked out too. Nobody can see us, I promise," Xander murmurs against my mouth before deepening the kiss.

I'm so caught up in him that I don't ask where we're going or what we're doing. When he breaks the kiss, I realize the car has stopped. Looking around, I spot the back of a building, but I'm not sure what it's to. The driver opens the door, and Xander and I get out. He guides us toward a backdoor. It opens and Ciara nods with a grin.

"You owe me," is all she says before opening the door farther and granting us access. "Second door on your right. Everything is set up."

"Thank you." Xander kisses her on the cheek, and Ciara rolls her eyes.

"You're welcome. Once you're done, just call the driver so he knows to return, and make sure you exit out this door."

We head down the hallway, but I have no clue where the hell we are. That is until I spot several movie posters along the walls. "Are you taking me to the movies?" I ask.

"Yep." Xander takes my hand in his, and my eyes dart around for anybody who might see the sweet gesture. "Nobody is here but us, so stop worrying."

We enter the door Ciara mentioned, and inside is a full size movie theater with previews playing on the screen. We walk up the steps until we reach the middle of the theater. And that's when I see a table full of food: boxes of candy, popcorn, nachos, two large drinks, and tons of other stuff.

"You did all this?" I ask in awe.

"It's our first date." Xander shrugs. "Doesn't everyone have their first date at the movies?" For us to be the only people here means he went through the trouble of renting out the entire theater just to take me on a date. And he did it because I'm not ready for us to go public yet.

We both grab a drink, some candy and popcorn, then make our way to the middle seats just as the previews end and the lights turn down, indicating the movie is about to start.

Not able to stand another second without touching him, I pull his face towards mine for a kiss, not giving two shits about whatever it is that he's picked for us to watch.

The only thing I care about right now is showing Xander how much him doing this tonight means to me.

And just like anytime Xander and I kiss, things quickly heat up, and before the opening lines of the movie are even spoken, I'm flipping the arm rest up and undoing his pants. I'm almost positive the tub of popcorn hits the floor, but I don't give a fuck. My lips wrap around the head of his cock, and my mouth moves down his hard length, inch by delicious inch, until I'm swallowing as much of him as I can down my throat. My nose grazes against Xander's neatly trimmed curls, and I can't help but inhale his musky scent. Xander lets out a low groan, but doesn't move a muscle as I begin to bob my head up and down over him. It doesn't take long before his hips begin to buck frantically as he drives his cock in and out of my mouth, meeting me thrust for thrust. My saliva drips down his dick as he fucks my mouth until he comes down my throat. Once I've sucked him clean, I sit up and wipe the spit from my lips while he tucks himself back into his pants.

"In case I didn't make it clear." I chuckle. "Thank you for tonight."

Xander throws his head back with a laugh. "If that's how all our dates are going to begin, you better believe I'm going to be taking you out often."

We spend the next couple hours eating way too much junk food, making out, somewhat watching the movie, and talking about random shit. The night is absolutely fucking perfect. When the credits come up, I'm sad that the night is coming to an end, and I think Xander is too, because he says, "We can do this again. Hell, next time I can rent the theatre for two movies." He chuckles, but I frown. If I wasn't so hellbent on keeping us a secret, we would be able to go out whenever we wanted. Here he is goiWng out of his way to show me how much this relationship means to him, and in return, I'm forcing us to hide.

"Thank you again for doing this."

"Of course." He smiles. "It's what boyfriends do." He shoots me a playful wink before he shows me with his hot, wet, talented mouth what else boyfriends do.

CHAPTER FIFTY

Xander

I'M STICKY AND SWEATY AND SORE AS FUCK, AND I CAN'T WAIT TO TAKE A hot shower and change out of my workout clothes. I considered rinsing off at the stadium but then figured if I waited until I got home, I might be able to convince Cole to join me. Training camp doesn't start for another month and a half, but I always start getting back into my routine weeks beforehand. That includes working out twice a day and eating only what's on my diet. My body is my vessel, and if I don't fuel it properly, it won't perform like I need it to.

When I unlock the front door, I immediately notice that it's dark and quiet. When you live with an infant, it's almost never quiet. I'm about to flick on a light when I spot several lit candles on the table and countertops.

"Cole?" I call out, but he doesn't answer. I walk into the kitchen and see aluminum covered dishes on the stove. It smells like Italian, and my stomach grumbles.

"Hey, you're back early." Cole pads into the kitchen in

nothing but a pair of sweats hanging low on his hips. His hair is still damp, which means he's just showered. Damn it. He gives me a chaste kiss then backs up slightly. "I made us dinner, but you stink. Why don't you shower while I finish heating the side dishes up, and then we can eat."

"You cooked?" I ask stunned because Cole doesn't cook... hell, Cole *can't* cook.

"Well, sort of." He chuckles softly. "I had your chef make it all and bring it over so all I would have to do is heat it up. Technically that means I made it." He shrugs with a big grin splayed across his face.

"Where's Zoey?" It's only five o'clock, so there's no way she's already down for the night.

"Joanne and John had to come into town for a business meeting. They asked if they could take Zoey for the night." He waggles his eyebrows, and I laugh. "She'll be home in the morning."

Grabbing the drawstrings to his pants, I pull him towards me until our bodies are almost flush. "Does that mean what I think it means?"

"A full twelve hours of sleep?" he deadpans. "Yes, it does."

I bark out a loud laugh. "Funny. More like a full twelve hours of me fucking you."

"More like six. The other six I'll be fucking you." He kisses me then starts to walk toward the stove. "But first you need to shower." He smacks my ass. "Now."

"I was hoping you would join me," I grumble. "It's the whole reason why I'm still all sweaty."

"I already took one." He laughs, shaking his head as he places a pan into the oven.

"Okay, then how about I dirty you up, then you can shower with me." I come up behind him and snake my arm around his waist, my hand running down his muscular torso and landing on the bulge in his pants. He lets out a low moan, and I know I have him.

"Fine, but we only have thirty minutes." He turns around. "That's how long the chicken will take to bake in the oven."

"Thirty minutes? I'm going to need way more time to do all the things I want to do to you. I'll take a quick shower while you...fake bake our dinner, and once we're done eating, we'll have all night." I cage Cole in my arms and give him a chaste kiss on his lips before I head out of the kitchen.

"I'm not fake baking!" he yells. "The oven is really on!"

"You're warming shit up!" I shout back through my laughter. "That doesn't fucking count."

After taking a quick shower, I meet Cole back in the dining room where he has everything set up for dinner. The food smells delicious, and I love that he called my chef to prepare it, knowing I'm back to eating healthy. We eat our chicken and salad while talking about our day, and it all feels so domestic, like something you see couples doing in the movies. Before Cole and Zoey moved in, it was just me. Sure, sometimes after practice, I would meet some of my teammates for dinner, but most of them are either married or seeing someone. And the ones who are single, are usually going out to find someone to hook up with. And since that wasn't something I was interested in doing, most of the time I found myself alone in my empty condo. At the time, I thought I was okay with that, but now that I know what it's like to have my home full of baby bottles and toys and swings, my bedroom littered with Cole's clothes, and my kitchen filled with junk food, I can't imagine it any other way. The truth is I'm dreading the season starting. The nights alone in the hotel rooms while I'm on the road for days at a time. I've gotten so used to sharing a bed with Cole. To Zoey's babbling in the early morning. I don't know how I'm going to go days without seeing them.

"Hey, you okay?" Cole asks, standing and taking my empty plate from in front of me.

"Yeah, thank you for dinner," I say, standing as well to help him. We enter the kitchen, and he places the dirty dishes into the sink and turns the water on. "Stella will be by tomorrow to clean. Just leave the dirty dishes and she'll handle them. I turn the water back off. Cole is about to object, but before he can, my hands grip his sides, and I bracket him with my arms.

"Are you sure you're okay?" he asks again, concern evident in his tone.

"Yeah, that's the thing." I rub my nose up and down along his jawline, taking in his scent. "Everything feels like it's perfect." My lips land on his neck, and I suck on his skin lightly. "I know there are going to be times when things aren't easy. Like my traveling, or us raising Zoey, but I just want you to know there's no one else I would rather be with than you." My mouth moves to his collarbone, and I trail kisses over his flesh. "I love you, Cole."

When he doesn't say anything, I raise my head to look at him. His eyes are glossy with unshed tears, and I'm afraid maybe I said something wrong. But then his hands frame my face, and he pulls me into a searing kiss before he backs up slightly. "I love you too, so fucking much."

CHAPTER FIFTY-ONE

Cole

"I'M SORRY, BUT I CAN'T GO."

"Are you fucking serious?" Xander shouts, and Zoey startles, her eyes going wide at never having heard anyone yell before. Xander stands frozen in his spot for a long beat before he throws his arms up in defeat. "Fine! I'll be home in a couple days." He slams the door behind him, and Zoey makes a small sound like she's about to cry.

"Shh...it's okay," I say softly to calm her down, and it works. I finish feeding her then pack our bags, needing to get out of this condo. I make the two-and-a-half hour drive to Brenton, and it isn't until I pull up to the Cross's ranch that I realize I should've called first. Stopping at the entrance, I call Joanne, and she answers on the first ring.

"Cole! It's so good to hear from you. How is my beautiful granddaughter doing?"

"That's actually why I'm calling. We were thinking about visiting today, but I wasn't sure if you were up for company."

"Oh, yes! Of course! What time are you thinking?"

"Uhh…" I chuckle softly. "How about now?"

"Now?" It takes her a few seconds to understand. "Are you here right now? Well, get in here!" She hangs up on me, and when I make it down the long driveway, I see her and John standing outside waiting. When I pull up, she rushes to the car to give me a hug before grabbing Zoey.

"Where's Xander?" she asks.

"He had to fly to Florida for a sponsorship event."

"Oh! Well, Florida is nice this time of year. Hot, but you can't beat the beaches." Yeah, that's exactly what he said when he begged me to tag along and make it a family trip. "How long will he be gone?"

"I think he said like four days or so."

"That's fun! Okay, come in and let's get this sweet angel out of this car seat." We make our way into their living room and have a seat. John grabs us all a drink while Joanne dotes on Zoey.

"So how have you been, Son?" John asks, and I'm not sure why—maybe it's him calling me son or the fact that they're the closest thing to parents I've had since my own died—but it's as if everything has reached the surface and finally tips over the edge.

"I'm in love with Xander," I blurt out. Both of them stop what they're doing and wait for me to continue. "I'm…I'm in love with him," I say again with a laugh. "I'm in love with him…and apparently that's all I'm capable of saying at the moment."

John chuckles, and Joanne sets Zoey down on her blanket. "I'll be right back," she says before leaving the room. A minute later she returns and hands me an envelope. "Delilah wrote you a letter. I was told to give it to you when you, and I quote, 'pull your head out of your ass.'"

I stare down at the white envelope that contains the last

words from the only woman I've ever loved. "Would you mind watching Zoey for a few minutes?"

"Take all the time you need," John says. I stand and start to head out the back when John calls out my name.

"Yeah?"

"I just want you to know I'm happy for you. That you found love. And I'm honored that my granddaughter will be raised by two strong and caring men who love her as much as they loved her mother. You don't need it, but you have our blessing."

"You both knew?" I ask in shock.

"Delilah used to tell us everything," Joanne says.

"I don't know what to say..."

John walks over and gives me a hug. "We meant it when we said we'll always be here for you and Xander. Just because Delilah isn't with us anymore doesn't mean we stop caring about you guys. Now, go read your letter, and we can talk after."

I walk out to the back of the ranch and head inside the old barn where Xander, Delilah, and I spent most of our days. Seeing the ladder is still there, I climb up to the second level. The haybed is still there, although the blankets have been removed. Feeling wrong to lay on it without Xander and Delilah, I sit on the ground against the barn wall and open the letter.

Cole,

If you're reading this, two things have happened. One, I've passed away and two, you finally admitted to being in love with Xander. I know what you're thinking. What if you never admitted to it? How would you have gotten your letter? Well, that's just it. I knew you would. (But before you get all bent out of shape, I wrote a second letter I told my mom she could give you after one year of my being dead in case I was totally wrong, but I wasn't). I wrote Xander's letter first, and while it was hard to write, writing a letter to you just might kill me (Sorry, too early for jokes?). First, let me start by saying thank you for being my best friend. You and I had a connection, a bond of some sort, I don't think I could've ever found with anyone else. The way you took care of me and loved me. It's like you always knew exactly what I needed even when I didn't know it myself. You believed I would survive more than anyone else. It was your love and confidence that got me through each diagnosis. You are truly one of a kind, Cole Andrews.

As I write this letter, you're asleep in our bed with our daughter in her bassinet next to you. I'm not sure how old Zoey will be when you read this, but it won't matter because regardless of her age, I know you're going to continue to be an amazing, loving father. Please know that I HATE that I left you to raise her without a mother. The only thing that helps me live with myself is knowing she won't only have one parent, but two. She will have you and Xander every step of the way as she grows up to be a precious little girl and then a beautiful young woman. She will have both of you when she graduates from high school and one day when she gets married. And no, I'm not specifying a sex because as a mother the only thing I would ever want for my daughter is for her to be happy, and I truly believe that's all your mom wanted for you. I can't know what she meant when she spoke to you that day, but I know you, and I imagine a sensitive, compassionate man probably comes from two parents who are equally sensitive and compassionate, so I choose to believe if your mom was here, she would be so happy her son has fallen in love. I know I am.

I watched for years as the two of you fell in love, and I'm sorry it took my death for you two to finally admit your feelings. We all know life is too short, so please don't waste a day of it. While I was getting my first round of chemo, I noticed a new quote on the hospital wall. I would love it if you could one day share it with Zoey: Do what makes you happy, be with who makes you smile, laugh as much as you breathe, love as long as you live.

Be happy, Cole. Love and laugh and smile and live. Do it for me, please. And also, if you could please keep wishing on shooting stars with our little girl, that would mean so much to me. I'll never forget the first night we met and you told me you knew what

I was wishing for. You're probably thinking I'm going to finally tell you what I've been wishing for after all these years, but I'm not going to because it was my wish, but I can tell you this much, it came true.

I love you, Cole. Please give Zoey and Xander a kiss for me, and tell our little girl her mommy will always be watching over her, especially when the stars come out at night.

Until we meet again,
Delilah

My first thought is to call Xander, but it's not enough. He's been doing everything in his power to show me he loves me while being patient, and instead of meeting him halfway, I've pushed him away every step of the way. I've been so caught up in what other people would think, how they would view two men together, raising a baby, that I allowed strangers to come before how I feel. I was so afraid to apply for the coaching jobs because I knew I would have to admit I'm gay, so instead I didn't apply. Then I got angry and took it out on Xander—choosing to run here instead of going with him and standing by his side.

Folding the letter up, I climb down the stairs and make my way back to the house. Joanne and John are still sitting in the living room giving Zoey all of their attention. When they notice I'm in the room, they look up.

"Are you okay?" Joanne asks.

"Yeah, but I was wondering if you could watch Zoey for a couple days. There's this guy, and he kind of owns my heart, and I treated him like crap."

"Of course. We'll be right here when you get back."

I give Zoey a kiss and go over her schedule with Joanne, then head out to the airport. I book my flight on the way, and once I'm there, I park in long-term parking then pick up my ticket and go through security. With twenty minutes until boarding, I pull the applications up on my phone and click submit. If somebody won't hire me because I'm gay then I don't want to work there anyway. I text Ciara and ask for the hotel where the function is being held, and she texts me back the time and address and tells me she'll have a car waiting for me when I arrive along with a suit in my size. That woman definitely deserves a raise.

CHAPTER FIFTY-TWO

Xander

I ARRIVED A COUPLE HOURS AGO IN FLORIDA FOR A SPONSORSHIP PARTY. I checked into my hotel and changed into a suit for the party. Luckily, I'm staying in the hotel where the party is being held. I've checked my phone a dozen times since landing, hoping to get a text or call from Cole. I've considered calling him, but I wouldn't even know what to say. He's not here because he's still refusing to go public with our relationship. I thought we were making progress, between our date to the movies and the night he surprised me with dinner, I thought it would only be a matter of time until he came around. But then this past week, it's as if he's taken ten steps back. He's been pissed off and cranky as fuck at the world and taking it out on me. I don't want to think it, but I'm starting to wonder if maybe, even though he loves me, this isn't the life he wants. I meant what I said before. If he doesn't want to be with me, I'll still raise Zoey with him. I just want Cole to be happy, even if it's not with me.

I'm walking around and socializing with everyone at this

party, thanking them for choosing me as their spokesperson, but I'm not really here. My body is, but my mind and heart are back in Texas. I left upset and didn't kiss Cole or Zoey goodbye. I shouldn't have left like that. He just needs time, and he needs me to be patient. Pulling out my phone, I shoot a text to Cole, telling him I'm sorry and that I love him, then I stare at my phone to see if he's going to respond. When he doesn't, I put my phone back in my pocket and head over to the bar.

"Coke, please," I ask him, then take my phone back out to check it again.

"Asshole still hasn't responded?" My head shoots up at the voice, and standing there in a three piece suit is none other than Cole.

"He's not an asshole," I say, "Just going through some shit."

"Nah." He chuckles. "He's definitely been acting like an asshole. It's a wonder his boyfriend even continues to put up with his shit." I look around to make sure nobody heard what he just said, when he closes the gap between us. We're standing way too close to just be considered friends, and I have to wonder if he's lost his mind. That is until he leans in and, gripping the sides of my face, kisses me right here in front of everyone. And now I know he's lost his mind. It's not a long kiss. Just a quick brush of our lips, but it's enough that if there's anybody watching, they'll know we're more than friends.

"You just kissed me," I point out, stunned.

"You left without kissing me goodbye." He shrugs. "Plus, I'm done hiding. I love you, and I'm proud to be in a relationship with you. I'm not going to keep it in a closet like it's a dirty secret any longer." His words hit me straight in my chest. I've waited for so fucking long for him to say this.

Gripping the back of his neck, I pull him into another kiss, this one harder and rougher than the one he initiated. "I love you, too," I murmur into his mouth. Then I repeat the same words he said to me the night he made us dinner. "So fucking much."

EPILOGUE

Xander

THREE MONTHS LATER

"HEY!" I HEAR COLE SHOUT OVER THE CROWD. HE'S SITTING COURTSIDE WITH Zoey in his lap. She spots me walking over and grins ear-to-ear. It's half-time and I should be heading into the locker-room, but I wanted to say hi to them before I do.

"Hey! I wasn't sure if you would be able to make it." I give Zoey a kiss on her cheek, and she squeals.

"Practice ended early, and I grabbed Zoey from Kacey and headed straight over here. We couldn't miss your first game of the season." Cole grins. After he told me he hadn't applied to any coaching positions in fear of having to admit he's gay, he also mentioned that while he was waiting for his flight to come see me, he applied to four job openings. The following week, he went on two interviews. He told both principals he's gay and was offered jobs by both. He accepted the one he wanted, becoming the new physical education teacher and varsity basketball head coach, and

I couldn't be more proud of him for following his dreams.

"Can you hold Zoey for a minute?" he asks, handing her to me.

"Uh, yeah, but I really need to get to the locker room."

"It will just be a second," he says. I take Zoey into my arms, and when I look back to Cole, I have to look down because he's kneeling...on one knee.

"Cole..." I begin to say as I glance around me, realizing the entire stadium has gone quiet. Even the music has stopped. I spot the television screens and see we're displayed on them. My eyes go back to Cole who is now holding a small box in his one hand.

"Some might think this is too soon, my asking you to marry me, but what they don't realize is that our story began thirteen years ago, under the stars in a barn where we promised to always be best friends. I've loved you since the day I met you, and I would love it if we could keep our story going with you as my husband. Xander Thompson, will you marry me?"

"Hell yes, I'll marry you."

Cole smiles and stands, placing the simple band on my ring finger. "Thank you." The crowd starts chanting kiss, kiss, kiss, so we give them what they want: a kiss, right there in the middle of the stadium with Zoey in our arms. And while most would thank God for blessing them with such happiness, I thank Delilah. It's because of her that I was able to find the love of my life.

♡ ♡ ♡

TEN YEARS LATER

"HOLY SHIT, THAT FEELS GOOD." XANDER GROANS, HIS VOICE MUFFLED FROM him being face down against the pillow. "Yes, right there."

"Shh…" I say, gripping the sides of his thighs tighter and pounding into him from behind. I watch as my cock disappears into his ass then glides back out almost all the way before I push it back in, making sure I hit as deep as I can go. Xander's been on the road for ten days—the team's longest block of away games—which means we have ten days to make up for before our daughter wakes up and comes knocking on our door, wanting breakfast. The last thing we need is her waking up early because she hears his voice.

"Don't you dare stroke your fucking dick," I threaten when I see his hand shifting under him. "The only place you're coming is in my mouth." And the thought of Xander's hard cock in my mouth has me losing control. My thrusts turn frantic, and seconds later, I'm coming. I pull out, and without even bothering to clean up, I slap his ass so he'll roll over onto his back. When he does so, his hard dick springs free, and I'm wrapping my mouth around it before he can even say hello.

Yeah, that's right. He walked in the door about thirty minutes ago, and I pretty much attacked him, stripping down his clothes and demanding to be inside of him. I can't help it, though. My need for Xander has only seemed to strengthen over the years.

My wet mouth glides up and down his shaft, my hand cupping his balls while massaging them gently. I know it won't be long until he's shooting his load down my throat. It never takes long after he's been on the road. I take him all the way down until the tip of his dick hits my throat, and his hips buck as he lets out a guttural groan, telling me he's about to come. I take him deep one more time and then, just as I expected, he's coming all over my tongue. Once I've licked him clean, I release him from my mouth.

"Welcome home," I joke, and he chuckles.

"Two more months, and I'll be home for good," he says just as there's a knock on the door.

"Dad! I'm awake. I know Pops is home," she shouts through the door, and I laugh at her new nickname for Xander. Since she was old enough to speak, she's called us both Dad. It just happened, and we were both completely okay with that. We're both her fathers. We've always been honest with her about the fact that I'm biologically her father and Delilah is her mother. A few months ago, though, while watching a movie, she heard the little girl call her dad 'Pops' and ever since, she's dubbed that name for Xander. It drives him insane, but he wouldn't dare tell her that.

"We really need to think of a new name for me," Xander says, heading to the bathroom to shower. "I'm only thirty-five years old, not sixty-five!"

Throwing on a pair of pants and a shirt, I head out to the kitchen to start breakfast. "Morning, sunshine." I give my daughter a kiss on her forehead before I pull the mixing bowl out of the cabinet.

"Morning." She jumps up onto the barstool and bounces in her seat, excitedly. "What time are we leaving?"

"Eleven," I say, heating up the skillet and mixing the pancake batter in a bowl. "Chocolate chips or blueberries?" I ask.

"Neither. Bananas, please."

"You got it." I grab a banana and start slicing. "Have you decided which dress you're going to wear today?" I ask, making conversation.

"Yep! The one grandma got me while she was in Hawaii with grandpa."

"That's a beautiful dress." I pour the batter onto the hot surface.

"Morning, sweet girl," I hear Xander say.

"Morning, Pops!" Zoey squeals, and out of the corner of my eye, I see her jump into his arms. He plants a kiss on her cheek and carries her over with him. I laugh at how tall she's gotten, her long legs wrapping around his torso—too tall to be carried, but Xander doesn't care. He leans in and gives me a quick kiss, then snags a couple slices of bananas and throws them into his mouth.

"Pops, want to see my dress?" Zoey wiggles her body to be let down, and Xander drops her to the ground.

"Yes, but let's eat first. We don't want to get any food on it." He hands her three plates for her to carry to the table.

"Fine." She huffs. "We're leaving at eleven."

"Sounds good."

After we eat breakfast, I jump in the shower and get dressed while Zoey does the same. Once she's dressed and Xander has taken no less than fifty photos of her in her new dress, we head out. It's a two-and-a-half hour drive, but Zoey makes it go by quick, telling Xander everything that he's missed while being gone. He listens and responds like it's the first time he's hearing everything, even though he video chats with us nightly.

When we get to the hospital, we immediately spot Joanne and John. Zoey runs over to them to give them a hug and show them her dress.

"Thank you for coming," Dr. Morton says, shaking our hands. "What you're doing here is amazing." He walks us over to the main area where they will be doing the ribbon-cutting ceremony.

"It's the least we can do," Xander says. Everybody gathers around, and Zoey comes running up to join us in the front along with Joanne and John.

"Thank you everyone for being here today as we officially open a new wing in Texas General Hospital," Dr. Morton begins. "This wing has been made possible by two men who I have had the privilege of getting to know over the years while I was treating their friend, Delilah Cross. Delilah was a fighter, and while she unfortunately lost her battle to cancer, I am so proud to announce the brand new children's oncology wing, which has been built in her memory and funded by the Delilah Cross Wish Upon a Star Organization. Not only will this mean the children who are treated here will get the best care possible and be more comfortable, but many families who may not have been able to otherwise seek treatment will now be able to. Without further ado, Zoey, cut the ribbon."

Using both hands, Zoey holds the big scissors and cuts the ribbon in half. Everyone claps and comes over, hugging and thanking us. When Xander mentioned wanting to start a charity in Delilah's honor, we both agreed the only one that would be fitting is one that raises money to help families who need financial help so their children can be treated. Delilah was fortunate that her parents could afford her treatment all those years, which is why she was able to live as long as she did. But what many people don't know is that one-quarter of cancer patients can't afford treatment.

"You did good, Mr. Thompson." I pull my husband into a hug and give him a quick kiss.

"We did good." He kisses me back. "I was thinking since we're in town, tonight we could take Zoey to the barn to watch for shooting stars." And that right there is why I love this man.

THE END.

ACKNOWLEDGMENTS

The first person I need to thank is Kaylee Ryan. This book wouldn't exist without you. Thank you for planting the seed, and then spending hours upon hours discussing the book, the details, the title, and the cover.

My children, thank you for supporting me in my passion and believing in me.

My crew who read this book as if it was their own, giving me their thoughts and opinions every step of the way to make sure the story in my head went onto the paper seamlessly: Stacey, Nicole, Brittany, Andrea, Tabitha, Ashley, Krysten, and anyone else I forgot because my memory sucks, thank you!

Readers and bloggers, if you made it this far, thank you for taking a chance on me, especially those of you who have read my other books. I know this book is different than what I've written, and it truly means the world to me that you gave it a chance.

Juliana, thank you for once again designing the perfect cover to do this book justice.

My Fight Club, I love you ladies (and gents) so much! Thank you for reading and loving my books, and for simply being you.

ABOUT THE AUTHOR

Reading is like breathing in, writing is like breathing out.—Pam Allyn

Nikki Ash resides in South Florida where she is an English teacher by day and a writer by night. When she's not writing, you can find her with a book in her hand. From the Boxcar Children, to Wuthering Heights, to the latest single parent romance, she has lived and breathed every type of book. While reading and writing are her passions, her two children are her entire world. You can probably find them at a Disney park before you would find them at home on the weekends!

www.authornikkiash.com

www.ingramcontent.com/pod-product-compliance
Lightning Source LLC
Chambersburg PA
CBHW060708010826
48976CB00025B/1860